Love Me Not

Love Me Not

M. J. ARLIDGE

PENGUIN BOOKS

PENGUIN BOOKS

UK | USA | Canada | Ireland | Australia
India | New Zealand | South Africa

Penguin Books is part of the Penguin Random House group of companies
whose addresses can be found at global.penguinrandomhouse.com.

Penguin Random House UK

First published by Michael Joseph 2017
Published in Penguin Books 2017
001

Typeset by Jouve (UK), Milton Keynes
Printed in Great Britain by Clays Ltd, St Ives plc

A CIP catalogue record for this book is available from the British Library

ISBN: 978-1-405-93789-4

www.greenpenguin.co.uk

MIX
Paper from
responsible sources
FSC® C018179

Penguin Random House is committed to a sustainable future for our business, our readers and our planet. This book is made from Forest Stewardship Council® certified paper.

1

07.05

Southampton glowed blood red. It was a fresh autumn morning, the frost still crisp on the ground, but a warm light was stealing over the city as the sun crept above the horizon. It was a stunningly beautiful sight and Sonia Smalling smiled to herself as she drove along the quiet country road. It was days like this that made you glad to be alive.

Sonia had worked in Southampton for nearly ten years, but had never chosen to live there, preferring the calm, unhurried rhythms of village life. She lived near Ashurst, on the edges of the New Forest, and loved nothing more than taking the dogs for a walk at first light. Her husband, Thomas, often accompanied her and occasionally the boys too, when they could be coaxed out of their beds. With the sun low in the sky, it would have been a glorious day to bound along the narrow, wooded paths with her two red setters, but Sonia had had to forgo that pleasure this morning. She had a new set of kids starting today and wanted to be in the office early to ensure that everything went off smoothly.

It wasn't a difficult commute, despite the inevitable traffic on the A336, and when Sonia was flying along the country roads like this, she was perfectly happy. She had her favourite radio station playing, the heating was cranked up to the max and she was enjoying the roar of her new Audi. Uncharacteristically for her, she hadn't gone for the basic model, raiding her savings to buy the sporty version instead. 'Live a little' was her argument to her rather bemused husband.

The road was clear, so she put her foot down. Despite the frost, her tyres gripped the road and the car sped along. She looked down at the clock – 7.05 a.m. – and realized that she would be at work even earlier than usual today. That should keep her boss off her back.

She flicked her eyes back up and immediately froze. A woman was standing in the road, dead ahead of her, shouting and waving her arms. Instinctively Sonia slammed on the brakes. But already she knew that it was too late – she would hit the woman and it would be her fault for driving too fast. In those few, precious seconds, she saw the whole thing – the horrible impact, her shattered body – but to her enormous surprise the car suddenly lurched to a halt, a few inches from the terrified woman.

Sonia sat stock still, her heart thumping, her head throbbing. But already the woman had rounded the car and was hammering on the window.

'Please, help me . . . You've *got* to help me.'

Sonia turned to her, trying to fathom what was happening. The woman was dressed in combat trousers and a trench coat. Through the open visor of her helmet, Sonia could see a small trickle of blood running down her temple.

'My boyfriend, he's come off his bike. He's not moving . . .'

Sonia stole a look down the road and got her second shock of the morning. Ahead of them was a crumpled motorbike and next to it a figure, lying motionless in the middle of the road.

The woman was crying, shaking and desperate, so, gesturing to her to move away from the car, Sonia unclipped her seatbelt and climbed out. Sonia was still pretty shaken herself, but as she'd been trained in first aid, it was her duty to help. Flicking a look behind her to check that the road was clear, she hurried over to the man, praying to herself that his injuries weren't severe. She had seen many things in her lifetime, but she had never had anyone die on her.

'Can you hear me?'

Kneeling down on the cold tarmac, Sonia gently rolled him on to his back. His visor was cracked, his eyes closed, and already Sonia feared the worst.

'Is he ok? Is he going to be ok?'

Sonia ignored the twittering girlfriend, raising his head off the ground. He still felt warm, which was something, but he remained unresponsive, his head heavy in her hand.

'Everything's going to be fine,' she continued to the injured man. 'But I need you to talk to me.'

Still no response. Sonia tried to ease his visor up, but it wouldn't budge.

'Can you hear what I'm saying?'

Still nothing, so she tried again, louder.

'Can you hear what I'm saying to y—'

His eyes shot open, locking on to hers.

'Loud and clear, sweetheart.'

Then he drove his fist into her face.

2

07.08

The underground car park was dark and gloomy. Before long it would be full of young professionals racing to their cars, but at this hour it was lifeless and unwelcoming, lit only by the flickering strip lights. Helen Grace cut a lonely figure as she walked across the oil-smeared concrete, the fluorescent lights dancing over her biking leathers.

She made her way quickly over to her new bike, which stood proud in bay 26. Helen was not prone to extravagance, but had decided to treat herself following her recent troubles. She had received a hefty sum in compensation, following her wrongful arrest and imprisonment, and had decided to make use of it. She'd given the majority of the money to a local children's charity, but had blown the rest on a single purchase – a new Kawasaki Ninja.

She was glad of its company this morning. Prison had not broken her, but it had left a deep mark. She struggled to sleep, finding the silence in her top-floor flat suffocating, and when she did manage to nod off, she was plagued by terrible nightmares. In these dreams, she was back in her cell, scared and desperate. Sometimes the ghosts of Holloway paraded before her – the murdered inmates castigating Helen for failing to save them. At other times, it was her sister, Marianne, who came to her, appealing to

Helen to join her in death. Hideously, Marianne appeared not as Helen liked to remember her, but as she was at the very end – the bullet hole in her forehead glistening wet.

Helen would wake disoriented and sweating, her fear lingering long after these awful visions had disappeared. She had always loved her little flat, but nine months on from her release, it often felt small, even oppressive. Helen knew it was all in her head, that her cosy home had always been her sanctuary, but there was no denying the shallowness of her breath or the furious beating of her heart as she awoke with a start from these fevered dreams. Helen hadn't had a full-on panic attack yet, but she sensed one was coming, so whenever she felt her anxiety levels rise, she fled. Down to the basement and on to her bike. Only when she was astride it did her dark feelings start to recede.

She was no longer a prisoner, but sometimes she just needed to get *out*. Which is why she looked forward to the dawn, when the day was new and waiting to be seized. Flicking off the stand, she waited for the gate to rise, then, pulling back the throttle, roared out and away into the light.

3

07.09

She scuttled backwards as fast as she could, scrabbling across the tarmac. Her legs were grazed, her nails cracked, but still Sonia kept going, as her attacker advanced upon her. Her head was spinning, her eyes were thick with tears and she could feel blood dripping off her chin. All she wanted to do was lie down and cry – but instinct drove her on. She had to get away from him.

She had been so shocked when he'd opened his eyes that she'd failed to see his fist flying towards her. Too late she'd realized the danger and moments later felt herself falling backwards. Her nose was broken for sure and the back of her head was sticky too, where it had connected with the road. She wanted to be sick, could feel the vomit rising in her throat, but she forced it back down, as she struggled to escape.

She tried to turn, to scramble on to all fours, but his boot connected sharply with her chest, forcing her on to her back once more. Still she kept moving, but her head was suddenly filled with visions of what he might do to her on this quiet country road – things she'd read about in the papers, things she'd come across in her line of work. She had met so many victims in her time, but she'd never thought she'd actually *be* one.

He was laughing now. The woman too. Hatred flared through Sonia. They had *no* right to do this to her. To lure her from her car. To beat her. To bully her in this way. She was a grown woman with a responsible job – a job which gave back. She was a wife too, a mother . . .

Her back jarred sharply with something behind her, snapping Sonia out of her bitter thoughts. Turning, she registered that she had collided with her own car, cutting off her escape route. Terrified, she returned her gaze to her attacker, who now came to a halt a couple of feet from her. He seemed perfectly calm, relaxed even. Suddenly Sonia felt petrified, his composure seeming only to threaten bad things.

'I can give you money . . .' she suddenly found herself saying. 'I've got cash, credit cards . . . Take the car, if you want to . . .'

She gestured to the Audi behind her, a weak, imploring smile on her face. But the man didn't react at all, staring at her intently.

'I've got jewellery, a diamond ring, a necklace. Take those, you can sell them, please . . . *please*, just let me go . . .'

The man looked at her for a moment, then gently shook his head.

'Can't do that, I'm afraid . . .'

As he spoke, he pulled something from inside his jacket and pointed it at her. To her horror, Sonia realized she was now staring down the barrels of a sawn-off shotgun. She tried to speak, but was robbed of breath and could only listen helplessly as he concluded:

'This is the end of the road, sweetheart.'

4

07.17

The wind ripped over her, buffeting her body. Helen was comfortably exceeding the speed limit, but still she did not relent. The road was clear and she was in command, of her machine, of herself.

Her life was so complicated, her job so demanding, that these moments early in the day were the only ones she had to herself. Her previous boss, Detective Superintendent Jonathan Gardam, had left the force just after Helen's release from prison. This had come as a massive relief to Helen, who had no desire to face him, but she hadn't foreseen the ensuing complications. Nine months on, the powers that be still hadn't appointed his successor, leaving Helen to cover that job, as well as her own.

Previously she might have shrugged this off, leaning on those below her to help shoulder the burden. Helen had always been a popular and effective team leader, but since her imprisonment everything had changed. A year ago, Helen had been investigated and arrested by her own team, DS Sanderson leading the charge to bring her to book for a triple murder. Perhaps it had been done with the best of intentions, but it had shaken Helen to the core. Her team – whom she had inspired, encouraged and in some cases promoted – had turned on her. Many of those involved still worked at Southampton Central, but now they struggled to meet her eye. Charlie Brooks was a notable exception – her faith in her friend had never wavered – but Helen found working with the rest of the team profoundly difficult. They were dutiful, responsive, loyal even – but it was hard for Helen to trust them, her sense of betrayal still keen. Maybe she should have moved on, but Southampton was her home so she'd elected to stay. More and more these days, she was questioning the wisdom of that decision.

It was these moments that kept her sane. When she could tear along the quiet country roads, when it was just her and the elements. Speed had always been her friend, seeming to alter the world around her, to diminish its importance. She loved the feeling that biking gave her, like she was floating on –

It came out of nowhere. The black hatchback roared towards her, with no intention of stopping. Helen only had a second to react, but dropping her body and yanking the handle bars to the right, she managed to dodge the impact by a whisker. The car rushed past, its jet stream further destabilizing Helen, as her bike lurched towards the verge at the side of the road. She was only seconds from impact now, but clutching the brakes, she jammed her left foot down, more in hope than expectation. The bike bucked and shook, the tyres screeching as she skidded across the tarmac, before eventually coming to a halt just short of the grassy bank.

Helen shot a furious look towards the receding car, whose driver seemed utterly unconcerned by this near miss. Turning her bike around, Helen prepared to roar after the offending vehicle, intent on bringing them to justice. But, as she did so, something made her stop. In her peripheral vision, she saw a shape in the road ahead. Her first instinct was that it was probably a badger or a fox, mown down by the reckless driver, but as she turned to take it in properly, Helen realized that it was a woman, lying flat on her back in the middle of the road.

Without hesitation, Helen turned her bike back around and sped towards her. She ate up the ground in seconds, leaping off her bike and running over to the prone figure. Her helmet removed, Helen bent down to minister to the injured woman, whose face was generously smeared with blood.

'It's ok. I'm a police officer. And I'm here to help you,' Helen said quietly, propping up the woman's head with one hand, while pulling out her police radio with the other.

The woman tried to respond, but a large quantity of blood spilled from her mouth. She was choking now and Helen tried to raise her up, to ease the pressure on her airways. As she did so, Helen's heart skipped a beat. Taking in the woman's injuries fully for the first time, Helen saw that there was a huge hole in her chest. This was no road accident.

Maintaining her gentle hold, Helen radioed for assistance, but already she knew it was hopeless. The woman's injuries were too severe – Helen had reached her too late. The woman was clinging to life, trying to whisper something to her. She raised her head, her bloody lips mouthing a breathless, incomprehensible word, then suddenly she fell back, collapsing in on herself. Helen continued to hold her, but the fight was over.

The woman was dead.

5

07.21

Her coffee was cold and her career colder still. Emilia Garanita sat hunched over her desk, staring at the monitor, unable to summon the energy to finish the dreary article she was working on. It was early, but the office at the *Southampton Evening News* was filling up quickly, the noise levels steadily rising, as the assembled journalists got to work. Most people found the atmosphere friendly, even exciting, but she didn't. Had you told her a year ago that she would be back in this place, she would have laughed in your face. Following her scoop on the infamous S&M murders case, which had led directly to Helen Grace's imprisonment, she had hightailed it to London to make her name. A glittering future awaited . . . until it turned out that she had backed the wrong horse. Sometimes Emilia sincerely wished she had never crossed paths with the irrepressible detective inspector.

The work for the broadsheets had dried up first, then shortly afterwards the tabloids had tired of her too. When she had the inside track on Helen Grace's life in prison, everyone wanted to speak to her, greedily printing the articles that eviscerated Grace's good name. When it transpired that the wronged officer was entirely innocent, then people couldn't drop Emilia fast enough.

She had stuck it out in the capital for as long as funds allowed, but as her numerous siblings still lived in Southampton and relied on her financially, she'd been forced to return home to beg her former editor for her old job back.

'How you getting on with that article?'

Emilia turned to find her boss standing in his office doorway, staring at her.

'Not long now,' Emilia replied, privately cursing his black heart.

He hadn't given her her old job back of course, as the post had already been filled. But he'd found something else for her – a glorified trainee's job – so he could gloat at her fall from grace. Her successor got all the juicy crime stories, while she had to content herself with articles on Neighbourhood Watch schemes or home security demos. The copy in front of her was about a recent spate of graffiti in Southampton – not something to set the reader's – or Emilia's – pulse racing.

Tapping his watch theatrically, her editor retreated to his office. He knew she was struggling with her article and just wanted to let her know that he knew. She waited until he had shut the door, then put her earphones back in. This was not just to discourage her colleagues from conversation; it was her way of amusing herself. She had recently located the frequency of the local police radio and passed the time listening to it, as she tried to conjure up the words to finish her tedious articles. It didn't help her much, as she wasn't supposed to follow up any of the juicy leads it threw up, but it did allow her to flummox her successor by casually making reference to breaking stories that he knew nothing about.

The radio traffic was quiet again this morning. Southampton seemed to have been in a news coma of late and Emilia was just debating whether to make herself a third cup of coffee, when she heard something which stopped her in her tracks.

'All units to proceed to Barton Lane. Fatal shooting. Unknown perpetrator still at large . . .'

Emilia didn't bother to turn the radio off – she simply threw down her earphones and ran.

6

07.44

'She's married.'

DS Charlie Brooks stared at the brutalized corpse. She had raced across town to join Helen and had swiftly set about sealing the scene. Important evidence could be lost through casual police work and Charlie had picked her way carefully over to the body, her eyes immediately fixing on the thick gold band that clung to her fourth finger.

'Her name's Sonia Smalling.'

Helen now joined her, handing Charlie a transparent evidence bag. Inside were a purse, a phone and a lanyard with the victim's work ID attached.

'She's a married mum of two, works for the local probation service out of Totton.'

An image of her own child – wilful toddler Jessica – immediately sprang into her mind, but Charlie pushed it away. She had been deeply shaken by the sight of the poor woman's body but had to focus on the job in hand.

'How did she get out here?'

'According to the DVLA, she owns a black Audi A3. There's no sign of it now and I nearly collided with one racing away from the scene. I've alerted the incident room, we'll see what they come up with.'

‘Where does she live?’

‘Ashurst.’

‘So this would be on her way to work,’ Charlie replied, doing the navigational maths.

‘Presumably.’

‘So what the hell happened?’

Helen turned and walked away, gesturing for Charlie to accompany her. Charlie stared at the corpse a moment longer, then followed. Helen pointed to a team of forensics officers who were crowded round a motorbike, concealed in foliage a few yards from the road.

‘It was stolen from Southampton city centre last night and seems to have sustained some damage.’

‘So what are you thinking? An accident? Some kind of altercation?’

‘Maybe . . .’ Helen responded, though she sounded unconvinced.

‘A robbery, then?’

‘If so, it was a pretty amateur job. They left her cash, phone, credit cards . . .’

‘A carjacking?’

The two women looked at each other. It was the most likely explanation, but these were unheard of in Southampton.

‘Perhaps it was a personal attack,’ Charlie continued. ‘If she works for the probation service . . .’

‘It’s a possibility, but she works with shoplifters and truants, not armed killers.’

Charlie turned away from Helen to look back at the body, as if Sonia Smalling herself could provide the answers, but it was hidden from view now by the hastily erected tent. The reasons for this savage murder were equally well obscured – such a brutal killing on a quiet country road defied logic and practice. It also raised some unsettling questions for Charlie and the rest of the team.

Where had the killer got hold of the gun? What was his motive? And, most importantly, where was he now?

7

07.59

He drummed his fingers on the steering wheel, as he waited for the lights to change. They had made good progress into Southampton, but were hitting morning rush hour and were now stuck in a queue of office workers and yummy mummies at the Charlotte Place roundabout. He was wearing gloves and enjoyed the feeling of leather on leather, as he tapped his fingers on the hand-stitched steering wheel, but still he was keen to be away. He had never been known for his patience.

'Look at those freaks.'

A huge, silver SUV had pulled up alongside them. A Slavic-looking woman, barely out of her teens, was at the wheel. Behind her sat her charges – two young boys watching TV screens, headphones firmly on.

'Fucking zombies . . .'

As if sensing his disapproval, one of the boys turned, looking directly at the man. He stared back and the boy swiftly looked away, alarmed by his hostile expression. Chuckling, he turned his attention to the others in the queue. Men in suits, women in suits, stressed mums, nannies who didn't give a shit – all stuck in their daily grind, totally oblivious to those around them. What would they think if they could see what he could see? A pair of shotguns lying in the foot well, expertly sawn off, primed and ready for action? Would they scream? Would they run? Or would they ask for a selfie?

'Muppets ...' his companion agreed, as she rifled through the car's glove compartment, ferreting out a half-eaten pack of Polos and a battered *A–Z*. Lowering the window, she tossed them out on to the road, to the evident disapproval of the pensioner in the neighbouring car.

The man turned away from her and his attention was now caught by something at the side of the road. A traffic camera was fixed to a nearby lamppost, casting its eye over this busy stretch of road. It seemed to be pointing right at him, as if it alone realized who was waiting patiently in the queue. The man stared at it intently, wondering what it could see. Could it make him out? Could it see her? How good *were* these cameras?

He wasn't one of those people who craved the spotlight. He knew a lot of folk did, girls especially, but that had never been his bag. In the past, he'd only been on people's radar when something had gone wrong, when he was up for something. But now, for the first time, he welcomed the attention.

Leaning forward into view, he glanced at the camera, then slowly raised his arm, before extending his middle finger so it was pointing directly at the lens. He had lived in the shadows for so long, ignored by a callous, blinkered world, but all that was about to change.

Soon everybody would know his name.

8

08.01

'Have we got anything yet?'

DS Sanderson's voice rang out across the incident room, prompting DC Edwards to look up from his terminal.

'Nothing yet,' he answered dolefully.

'Uniform seen anything?'

'Loads of Audi spots, but none of our vehicle so far. Are we certain our perpetrator has headed into the city? He hasn't dumped the car and run?'

'That's what I was hoping you'd tell me,' Sanderson returned, moving away towards Helen's office.

The call from Helen had come through just after 7.20 a.m. Sanderson was still in her flat, but had made it to Southampton Central in record time. Helen was already at the crime scene and Charlie had headed straight there, leaving Sanderson as the most senior MIT officer in the building. Accordingly, she had hurried up to the Major Incident Team's offices on the seventh floor and set about establishing an incident room – standard procedure for a crime of this magnitude.

Edwards was already in, as was McAndrew, and more officers were turning up every minute. Everyone could sense that this was going to be a big number – if for no other reason than that the shooter was still at large. Forensics, witness statements and local CCTV would fall to Helen and the other officers at the scene. Sanderson's job was to track the fugitive, which in the short term meant finding the missing Audi.

She had immediately initiated an Automatic Number Plate Recognition Search. As soon as a traffic camera got a good look at the Audi plates, it would ping up on their system. The system was not foolproof, as there was a slight delay, and if the vehicle was moving fast it was hard to pinpoint its *exact* location, but it would tell them roughly where it was and what direction it was heading in. Officers on the ground could then be deployed, along with the chopper and Armed Response Units, to bring their fugitive in.

That was the theory at least. But so far they had had no sightings or flags. Sanderson had questioned whether they should put out a general alert, but Helen had slapped that idea down, insisting she didn't want members of the public getting involved, when the threat level was so high. It was a fair point of course, but the vigour with which it had been made had unsettled Sanderson.

The truth was that things hadn't been right between her and Helen since the latter's release from prison. Sanderson had played a key role in helping Charlie bring Helen's nephew to book, thus ensuring her release, but this couldn't disguise the fact that prior to this she had believed her boss capable of cold-blooded murder. During their investigation into the S&M murders, suspicion had fallen on Helen and Sanderson had run with it, failing to realize that her boss was being framed. Unwittingly, she had helped condemn an innocent woman to three months of hell in Holloway Prison. She had pursued the case honestly and professionally, but Sanderson had got promoted off the back of it, taking Helen's job temporarily. Furthermore, it implied a basic lack of trust in Helen which was hard to erase from the collective memory.

A CID team is a tight unit and though logically Helen should have applauded her junior officer for following the evidence, emotionally things were rather more complicated than that. In Sanderson's eyes, Helen cleaved even closer to Charlie now, to the exclusion of others, herself most noticeably. Sanderson wasn't the paranoid sort and she was sure she wasn't imagining the constant slights and apparent disregard for her skills. She was being frozen out, punished for her disloyalty.

The team seemed fully engaged on their tasks, so Sanderson now slipped inside Helen's office. It had been hers for a few months, but was Helen's once more, all signs of Sanderson's brief occupancy having been removed. Sanderson suspected *she* might be removed too before long, from the team, perhaps even from Hampshire Police. Which is why she now took an envelope from inside her jacket and placed it carefully in Helen's in-tray. She liked the team here, she liked Southampton and a few months back would never have envisaged herself handing in a formal transfer request. But circumstances had changed and she knew that she would have to leave her beloved Southampton Central if she was to prosper. It wasn't what she wanted, but there was nothing to be done. So, with a heavy heart, she turned and left Helen's office, closing the door quietly behind her.

9

08.13

'I'm not asking for special treatment. I just need five minut—'

'That's exactly what you're asking for. And it ain't going to happen.'

'I'll be discreet. A couple of photos of the scene and then –'

'Are you insane? Have you seen how many officers are out there? You'll be in cuffs before you get anywhere *near* the –'

'Let *me* take that risk.'

'And have it come back on my head? No, thank you.'

Emilia suppressed a scowl, faking a smile instead. On arriving at the police cordon, she had been pleased to find PC Alan Stark in attendance. He had been very helpful during previous investigations, always willing to trade information for cash. Today, however, he was being surprisingly uncooperative.

'We can come back to that,' Emilia continued brightly. 'Let's just get the basics sorted for now. I know that we've got one fatality, a gunshot victim –'

'How the hell do you know that?'

'What I don't have is a name . . .'

'Planning to ring the family, are you? Offer your condolences?'

Emilia stared at him. She didn't like the scorn that was creeping into his tone – he had never been like this with her before. The fact that that was *exactly* what she was planning was neither here nor there.

'Look, Alan, this is a necessary evil,' she went on. 'So let's not make it more difficult than it has to be. I've got cash and – just this once – I can raise your rate, so we both profit from –'

'I don't want your money.'

'Really? Had a change of luck, have you? The horses finally been good to you . . . ?'

'I've knocked it on the head.'

Now Emilia was speechless. Alan Stark was an inveterate gambler, constantly in hock to the bookies. Emilia's cash had got him out of a number of awkward spots in the past and she was stunned that he was refusing her handouts now.

'Come on, Alan, I know we haven't been in touch for a while, but there's no need to be like this about it. What do you want – two hundred, three hundred? I need that name.'

Emilia reached into her bag for her purse, but Stark grabbed her wrist, stopping her in her tracks and pulling her in close.

'Why won't you listen to me?' he whispered harshly, his voice shaking with emotion. 'I don't do that any more. I have made a promise . . . to my wife, to my daughter . . . and I will not break my word for you, or anyone else. So why don't you just bugger off and leave me alone.'

With that, he shoved her forcefully away. Emilia could see tears welling in his eyes and she suddenly realized how badly she'd misjudged the situation, how desperately determined he was to beat his addiction. Holding her hands up in surrender, she moved further down the cordon, slipping out of view among the assortment of journalists, motorists and gawpers who made up the growing crowd. She stared up the road, irritated that the crime scene was just out of view around the corner and frustrated by her lack of progress. She had expected big things of this story, but was leaving empty-handed thanks to Stark's intransigence. Clearly his personal circumstances had changed – as had hers. Before, when she was the rising star of crime reporting, officers had been happy to take her bribes. Now that she was a glorified trainee, nobody would give her the time of day.

For now at least, she remained on the outside, looking in.

10

08.20

Helen closed the tent flap, shutting out the world. The road was crawling with forensics officers, scouring the roadside and verges for evidence, examining the tread patterns of the skid marks on the road, as they tried to piece together a narrative of the morning's awful events. Inside the tent, things were rather quieter. The forensics officers had completed their initial sweep around the body and were now packaging their evidence for analysis, leaving their boss alone in the tent.

Helen joined Meredith Walker, who offered her two shotgun cartridges, sealed in an evidence bag.

'They're from a Webley twelve-gauge shotgun,' she said, as Helen took it from her.

'How common are they?' Helen asked, fearing she already knew the answer.

'Very. They're used by farmers, on shoots, at gun clubs. They're a reliable British brand and not too expensive. There are probably over twenty thousand registered in Hampshire alone.'

'Right,' Helen replied, trying not to sound downcast.

'If you get me the gun, I might be able to match it to the discharged cartridges, but there's no way of tracking it from this, I'm afraid.'

'Did you find any prints on the cartridges?'

'Nothing so far, but we'll double-check at the lab.'

'What can you tell me about the injuries?'

Meredith turned away from Helen to look down at the crumpled body.

'She was shot twice, at point-blank range. The perpetrator was standing no more than five feet from her.'

Meredith took up a stance in front of the body, raising her arms and pointing them at the victim, as if firing a shotgun.

'He fired directly at her, the shots striking her once, twice in the chest, pretty much in the same place. The impact would have been extreme – if the shock didn't kill her, the internal haemorrhage would have. It would have been quick.'

If this was supposed to comfort Helen, it didn't. Thanking Meredith, she left the tent and walked away down the road. There was little more she could do here, it was time to get back to base, but still she hesitated. The sun was beaming down on Southampton and normally this would have been a beautiful scene, the autumn leaves glowing in the warm light. But instead this quiet spot had been the scene of . . . what? An unprovoked attack? A brutal robbery? An ambush? The remote setting, the use of a shotgun . . . it reminded Helen of the crimes of old – a highwayman lying in wait on a secluded road. But was such a thing possible in the twenty-first century? Moreover, if robbery was the motive, why had her attacker left her money and jewellery behind? Had Sonia Smalling perhaps seen or heard something which meant she had to be silenced? Conversely, if it *was* a personal attack – revenge of some kind – why steal her car? A car which would inevitably be traced?

There were so many questions unanswered, but one was uppermost in Helen's mind. Had the killer deliberately set out to kill Sonia Smalling this morning or had he just killed her because he *could*? This brutal crime felt like an execution and it had set Helen's nerves jangling. Southampton had been quiet of late, but as she stood alone on the once tranquil country lane, Helen had the distinct feeling that this peace was about to be brutally shattered.

11

08.46

The radio was still playing as they pulled into a parking bay in the city centre. The Audi's former owner clearly liked her hits golden – her chosen station pumping out an endless slew of seventies and eighties 'classics'. Bob Geldof's voice filled the car now as 'I Don't Like Mondays' bounced off the windows. The driver paused for a moment to enjoy it, watching his companion jigging along in the seat next to him, before he abruptly turned it off.

'I was enjoying that,' she moaned.

Shaking his head good-humouredly, the driver wrenched the door open and climbed out. As he walked towards the back of the car, he took in the people passing by. The sun was climbing in the sky and what had started out as a cold day was now becoming decidedly warm. Most people had already stripped down to puffa waistcoats or cardigans and he knew that the pair of them risked standing out with their long, heavy overcoats, so he didn't linger, flicking open the boot. His companion joined him, but she said nothing. She could sense the change in his mood.

Darting a look left and right to check that no one was close by, he removed the rug that concealed the contents of the boot, tossing it casually on to the ground. Now he reached inside, grabbing a handful of shells and shoving them into his pocket. She did likewise, until all that was left inside was a large hunting knife. Snatching it up quickly, he strapped it to his chest, then buttoned up his coat, hiding the weapon from view.

'You look like something out of your video games,' she said, her local accent twanging through, despite her attempt to sound American.

He shrugged, but was pleased at the compliment. He'd always fancied himself as a warrior and now he looked the part. Tossing the car keys into the boot, he slammed it shut and turned to face her.

'Ready?'

She shook her head slowly.

'There's something we've got to do first . . .' she teased, pulling a small bottle from her coat pocket.

Unscrewing the safety cap, she deposited two amphetamines in his hand, watching as he tossed them carelessly into his mouth. She did the same, then drew a third from the half-full bottle.

'One more for luck.'

Carefully she placed the small white pill on the tip of her tongue. Then putting her arms round her companion, she pulled him down towards her. He opened his mouth obligingly and she slipped her tongue inside. Now they kissed, long and passionate, letting the pill slowly dissolve. They could already feel the effects of the first two kicking in and they held on to each other tightly, lost in the exhilaration. Then slowly, reluctantly, he broke away. He paused to remove a stray hair from her face, ran his finger down her nose, then turned away, rapping the boot of the car with his knuckles.

'Come on, babes, we've got work to do.'

He was already striding ahead, full of energy and purpose. She stood and watched him for a second, then moved swiftly away from the vehicle, following her lover towards the parade of shops.

12

08.57

She wasn't sure what she'd been expecting, but it wasn't *that*.

The photos that had just been thrust into her hand were of a woman lying naked on a stainless-steel slab. Not your everyday pics, but the kind that Emilia had seen often enough thanks to her carefully cultivated contacts in Southampton's police mortuary. These, however, were something else. The woman's skin was pale, her eyes closed and the image would almost have looked peaceful, were it not for the huge, scarlet hole in the centre of her chest. It looked as if she had been opened up for surgery, rather than simply murdered, such was the violence of the impact.

'Shotgun?' Emilia queried.

David Spivack nodded. He was a thin, bald man, dressed in mortician's scrubs. Working as an assistant to the Senior Pathologist, Jim Grieves, he had full access to the mortuary's varied cast of cadavers – indeed, he had sewn up most of them – but possessed little of his boss's morality or discretion.

'Point-blank range,' he eventually elaborated, casting an eye over his shoulder to the mortuary's fire exit. He was standing with the journalist on the metal staircase, and though he was out of sight, could not be sure that he was out of earshot.

'One shot or two?'

'Two. Almost blew a hole clean through her.'

Emilia smiled to herself. Spivack was not a man who wasted words on sentiment. Whether this was because he was heartless or just in a hurry, she wasn't sure.

'Any post mortem abuse or sexual assault?'

'Too early to say.'

'Was the body clothed?'

'Sure. And they'd left her wedding ring and other valuables on her.'

'Who found her?'

'DI Grace. The killer drove straight past her apparently . . .'

Another salient detail, which Emilia hoped to make the most of.

'And do we know who she is?'

Spivack quickly filled her in on the details, Emilia stopping him occasionally to check that she'd heard him right. A married mum in a socially responsible job, slain on a quiet, country road – if anything was going to put the wind up the good folk of Southampton, this would. Even better, the killer was still at large . . .

'That's as much as I know,' Spivack now concluded. 'But I can get you next-of-kin details if you're keen.'

His eyes fell on her purse and Emilia had no hesitation in unzipping it once more. She had been in the doldrums for so long now, so out of the game, that she had begun to wonder if she would ever get a second chance. But Sonia

Smalling, a nutter with a gun and a loose-lipped mortician had given her her opportunity.

As Emilia pressed another hundred pounds into Spivack's hand, she offered up a silent prayer for weak men everywhere.

13

09.11

He looked like he was about to collapse. Charlie had just broken the news to Peter Smalling and they were now standing in his cosy living room, staring silently at each other. His hands were shaking, he seemed to be having trouble breathing, so, gesturing to the Family Liaison Officer to help, Charlie took him by the arm, guiding Sonia's stunned husband down on to the nearest sofa.

He hadn't said a word since their arrival. As soon as he'd seen their warrant cards, he'd seemed to know what they'd come to say. Charlie had done this many times before and cut straight to the chase, filling him in on the basic details, omitting the more unpleasant elements. Peter had listened, nodded, then walked into the living room. Charlie had followed to find him standing in the middle of the room, seemingly dumbfounded as to what to do next. The FLO had tried to get a response from him, asking him where his boys were and if there was anyone he would like her to contact, but he looked at her as if she was speaking gibberish. He seemed to be on the verge of hyperventilating, so, having got him on to the sofa, Charlie sent the FLO off to make a cup of tea. What Peter Smalling needed now was space to breathe.

Ten minutes later, his cup of tea half drunk, he seemed

to recover his voice. He was clearly a shy man, a tech journalist who spent most of the day tucked away in his home office, but Charlie had to get him to talk and gently coaxed him out of his shock.

'I know how hard this is. I appreciate that talking to me is probably the last thing you want to do, but I need to ask you some questions, Peter. Would that be ok?'

'Yes,' he whispered eventually, staring into his tea.

'How was Sonia this morning? Was she worried about anything, distracted?'

'No, no . . . She wanted to be in work early this morning, didn't have time to walk the dogs, but other than that . . .'

'Your boys were here?'

'Yes, and she got them up as usual. That takes a bit of doing these days . . .'

'And then?'

'She had a shower, grabbed a bit of breakfast and left.'

'And you?'

'I . . . I dropped the boys off at school, then took the dogs out . . .'

Right on cue, two boisterous red setters bounded into the living room, pursued by the flustered FLO.

'Sorry, I was trying to keep them in the kitchen, but . . .'

'It's ok,' Charlie told her. 'They're fine in here.'

The dogs had bounced up to Peter and were smothering him with affection. He fussed them, stroking their long ears, and Charlie was moved to see tears forming in his eyes. The uncomplicated devotion and love of his dogs were cutting through his shock, revealing the true extent of his devastation.

'And the route Sonia took this morning, is that her normal commute?' Charlie said, knowing she needed to press on now, before she lost him entirely.

'Yes,' Peter replied, wiping his eyes. 'She swore it was the quickest way.'

'And why was she so keen to be in early?'

'She had a new lot of kids starting Community Payback today.'

'These are youth offenders, right?'

'Yes, Sonia is a probation officer. She works with young people who've made bad decisions, helps them get back on track.'

'And has she ever experienced problems at work? Received threats? Been the victim of violence . . . ?'

Peter looked up at her, seemingly surprised by the question.

'You think someone did this . . . *deliberately*?' he said, as if the thought hadn't occurred to him before.

'That's what we're trying to find out. Had she spoken to you recently about her work, shared any concerns with you?'

'No, nothing like that. The kids are unreliable, occasionally abusive, but . . . they're just kids. Once you talk to them, give them a bit of attention, something to work towards . . . I know people think they're bad apples, but they're not.'

'In the past then? Going back months, years even?'

Peter shook his head once more. 'Some kids were better than others, but they respected Sonia. She'd accompany them when they had to make amends to their victims, helped them learn new skills while they were doing their community service. They *liked* her . . . and she liked them.'

'What about her domestic situation then? Any family issues? Problems with neighbours?'

'No, no . . .' Peter intoned, looking more bemused than ever.

'And your marriage was a happy one?'

'Of course.'

'No problems, no stresses?'

'No, she loved me, she loved the boys. She missed her family back in Poland, her mother particularly –'

'So your wife's not from here originally?'

'No, what of it? Why are you asking me all this stuff? It has to be an accident. Mistaken identity or road rage. You hear about that kind of thing all the time in the papers.'

And now he broke down, hiding his face in his hands. The image of his wife, dead on a country road, had forced its way into his consciousness and the horror of it was overwhelming him. The dogs were picking up on his mood now, turning nervously in circles, wanting his attention, but sensing something was wrong. Peter was weeping silently, his upper body convulsing. There was nothing Charlie could do but watch, as his nice, ordered life collapsed in ruins. She wanted to offer him comfort, but what could she do? His wife was dead, his sons had lost their mother and the whys and wherefores of this brutal crime remained as opaque as ever.

14

09.12

'I can't see it properly. Have we got anything better?'

Helen was back in the incident room at Southampton Central. A snatched, black-and-white image from a traffic camera was up on the screen, but it was blurred and unclear.

'The tech boys are working on it, but this is the best we can do for now,' DC McAndrew replied carefully.

Helen returned her attention to the image. It had been taken by a camera at the Charlotte Place roundabout, towards the north of the city. The wider shots clearly showed the missing Audi waiting at the lights before moving off north towards Bevois Mount and Portswood. This enhanced close-up appeared to show the driver gesturing towards the camera. But that was all that could be said for sure, as the image was difficult to decipher, the glare on the car's windscreen making it hard to discern his features.

'Are we sure it's a bloke?' Edwards piped up.

'Looks like it,' Helen responded quickly. 'His build, the length of his reach and, here, that mark on his neck as he moves forward –'

'His Adam's apple,' DC Reid added.

'Exactly. Can we zoom in on that dark patch there?'

Helen indicated a small black spot at the base of the driver's neck. McAndrew obliged but the image was still indistinct.

'What is that? A tattoo?' Helen asked.

'Or a scar?'

'It's too dark for a scar.'

'An injury then? Is he bleeding?' Sanderson suggested, glad to be able to make some contribution to the debate.

'There's no evidence that Sonia Smalling's killer was injured in the attack,' Helen replied. 'So my guess is that it's a tattoo of some kind. Let's start drawing up a list of all the probationers that Sonia Smalling worked with, focusing on the males. Look at their mugshots, see if any of them had tattoos on their necks.'

Helen knew it was a long shot, but they were clutching at straws at the moment and any lead would have to be chased down. McAndrew zoomed out the image and Helen was about to continue her briefing, when DC Reid suddenly interjected:

'What's that?'

'What's what?'

'*That*,' Reid insisted, walking up to the image, indicating a shadow to the left of the driver.

Helen and the team crowded round. Reid was right, there was a small, dark shape on the dashboard by the passenger seat.

'Zoom right in.'

McAndrew obliged and the image became slightly clearer. It was too dark to be skin, too unreflective, yet the shape looked like . . . fingers. Five gloved fingers resting on the passenger-side dashboard.

'You'd better let uniform know that we are looking for *two* suspects,' Helen said decisively, turning to Sanderson. 'And remind them to proceed with extreme caution.'

Sanderson hurried off to do her bidding, while McAndrew marshalled the troops to run down leads relating to Sonia Smalling's work. They were making some progress – she had directed all uniformed beat coppers to the north of the city and armed units were patrolling Portswood, St Denys, Bevois Mount and beyond – but the perpetrators remained at large. The question was, what would they do next?

Would they run? Or would they hide?

15

09.13

Alan Sansom had worked in Portswood for over thirty years. He had diligently helped his father run the family pharmacy, before eventually taking over management of the shop when it became too much for him. As a young man, he'd had visions of expanding their business, of opening more branches, perhaps becoming the Lloyds of the south. It hadn't panned out that way, but he wasn't one to grumble, and it still gave him a small thrill to see his family's name above the door.

Day after day, year on year, the shoppers of Portswood had encountered Alan, stationed behind the pharmacist's counter in his white coat, and during that time he had seen it all. Portswood was slowly gentrifying itself, but it was still a major magnet for students, immigrants and the like. There was a ready supply of cheap, rented accommodation available locally, young people living cheek by jowl in shoddily converted houses. You got your rough elements of course and many of them had found their way into Alan's shop at some time or other. Junkies begging for drugs, care-in-the-community types railing at God, schoolchildren filling their pockets with sweets, the list was endless. It was Alan's vocation to do good, but some days he really despaired of humanity.

This morning his eyes were glued to a couple hanging around by the entrance. They had been in the shop for a little while now but seemed in no hurry to make a purchase. The woman had her back to him and was loitering by the sunglasses stand, twirling it round and giggling as she tried on different pairs. She looked like she was just killing time . . . but he was less sure about the man. He was hidden from view and Alan couldn't quite see what he was up to, which made him nervous. He had a good radar for these things and his instincts were telling him that something about this pair wasn't right. It was a nice day, but both were wearing heavy, knee-length coats – a common ploy of shoplifters the world over.

Normally he might have observed them for a little longer before making his move, but he was tired and irritable today after another bad night's sleep. So, lifting up the counter hatch, he walked briskly across the store. It was a large space, generally popular and well patronized, but it was too early for the morning rush, and Alan hoped to deal with the pair swiftly and discreetly. This was his shop and he would not be made a fool of.

'Ok, you two, I'm going to have to ask you to buy something or clear off. This isn't an amusement arcade.'

He had used this line before and it usually had the right effect. This time it seemed not to do the trick, however. Indeed it only seemed to make the man smile. Sansom took him in properly for the first time. He was a big brute of a guy, unshaven, with a tattoo on his neck.

'On your way. This isn't a refuge or a charity and I have better things to do than –'

'Take it easy, fella,' the man replied, pulling a shotgun

from his coat and pointing it straight at the stunned pharmacist. 'You're closing early today.'

Alan stood stock still, too shocked to react. But the young woman was on the move already and to his horror he saw her reach up and turn the key in the security lock just above the shop entrance. With a deep, metallic groan, the security shutters started to descend, juddering to a halt as they eventually hit the floor.

16

09.35

His eyes were glued to the screen. The dogs were getting restless, confused by the lack of activity, but he ignored them. The image on the screen in front of him demanded his attention, sickening though it was. A press helicopter had managed to get above the site of the 'police incident' and was beaming live pictures from the scene. Peter Smalling took in the white tent, the forensics team, the uniformed officers guarding the area, full of purpose and self-importance. Too fucking late, he thought to himself bitterly.

It was just gone nine thirty. How much life can change in a couple of hours. He had been so content this morning, him and the dogs bounding through the woods. He'd been full of ideas, full of schemes, thinking how he could pack the boys off to his sister's the following weekend, so that he and Sonia could get away for their anniversary. He had worked it through in his head, had a couple of nice B&Bs in mind – it seemed utterly impossible to him that they wouldn't celebrate another milestone.

He had been watching the news since the police officers left. He hadn't called anyone, though they'd urged him to do so. They'd said that people find it hard to focus when in shock, that it's dangerous to drive and had gently suggested that his sister might pick the boys up today. But there was no way he was going to let that happen. It was his responsibility to break the news to them, though what he was going to say he had no idea. What *could* he say?

The newsreader was saying that it was a robbery, though the officer – DS Brooks – had deliberately avoided confirming that. She suspected it was something else – something more targeted – though she wouldn't say what. Her caution had unnerved him, hinting as it did at darker motives. They had taken her car – were perhaps joyriding around Southampton even now – it had to be robbery, didn't it? And yet they *had* left her purse, her jewellery . . .

A tear dropped on to his hand and Peter realized he was crying again. Sonia had never been one for flashy jewellery, but she had treasured her wedding ring. They'd found a small jeweller's in Portsmouth they liked and had had their rings made there. Matching ones in white gold, slightly squared in shape to make them more distinctive, with their joint initials etched on the inside, so they could always be close to each other, even when apart.

The rings had been very special to them, symbols of the unspoken commitment they had made to each other. They'd planned to grow old and fat together, but the woman he'd loved more than life itself was now lying dead in a police mortuary. And the ring she'd so cherished was being tugged from her finger by a faceless mortician.

It was an image that punched him in the heart and Peter dropped his head and wept.

17

09.40

'Do we have any sightings? Do we have any idea which direction they went in?'

Helen was standing by Sonia Smalling's Audi, flanked by Charlie and Sanderson. An eagle-eyed PC had spotted the abandoned vehicle in a disabled parking bay in central Portswood and had called it in immediately.

'Nothing so far,' the PC answered. 'We've asked in Sainsbury's, a couple of the newsagents and off licences, but nobody's seen anything . . .'

Thanking the PC, Helen turned to his superior, Sergeant MacDonald, who stood nearby, flanked by a sea of blue uniforms.

'I want your officers to visit every shop, business and residence within a half-mile of the abandoned car. We're looking for two suspects – they'll be pumped up, potentially acting aggressively. Tell your officers to proceed with caution. One or both of them may be armed.'

As the sergeant set about organizing his search team, Helen turned to Charlie.

'Are there any probation offices around here?'

'No, they're all down in Totton.'

'Any of Smalling's probationers – past or present – from this neck of the woods?'

'No, she works with those from the south of the city.'

'So why have they come *here*?'

Charlie shrugged, as Helen looked once more at the car. The parking bay in which the car had been abandoned was intended to allow disabled shoppers easy access to the nearby pedestrianized precinct and Helen's gaze drifted that way now. It was still early in the day but already the shops were busy, the central avenue clogged with pensioners, mums and young professionals.

'You and I will take the precinct,' she told Charlie. 'It's a decent place to lose yourself in the crowds, plus there's plenty of shops if they need to lift some supplies –'

'And plenty of potential hostages too.'

'Exactly. In the meantime,' Helen continued, turning to Sanderson, 'I'll need you to chase down CCTV. Try not to tread on the toes of uniform, but some of the businesses round here must have cameras. I want a good image of our suspects.'

'Wouldn't I be more use assisting y—'

'Now, please.'

Reluctantly, Sanderson withdrew. Helen could tell she wasn't happy, but she didn't have time to consider her feelings – not when the stakes were so high. Gesturing to Charlie to follow, Helen hurried across the road in the direction of the shopping precinct. Instead of leaving Southampton altogether, the fugitives had fled to a densely populated, residential area and she wanted to know why.

18

09.41

Sweat was crawling down his temples, his heart beating out a furious rhythm, but Alan Sansom told himself to keep calm. He had been trained for this and knew the drill – in the event of a robbery, you do as you're told and wait until the perpetrators are long gone before calling the police. Training, however, was one thing, the reality something else. He had never been threatened with a *real* gun before.

He was kneeling down, his hands tied firmly behind his back. The huge brute of a man had marched him at gunpoint to the back office and forced him to open the safe. It had been duly emptied and the man was now rifling through the pharmaceuticals that were stored here out of harm's way. Alan had been ordered to face the wall, which was a mere two inches from his nose, but out of the corner of his eye, he could see the man at work. Predictably, he was ignoring all the bog standard products – ibuprofen, decongestants, energy powders – in favour of the more valuable products. Methadone, amphetamines, maximum-strength codeine tablets – he seemed to be zeroing in on these, shoving packets of them into a canvas holdall.

The woman stood by the door, her back to him as she kept an eye on the shop beyond. Of the two, she seemed the keener to get going, while the man was clearly enjoying himself. He looked like a kid in a sweet shop, picking up the boxes of drugs and kissing them, before dropping them in his bag.

'Hurry up, babe,' she hissed at her accomplice, 'we haven't got all day.'

Alan knew he was powerless here, but still it made his blood boil. This was his shop, his business. What right did they have to come in here, truss him up, order him around? He was a respectable businessman, someone who contributed to society and what were they? A pair of thugs.

Suddenly Alan was filled with a desire to bring this pair to book, to call them to account when the time came. He had a decent idea of what the bloke looked like, but he hadn't had a proper look at the woman. She had commandeered a pair of faux aviator sunglasses from his stand, which were offset by a candy-pink baseball cap. It was a pretty colourful way to conceal your identity but it worked. If asked to identify her, he wouldn't have been able to provide a single salient detail, apart from her long, blonde hair of course.

The woman still had her back to him, so he decided to chance his arm. Better that than sitting here like a dummy, as his shop was looted. It wouldn't do to be caught staring, however, so very slowly, inch by inch, he began to rotate his head. With just a quarter-turn, she would be in his line of sight. He could note her particulars, while she was busy scanning the store, then return his gaze to the wall until this awful ordeal was over.

The woman had gone very quiet now, so Alan paused

briefly, fearful of detection. But no abuse came his way, so he continued to move.

And now he saw her. But, to his surprise, she was not keeping an eye on the shop. She was looking directly at him.

Smiling, she peered over the rim of her aviators and said:

'You looking at *me*, honey?'

19

09.43

'Jesus Christ!'

Martin Gardener virtually spat his coffee over his desk, as he took in the pre-autopsy photos that Emilia had laid in front of him.

'How the hell did you get these?' he asked.

'A resourceful journalist has her ways . . .' Emilia replied, trying not to sound too smug.

'We can't print them.'

'Obviously not, but I thought you'd want to see them anyway. Sonia Smalling was married, had two kids, a worthy job . . . and someone's blown a bloody great hole in her. Two to be precise, but it looks like one because –'

'All right, all right . . .'

Gardener was a dick, but he was married with children and was clearly affected by the images in front of him. Which is what Emilia had been counting on.

'Anything from the widower?'

'He's not answering his phone and there are uniformed officers front and back at the house.'

'I thought you had the plod wrapped around your little finger,' Gardener commented, a little too sarcastically for Emilia's liking.

'But he will have to pick up his boys from St George's

Prep School.' Emilia ignored the jibe. 'So I'm hoping to grab a word with him there.'

'Make sure you get pictures.'

'What do you take me for?'

Gardener declined to answer that one, so Emilia pressed on:

'I've roughed out a shape for the copy, but I'm going to need the first three pages. On the front, I want to go big on the peaceful country road, lone woman, brutal shooting, death on a quiet autumn day. On the inside pages we'll focus on her and her family. Get testimonials from some of the people she's helped, colleagues, friends and then a paragraph about the people she's left behind, the boys growing up without a mother. The husband seems clean – never even had a parking ticket. I'm not sure we're going to get much from that angle, so we'll major on the family torn in two, the sense of shock in her village –'

'"We"?'

'Yes, "we",' Emilia responded quickly, stung by the implication. 'I was first on the scene, this is my story.'

'But this is *my* paper.'

'Come on, Martin,' she cajoled, softening her tone. 'I know I was a bit of an idiot before, but I'm better than the stuff I'm being asked to do. Jonathan wasn't even aware of this story, until I told him about it. I think I have a right to have my name on the byline. If I have to share it, then so be it, but –'

'You're sharing nothing,' Gardener barked back. 'Your name won't be on the byline.'

'But –'

'You are not our Senior Crime Reporter. That position

is held by Jonathan Simmons. Which is why *he* will be writing this story.'

'That's not fair,' Emilia moaned, fully aware that she sounded like a five-year-old.

'It's entirely fair, given your disloyalty to this paper. More than that, it's what's going to happen.'

Gardener walked round his desk, thrusting the photos back into Emilia's hands, invading her personal space.

'You may think you're a hotshot, Emilia, but know this. You are going to have to bring me a hatful of these stories before you are back in my good graces . . .'

He paused before he delivered the punchline:

'No pun intended.'

20

09.44

Helen weaved through the crowds of shoppers, scanning the pedestrianized walkway. Charlie was close behind her, but was struggling to keep up due to the myriad obstacles in her path. Pensioners were stopping to chat, toddlers were darting here and there and young schoolgirls pretty much walked right into her, scarcely looking up from their phones as they did so. In the midst of all this, Helen stood tall, craning to get a look at the faces passing by.

Everything seemed calm, relaxed even. What had she been expecting? A gunfight? A trail of destruction? Truth be told, they weren't even sure yet what they were looking for. Two men? A man and a woman? They had no physical description, no clear idea even of what their perpetrators were wearing.

'See anything?'

'Nothing,' Charlie answered, from just behind her. 'You?'

Helen shook her head. The scene in front of her was so normal, so workaday, that Helen started to wonder if the killers had come here to lie low. Maybe they had friends who lived round here or had rented a place, knowing they would need a bolt-hole? Perhaps Helen's instincts earlier had been wrong, perhaps this morning's murder was unplanned – a moment of rage or a terrible aberration – and now the suspects just wanted to disappear, to get their heads together, while they worked out what to do next.

But now as Helen surveyed the scene, she spotted it. This was a popular precinct, where all the shops did a good trade. Which is why it struck her as odd that one of the most centrally placed outlets was closed. The shops that flanked it were warm and welcoming, very much open for business, but the dirty shutters at Sansom's pharmacy were firmly closed. It looked odd, out of place, like the first tooth in a toddler's mouth. A couple of bemused shoppers stood outside chatting, clearly surprised that their plans had been disrupted.

Helen changed course abruptly, heading directly towards the shop. Instinct was guiding her now, the sense that something was wrong. She hoped she was mistaken, that there was a mundane, logical explanation for the shop's closure. But as she neared the shop front, her hopes were suddenly extinguished. A loud bang rang out, muffled by the shutters, but still clearly audible. Then another, harsh and percussive. The shoppers were already moving away, alarmed and confused by this strange noise, but Helen brushed past them, sprinting in the opposite direction.

She knew exactly what it was.

21

09.46

Melissa Hill crouched down behind the display, barely daring to look.

She had been hiding back here since it started. She had popped into the chemist's straight after breakfast, as they were out of both formula milk *and* nappies. The baby section was at the rear of the shop, round an L-shaped corner, and at first she hadn't noticed the confrontation by the entrance. Then she'd heard shouting and to her horror had witnessed the shop's owner being marched towards the back of the store at gunpoint.

After that, things had gone quiet for a while. Melissa had no idea what was happening back there – she didn't really want to know – but she did want to get out of this shop. The security shutters were shut, however, and she wondered whether those robbing the store had the key. Either way, it seemed as if there was little chance of her reaching the front unnoticed – the woman was keeping a watchful eye on the interior of the shop.

It had been slow torture, sitting there doing nothing, but Melissa had no choice. So she'd kept herself out of sight, gently jigging Isla up and down in her sling to keep her asleep. Things had seemed relatively peaceful out back and for a moment Melissa wondered if the situation had calmed down a little. Then suddenly she heard raised voices and seconds later a deafening bang, then another, followed by a horrible silence.

Moments later, the two figures had bolted from the back office, upsetting a carousel of DVDs as they went. It crashed to the ground with a heavy thump and it was then, as Melissa backed ever closer to the display cabinet, that Isla started to stir.

'No, no, no . . .' Melissa whispered, jigging her baby up and down.

But the reverberation from the fallen carousel seemed to fill the room and Isla screwed up her face, upset and angry to have been disturbed. Melissa was scrambling for a dummy. She knew she had one somewhere and rummaged in her pockets for it. If she could keep Isla quiet, maybe they wouldn't notice her, maybe they would just leave . . .

Isla was making small moaning sounds now, so Melissa searched increasingly frantically. The wretched dummy wasn't in her coat pocket, so she tried her jeans, before remembering that she had stuck it in the side pocket of her rucksack. Thrusting her hand backwards, she shoved it into the netting and breathed a sigh of relief as her fingers settled on the gummy, plastic teat. Ripping it out, she brought it up to her baby's mouth.

But she was a second too late and Isla let out a piercing, agonized cry.

22

09.48

Emilia stormed back to her desk, cursing her life. She knew she had been reckless and selfish at times, but did she really deserve *this*? Sweating under the yoke of a mediocre editor at a regional newspaper? She had more journalistic instinct in her little finger than he did in his entire body. She had broken several major stories. What had he ever done? Increase their advertising revenue? He was a failed reporter masquerading as an editor and it made her sick to her stomach. Perhaps it was time to get out of journalism altogether – she was damned if she was going to demean herself in a role that was traditionally given to graduates, who in her experience had neither wit nor wisdom.

The rest of the newsroom was aware of both her progress and her mood as she stomped back to her desk. Looking up, she caught Jonathan Simmons's eye, but he wisely dropped his gaze to his monitor. He was nominally her line manager, but after his first attempt to assert himself – which had been firmly, and obscenely, rebuffed – had decided on a softly, softly approach. In truth, he now avoided Emilia, feeding off the scraps of stories handed to him by the police and other agencies, leaving her to please herself. Emilia suspected his strategy was to starve her out – and it was working. Her patience was wearing thin and she was a whisker away from jacking the whole thing in.

Landing on her chair with a thud, she flicked open her laptop. She was tempted to do it there and then – to pen a brief, cutting resignation letter. She had fantasized about this many times and it was only the thought of her family that stopped her. In times gone by they had had a good life, especially when she was commanding decent fees from the nationals, but now she was on a trainee's wage, life was considerably harder. She had several younger siblings, all of whom had come to rely on her since their father had been incarcerated. For Emilia this had been a price worth paying – she loathed the worthless bastard – but the responsibility occasionally ground her down. She loved her brothers and sisters, but they were feckless, seemingly incapable of holding down a job or contributing to the running of the household.

She closed her laptop, knowing full well that she wouldn't be writing a resignation letter today. Kicking her bin over peevishly, she slumped in her chair, defeated. She would have to finish her article today, but somehow she couldn't face it. Perhaps she needed a smoke? Or another coffee? Even these options bored her, so instead she picked up her earphones, which she now realized were still burbling away to themselves. Popping them into her ears, she leant back and closed her eyes, wanting to lose herself in the staccato drama of their despatches.

'Shots fired at Sansom's pharmacy. All Armed Response Units to proceed to Folly Lane shopping precinct. Two shots have been reported . . .'

Emilia sat bolt upright. Across the way, Jonathan Simmons was writing up *her* piece, but suddenly she didn't care. Scooping up her laptop, she killed the police feed, then tiptoed away from her desk as quietly as she could.

23

09.49

Helen tugged at the shutters for all she was worth, but still they refused to budge. The owner was clearly a stickler for security – this had presumably provided him with reassurance in the past, but what would it cost him now? Helen tugged again, but the stubborn defences refused to yield.

Helen heard footsteps behind her and she and Charlie were joined by two uniformed officers, breathless and overexcited.

'Help us get this thing open.'

The officers did as she'd instructed and now the shutters groaned but still resisted, as if determined to fight to the bitter end. Cursing, Helen redoubled her efforts and slowly they started to shift, lurching up a couple of inches. It wasn't enough and Helen urged them to try harder. A few more inches and one of them might be able to slide underneath.

As they heaved, she listened intently for sounds from within. But she could hear nothing. Was this a good sign or a bad sign? Were they too late? Had the shooters departed? Or were they lying in wait, preparing an ambush for them? Helen clocked a mobile Armed Response Unit pulling up across the way and beckoned them over. She cared little for her own safety, but even she baulked at facing two armed assailants with nothing but her radio and baton for protection. Best to let the professionals take point on this one – Helen had the distinct feeling she would be needed to deal with the aftermath.

Four armed officers raced over, their carbines cradled in their hands. They were ready to go in, but still the shutters refused to rise sufficiently, determined to shield those within from view. Every second counted, so Helen stepped aside, ordering the burly officers to pitch in.

'Over to you,' she barked. 'I need this open NOW.'

24

09.50

'Please don't hurt us. Please don't hurt us . . .'

Melissa couldn't stop herself, pleading for her life, for her baby's life, as the killers loomed over her. As soon as Isla had begun to cry, Melissa had panicked, dropping the dummy and clamping her hand over her baby's tiny mouth. This had only alarmed her daughter further and after that it was impossible to keep her quiet. She had shrieked and shrieked, growing ever more puce, and in the end Melissa had given up trying to stop her, dissolving into tears herself instead.

She had only stopped when she heard footsteps, fear forcing her to swallow her sobs. Slowly, casually, the man and woman had walked around the display to stand in front of her.

'What have we here?'

The man – six foot plus, with piercing blue eyes and a mocking expression – seemed to be enjoying himself, despite the blood he had just spilled. He seemed drunk on power, determined to milk the experience for all it was worth. The woman, who was significantly shorter and skinny with it, hung on his shoulder.

'A stowaway,' the man continued, smiling. 'Did we wake baby?'

Melissa stared back at him, tears staining her cheeks. She was too shocked, too terrified to respond.

'Bang!'

The man roared the word at them, provoking more shrieking from Isla.

'Shh, baby, everything's going to be ok,' Melissa whispered, burying Isla's face in her neck, furious that this man should taunt her child. What kind of animal was he?

'Get her purse,' the man ordered.

The woman obliged, wrenching Melissa's rucksack from her and rifling through the contents until she found her purse. Grimacing at the paltry contents of the latter, she tossed it into the holdall nevertheless.

'Well, that's us done,' the man resumed, arrowing a glance towards the security shutters.

Then Melissa became aware of noises outside. The shop had been deathly quiet since the initial burst of shooting, but now there were voices. And with them the sound of the security shutters straining. The rescue party had arrived.

Turning away from the shutters, Melissa realized that the man was staring straight at her. A thin smile stole over his face as he took her in. He seemed to be feeding off her fear, enjoying her discomfort.

'Now . . .' he said languorously. 'Which one of you wants to go first?'

Melissa stared at him. Surely he should be fleeing? Why would he linger?

'Please don't do this. You don't have to do this . . .'

But the man seemed not to hear her, raising his shotgun to Melissa's eye-level. Cowering, Melissa pulled her hands across her chest, determined to shield her baby from the shot. But the barrels of the gun swung lower, pointing directly towards Isla.

'No, no . . . she's just a baby . . . she can't tell them anything . . .'

The barrels swung back up to Melissa's face. A moment's relief, then the man turned them back towards the baby once more.

'Do what you want to me, but let her go.'

Melissa was desperate now, praying for the rescue party to burst in and save her, but still they didn't come.

'Maybe I will, maybe I won't,' the man said, raising the barrels back to Melissa's eye-line again and taking a step towards her.

Melissa was whimpering, her whole body shaking. She was desperate to live, but she was backed into a corner. So, shielding her baby, she closed her eyes and braced herself for what was to come.

25

09.58

'Get back. Will you please just get back!'

Sanderson's voice was hoarse from shouting, but she renewed her efforts, desperate to keep the gawpers away from the pharmacy. The Armed Response Unit still hadn't gained entry to the premises and the situation was live, but nevertheless passing shoppers couldn't help getting involved. Some of them already had their phones out, ready to start filming, despite having no idea what was actually going on.

Things were still chaotic outside, officers descending on the precinct from various parts of the city, and with Helen and Charlie on the front line it fell to Sanderson to marshal the reinforcements as best she could. She had sent some of them to support the armed officers but had deployed the rest as a human cordon, ringing the area outside the pharmacy to keep the public at a safe distance. Their numbers were few and the line stretched, but to her relief Sanderson saw another handful of uniformed officers hurrying towards her.

'Form up along here and get these people *back*,' she ordered.

They obliged and now, finally, they started to get a bit of traction, pushing the steadily growing crowd away from danger.

'Here, watch it!'

'Easy now!'

'What you doing? It's a free country . . .'

The usual complaints, accompanied by the customary insults. It infuriated Sanderson that these people didn't get it – she was trying to *protect* them – but all they were worried about was missing out. Did they really have so little in their lives that they would willingly put themselves in danger to get themselves on the news? It was a feature of modern life that Sanderson hated – everybody thought they were an eyewitness now, everybody a journalist. Nowadays when people should be intervening to stop a crime, or in this instance getting the hell out of the way, instead they wanted to record it, as if the whole thing were entertainment laid on for their benefit.

One of the officers had located some police tape and was passing it down the line. Sanderson grabbed it gratefully and passed it on. A couple of minutes later and the job was done – the scene was effectively sealed off. Just in time too, for, with a shower of sparks and a groan of metal, the security shutters finally gave up the fight. The team had decided to cut their way through using specialist equipment and, turning, Sanderson saw the Armed Response officers ready themselves for entry.

'What's going on in there?'

Sanderson turned back to find an elderly shopper had grabbed her by the arm.

'Are those *guns* they are carrying?'

'I can't tell you anything at this sta—'

'Has anyone been hurt?'

'What's happening?'

'Is it Mr Sansom?'

The questions rained down on Sanderson. She deflected them as best she could, telling them nothing, because she *knew* nothing. She had been trying – and failing – to source some CCTV of the fugitives when Helen had suddenly radioed through, ordering all CID officers back to the pharmacy. Sanderson had immediately been assigned crowd control duty, a job for a DC really, and had remained on the periphery ever since. She was aware that shots had been fired – though how many and with what impact she wasn't sure.

Each question seemed to underline her sense of impotence and ignorance, reminding her how far she'd fallen in the pecking order. Once she'd possessed Helen's confidence, but through her rash actions she had destroyed all her good work and nothing she did – *nothing* – seemed to make the situation any better.

She would remain in exile for good.

26

10.00

Inspector Sean O'Neill ducked through the gaping hole and ran to the nearest display case. Crouching down behind it, he paused, counting silently to ten, before moving around the display case and slowly forwards. Reaching the end, he held out a mirror to peer round the corner, then, satisfied that there was no movement, darted a look around.

Everything was still, the atmosphere hushed and heavy. Turning, he beckoned to his second-in-command to follow. Sergeant Ed McGarvey darted inside and made his way quickly over to his colleague, before signalling to the other two members of Red Team to join him. O'Neill watched with satisfaction as they made their way over to him swiftly but carefully, taking advantage of the cover provided. They had been working together as a unit for over a year now and during that time had seen their fair share of action. None of them had had to discharge their weapon – thankfully, given the paperwork that generated – but they had been in plenty of tense situations. Disarming a man with a machete, seizing a shipment of firearms, bringing in an entire gang at one point. These experiences had bonded them together, making them a slick and effective unit.

O'Neill turned back to the shop and considered his next move. Normally, he would announce the presence of armed police officers and ask anyone present to step forward with their arms in the air. But the threat of ambush was too great here, the evidence of the shooters' disdain for human life too evident, to do that. There was little to be gained by giving away their position.

He scrutinized the back of the shop once more, then gestured for his colleagues to fan out. He would take point as usual, but they would assume defensive positions either side of him, returning fire if necessary. They had spent years training for this and O'Neill knew that they wouldn't panic if the sound of shotgun fire suddenly rang out.

Easing the safety catch off his weapon, he took a step forward. Then another, then another. He was abreast now of another display and, crouching down, swung round the end of it. His weapon was raised and ready . . . but there was no one there. Now he moved forward more quickly, shadowed all the while by his team. There was a storeroom at the rear of the shop that he wanted to check out, but to get to it he would have to pass the final display cases, which might also provide good cover.

He moved forward cautiously, then suddenly stopped dead. He hadn't seen anything but had *sensed* movement, towards the rear of the shop, on the left. Someone raising a weapon? Readying themselves to strike? He inched forward, his eyes darting this way and that, calculating where and when the shooters might pop up. His gun was raised to eye-level, he was looking right down the sight, ready to pull the trigger, confident he could drop them if need be. He had been lucky so far in his career.

Without a word being spoken, the quartet moved forward in sync, padding closer, closer, closer to the final display case. Now a tiny noise ahead – something being nudged or dislodged perhaps – and Inspector O'Neill didn't hesitate. With lightning speed, he moved forward, rounding the end of the display.

'Armed poli—'

He was cut off by a high-pitched scream. In front of him was a trembling woman, with a finger jammed in a baby's mouth, rocking back and forth on the floor.

'Don't shoot,' she yelled. 'Please don't shoot . . .'

Peering intently towards the back of the shop to confirm that the coast was clear, O'Neill moved forward, scooping the woman up. Still cradling her baby, she collapsed into his arms.

'Are you ok? Are you or your baby injured?'

The woman didn't say anything.

'Can you tell me where the shooters are?' he continued.

But the woman just snuggled in closer to him and when she did speak, it was just to whisper:

'Please don't shoot . . .'

27

10.07

'Watch it! What do you think you're doing?'

Emilia turned to the lumbering oaf next to her and gave him her most withering stare, flashing her press pass at him. Reluctantly he backed down, moving an inch sideways in order to allow her to push towards the front of the cordon.

She had sped over to Portswood as fast as she could and was distressed to find a large crowd had already gathered outside the pharmacy. Putting her head down and her elbows out, she had managed to bully her way past the prams and pensioners, but on reaching the front realized that it had been a pointless endeavour. The cordon was a fair distance from the pharmacy, a strategically placed line of uniformed coppers shielding the shop front from view. Strain as she might, there was nothing she could see from this position.

Hugging her camera to her chest, she moved away from the cordon. She was now pushing past the very same people she had barged aside seconds earlier, with predictable results. She was accompanied by complaints and abuse all the way, but she ignored their vitriol. She had abandoned the newsroom, left her article unfinished and knew she had to return with more than third-hand testimony if she was to placate Gardener.

Breaking free from the crowd, she gazed at the scene. The line of officers near the shop was tightening up, linking arms and pulling their 'screen' even closer together. Behind them she could make out movement, though what was happening and who was involved she couldn't say. Nevertheless, she sensed that it was something significant, given the officers' reactions, so she scouted around for some way to gain a better view of proceedings. But there were no obvious solutions, the line of officers, plus the parked police vehicles, providing a natural barrier . . .

Now Emilia was on the move, having noticed that the nearest vehicle, a high-sided police van, was unattended and, better still, unlocked. Presumably in the rush to apprehend the perpetrators, the driver had forgotten to lock up. Emilia marched towards it, yanking open the driver's door. Hopping up into the cab, she put one hand on the top of the open door then, placing both feet on the driver's seat, eased herself upwards. Rising, she planted both hands on top of the roof, then lifted her foot on to the dashboard and pushed hard.

Within moments, she was on the roof. She would be clearly visible now to those below, should they chance to look this way, so she dropped on to her belly and wriggled forward. Reaching the edge of the roof, she peered over and was pleased to see that she had an unobstructed view of the shop entrance. Helen Grace was there, hovering by a hole that had been cut in the metal shutters, but she moved back quickly, as armed officers started to emerge. Grabbing her camera from her bag, Emilia teased off the lens cap and readied herself to shoot. She was expecting the culprits to be led out in cuffs, but to her surprise a young woman now emerged, supported by one of the armed officers.

Click, click, click.

Emilia fired off shots and was delighted to see as she did so that the woman had a baby strapped to her chest. The woman was saying nothing, just cradling her baby, but the image said it all and Emilia snapped away contentedly. The woman was ashen, her face startlingly white, and she looked very, very scared.

28

10.15

It was a sickening sight.

The Armed Response Unit had declared the building safe – the fugitives long gone – so Helen had headed quickly inside the pharmacy. She'd been told to go straight to the back office and proceeded there without delay, aware that a distressing discovery awaited her. Years of service had hardened her, but even so her hand went to her mouth, as she entered the small room. A middle-aged man was slumped forward on his knees, his jaw and half of his face blown away, his blood and brains decorating the floor around him. Helen took in the awful details – the impact burn, the clogged hair, the blood seeping into the fabric of his trousers – before raising her eyes to the empty safe. Why had his attackers done this when their captive was clearly cooperating?

'They went out the back way.'

Helen turned to find Charlie standing in the doorway.

'They pushed a couple of packing cases together in the yard, hopped over the back wall,' her junior explained. 'Sanderson's round there with uniform now, but . . .'

Helen nodded, returning her eyes to the scene in front of her.

'They didn't leave empty-handed,' she said eventually. 'They've emptied the safe and taken most of the good stuff.'

'So what are they? Thrill seekers? Junkies?' Charlie asked, taking in the packets of amphetamines that lay discarded on the floor around the owner's corpse.

'They certainly have a taste for rocket fuel. But that's not what's driving them. Everything that's happened so far has been well planned. They lie in wait for Sonia Smalling, then ambush her. They head here, lock themselves in, calmly go about their business. They kill a man in cold blood, even though it looks like he was cooperating with them –'

'You think they've killed before? That they have experience of this sort of thing?'

'The world is full of self-starters these days,' Helen countered. 'People who want to be famous, people who believe in a cause. Normally I'd be calling in anti-terrorism now, but the robbery element counts against that –'

'There must be easier ways to rob people though, surely?' Charlie interjected. 'They're looking at life sentences here.'

'So maybe it *was* personal. The victim's name is Alan Sansom,' Helen continued, looking down at the body once more. 'What connects him to Sonia Smalling? The latter dealt with junkies and thieves day in, day out. Is that the link? Was Sansom burgled at any point, did he dismiss any members of staff, did anyone have a grudge against him? This place is a long way from the scene of Smalling's murder, so it's an odd place to head to.'

'What if they just saw it en route? What if they were fleeing the first murder and saw an opportunity to stock up on drugs, cash. The chance to have a little fun . . .'

'If that's the case, we'll have to face up to it, but for now

I want us to search for *connections*. In the meantime, we need a better description of the killers. The CCTV in here is knackered – the wire feed has been cut – so we'll have to hope our survivor can enlighten us.'

Nodding, Charlie walked away, but Helen lingered a moment, taking in the brutalized corpse in front of her. She had hoped – prayed – that this morning's murder had been a one-off. But here was the proof that she was now confronting something darker, something bigger. She didn't feel ready for it, didn't have the strength for it, but she was once more being sucked into a nightmare. These killers were cold-blooded, clinical and utterly without mercy.

Though she might not realize it yet, Melissa Hill had just had a very lucky escape.

29

10.18

'I'm her sister! For God's sake, let me through . . .'

The police constable barring her way was eighteen, nineteen at the very most, and looked like a rabbit caught in headlights.

'I'm not supposed to –'

'Look at her, for God's sake,' Emilia persisted, gesturing to the young mother, who sat in the back of an ambulance, still cradling her baby. 'She needs me.'

The PC stared at the woman, swathed in a police blanket, then back at Emilia.

'Ok, give me your name, rank and number. I'm going to make a complaint to the Chief Constable. I have run all the way here, been worried out of my mind, I just want to make sure that she's ok.'

'All right, all right.' The officer gave in and ushered her through the cordon. 'But if anyone asks, it wasn't me . . .'

Emilia barely heard him. She was already marching over to the ambulance, keen to get there before someone more experienced recognized her. Climbing into it, she sat down on the bench – only then did the woman look up.

'How are you?' Emilia asked, full of concern.

'Ok . . . we're ok . . .' Melissa replied, looking a little confused.

'I'm so relieved to hear it. You've been through a terrible ordeal.'

The woman nodded but said nothing, returning her attention to her baby, who had quietened down at last.

'How many were there?'

'Two,' Melissa replied hesitantly, seemingly wrong-footed by the question.

'Two men? A man and a woman?'

'Who are you?'

Emilia plucked a card from her bag – it was one of her old cards, with *Chief Crime Reporter* embossed on it – and handed it to Melissa.

'I'm a journalist with the *News*. You've been through hell, but you're the sole witness to an awful tragedy,' Emilia said quickly, fully aware she was busking it now. 'And our readers will be very keen to hear about your experiences. We don't need to mention your child's name if you don't want to, but they'll want to hear about how you saved your little girl's life, how brave you've been –'

'Look, I'm not ready to talk to anyone –'

'Five minutes, that's all it'll take.'

'I haven't even spoken to the police properly yet, I can't be talking to the press.'

'I understand that and we can definitely pick this up later. How about I grab a quick picture of the pair of you and then –'

'OUT!'

Emilia turned to find a furious Charlie Brooks marching towards her.

'Charlie. How nice to see you agai—'

'I don't know how you got in here, but you're leaving.'

Charlie grabbed Emilia's sleeve and hauled her out of the ambulance.

'Steady on . . .'

'I'm sorry about this,' Charlie said, addressing Melissa now. 'There won't be any more intrusions.'

Emilia wanted to tell her where to go, but instead smiled sweetly, as an irate Charlie turned to her.

'Is it true that DI Grace let the perpetrators drive straight past her? After the Sonia Smalling murder?'

'Get out of my sight.'

'Any comment you'd like to make? I understand there were two perps –'

Now Emilia felt herself being propelled towards the police cordon, Charlie having taken her roughly by the collar.

'If I see you near a witness again, I'll have you arrested,' Charlie hissed, releasing Emilia suddenly.

The journalist stumbled a little, then regained her balance and composure. Smoothing down her jacket, she replied:

'Don't be a stranger, Charlie. There's more that unites us than divides us.'

Charlie was about to respond – forcefully – but Emilia had already turned and walked off. Win or lose, she always liked to have the last word.

30

10.28

It's amazing what some people will do.

Matthew Pritchard had risen late, after a heavy night's drinking. He was a third-year psychology student at Southampton University and last night had been the department's Freshers' bash. Usually this provided rich pickings for the older students, who appeared sophisticated and knowledgeable in the eyes of young women who were away from home for the first time. Many of his mates had gone back with company but – for reasons he couldn't fathom – he had not. He had tucked into the whisky as a result, drowning his sorrows, and had woken feeling dehydrated, lethargic and generally irritable. Three cups of fennel tea and a long shower had helped a bit but he still felt washed out. Which is why he was now perched by his first-floor window, watching the world go by.

This was something he enjoyed. All sorts of folk drifted by on the street below – mums, pensioners, students, crooks, coppers, even the occasional junkie or prostitute, wandering home after a busy night. You could tell so much about someone just by the way they looked, the way they moved, and Matthew liked to make up stories for them, imagining what their lives were like. He pictured where they lived, their families, and invented places they were going, things that they were trying to achieve. Sometimes people surprised him by actually doing something interesting – vomiting, shrieking with laughter, even attempting to snatch a bag – but the two in front of him now really took the biscuit.

He had spotted them when they were still fifty yards away. Something about them seemed weird – perhaps it was the long coats they were both wearing, or her odd combination of mirrored aviators and pink baseball cap. They looked as if they had dressed up for the day in costumes that didn't quite fit the occasion.

They certainly looked like trouble, walking fast along the street, casting occasional glances behind them. At one point, Matthew thought they had looked straight up at him and he had withdrawn slightly, but they had carried on unperturbed, so perhaps he was imagining it. He had been expecting them to march straight past his flat, but to his surprise they had suddenly come to an abrupt halt. Then, having cast quickly around to check that the coast was clear, they set about breaking into the small Fiat parked just outside his front door. Bold as brass. Having failed to pop the lock, the burly-looking guy grabbed the upper rim of the passenger's door and started to bend it back. It seemed to give relatively easily and soon the man was able to reach in and unlock the door from the inside. This would have been harder if the car had had an alarm, but of course all the cars round here were owned by students.

It all happened so quickly that it was only now that Matthew thought to grab his phone. Snatching it up, he opened the camera app, flicked it to 'video' and hit 'record'. The pair were in his viewfinder and he watched on as they pulled open the door. They paused to kiss briefly, then climbed inside, the bloke immediately getting stuck into the task of hotwiring the aged vehicle.

Within two minutes they were gone. Matthew stopped his recording, both shocked *and* impressed. He had witnessed a number of criminal acts in this neighbourhood, but few that had been executed with such practised ease. The thieves were clearly not amateurs and presumably knew which roads to target. It just served to confirm what he had long suspected – you couldn't trust anyone in this part of town.

31

10.31

'Tell me exactly what happened.'

Melissa Hill was cradling a cup of tea as she sat in the back of the ambulance with Helen. Melissa's baby was now being cared for by a paramedic, who was bouncing the little girl up and down on her knee. She seemed to have forgotten her terror and was gurgling and smiling at her playmate, which moved and surprised Helen in equal measure.

'I . . . I'd just popped in to get some things for Isla. Formula, nappies, y'know . . .' Melissa began faltering. 'I hadn't even got anything yet, I'd just come in when the owner walks past. Didn't even see me, he wanted to talk to two people who were messing around with the sunglasses.'

'Describe them to me.'

Melissa closed her eyes for a moment, her body shaking slightly. Helen could tell that she was back in that shop with them and laid a comforting hand on her arm.

'Take your time . . .'

Melissa exhaled – long and slow.

'A man and a woman. He's tall, six feet or more, she's shorter, five two, five three . . .'

'White, black, Asian . . . ?'

'Both white. He's got short, brownish hair, she's got shoulder-length blonde hair.'

Helen nodded and shot a look at Charlie. This was better.

'How old are they?'

'He's early twenties probably, she's late teens.'

'And what were they wearing?'

'Both were wearing trench coats, knee-length, khaki colour. He was bareheaded, she was wearing a pink baseball cap and aviators. And he had a knife . . . a kind of hunting knife strapped to his chest.'

Tears pricked Melissa's eyes now, as the terror took hold once more. Helen stroked her arm, comforting her as best she could.

'You're doing really well, Melissa.'

Melissa gave a grateful smile and tried to gather herself.

'Were they both armed?'

Melissa nodded.

'With shotguns?'

'Yes, but they were sawn off.'

'Did they threaten you and Isla?'

Melissa nodded again, clutching Helen's hand a little tighter.

'They . . . he wanted to kill me. He joked . . . he joked about who he would shoot first, me or Isla . . .' she continued, her voice quivering.

'Why do you think he didn't do it? Was he disturbed? Did we scare him off?'

Melissa shook her head vigorously.

'I could hear you trying to get in, *they* could hear, but he didn't seem to care. He was going to do it, then *she* stopped him.'

Helen nodded.

'How did she do that?'

'She just grabbed him by the arm and told him not to bother.'

'Exact words, please, Melissa.'

Melissa closed her eyes once more, unwillingly returning to her trauma.

'She put her hand on his arm and said, "Come on, J, she's not worth it."'

And, with that, Melissa Hill broke down.

32

10.35

Helen marched away from the ambulance, Charlie by her side. Melissa had told them all she could, so she'd organized for her to be reunited with her husband and returned home under police guard. They would have to talk to her again in due course – to get a formal statement – but she had done more than enough for now.

Reaching the end of the shopping precinct, the pair cut right, before turning right again shortly afterwards, bringing them around to the back of the pharmacy. The shop backed on to a quiet residential street, characterized by rather tired-looking Victorian houses and a scattering of low-end cars. Helen surmised that this road would normally be dead but today it was busy with uniformed officers, knocking on doors and stopping passers-by.

Sanderson was standing in the middle of the street, marshalling their efforts. Helen didn't dawdle, marching straight up to her.

'What have we got?' Helen asked.

'A pensioner in number twenty-two saw a man hurrying down the road about half an hour ago, but she swears he was by himself. So it's possible that they've split up.'

'Did she describe what he was wearing?'

'T-shirt and jeans, she said.'

'Carrying anything?'

'Not that she remembers.'

'Sounds like a dead end. Our guys are tooled up, wearing long coats, carrying stuff they've taken from the pharmacy . . . And, besides, I don't think our pair will split up willingly. It was probably just someone who heard the shots or the sirens. Have any vehicles been taken?'

'A student at number five says she saw a dark saloon pull away sharply. It would be around the right time, but she wasn't able to see who was in the vehicle –'

'Make? Model?'

'She's not sure and she didn't get the plate –'

'What else?'

'We're still knocking on doors –'

'So we've no idea which direction they headed in, nor whether they're in a vehicle or on foot?'

'Not yet. But give us time –'

'We don't have time,' Helen shot back. 'This pair have killed twice in a matter of hours and my guess is that they're not finished yet. Get me some concrete information, something I can *work* with . . .'

Nodding, Sanderson hurried off to confer with her uniformed colleagues. Helen watched her, seething with frustration at their lack of progress. A pair of killers were at large in Southampton, committing acts of murder with impunity, and nobody had witnessed *anything*. Were the perpetrators lucky or cunning? Time would tell, but for now they seemed to be able to ghost into people's lives, kill and then vanish without a trace.

33

10.57

The car came to a gentle stop and he killed the engine. They were out of sight now, parked up in an alleyway near South Hants Hospital. A long line of lock-ups flanked them – lock-ups that were seldom visited. It was the perfect place to hide away for an hour or so, until things quietened down a bit.

They had listened to the radio as they drove. Reports were filtering through of a 'major incident' in Portswood – he'd loved that – and local journalists were starting to make the connection with the earlier road closure near Ashurst. Information was thin on the ground, but you could sense the fear and excitement in the newscasters' voices – something big was starting.

Turning off the radio, he got out of the car. His companion did likewise, crossing to him quickly. She grabbed him by the collar, kissing him fiercely. He responded, his hands straying to her bottom, pulling her towards him, when a sudden noise made him stop.

It was a deep, dull noise, loud and repetitive. *Thunk*, *thunk*, *thunk*. He was bemused at first – feeling the first sudden stab of fear – then slowly he started to raise his gaze, following the direction of the sound.

'Look, babes . . .'

She had spotted it and now he did too. And the sight brought a big smile to his face.

'They've sent a chopper after us . . .'

Helicopters weren't an uncommon sight in Southampton. There were the few rich tossers who flew to the docks and the inevitable traffic choppers. But these moved fast and on well-prescribed routes – this one was taking its time, circling the city, searching, searching, searching . . .

The sound seemed to be getting louder, so instinctively he withdrew, pulling her with him. They hid beneath the lip of a lock-up roof, remaining perfectly still as their eyes followed the helicopter's slow, measured progress. It seemed to linger over them, turning circles, before eventually it cut west, away from the hospital environs. Neither moved until its gentle thrum was a distant sound once more.

She giggled and he responded. It seemed crazy that a helicopter had been scrambled to search for them – it was beyond what they had hoped for – and it was thrilling to think that they were now the objects of a police manhunt. Had the cops circulated descriptions of them? What did they know? At first he had regretted leaving a witness alive, but it had definitely upped the stakes. Would they catch them now they had something to play with? Or would the fugitives continue to slip through their fingers?

He was suddenly filled with a feeling of power, of certainty. Like they were untouchable. Able to do whatever they wanted, *whenever* they wanted. Turning to her, he took her in his arms. She seemed to be feeling it too. Perhaps it was the uppers. Perhaps it was the adrenaline. Both felt exhilarated and free.

She kissed him again and this time he didn't hold back. Their tongues locked and, as he ran his hands down her back, he felt his arousal growing. Pushing her back on the bonnet, he peeled off her coat, pulled open the buttons on her shirt and thrust his hand inside. She responded, biting his ear. She was hungry like him, exhilarated. And now she took control, sliding off her trousers and knickers in one fluid movement, before pulling her lover on to her.

34

11.01

The vibrations seemed to ripple through her, as the helicopter passed overhead. Anna Sansom was stuck in a traffic jam, her car boxed in, and she had felt the helicopter's approach before she saw it. It was flying very low, its rotary blades beating angrily, and the whole car seemed to shake as it swept over her and away. Her nerves were jangling enough as it was and it had left her feeling shaken and uneasy.

She had been trying to get hold of Alan for nearly an hour now, but her calls kept going to voicemail. That wasn't like him, Alan's phone was always charged and by his side, in case a supplier or customer tried to contact him. She hoped that he just had no signal, but she was starting to wonder. A neighbour had popped round, telling her that there had been 'an incident' at the shopping precinct, enquiring if Alan was ok. Anna didn't listen to the radio much and had been confused at first, hardly taking in what Joan was saying. Her neighbour had a tendency to exaggerate, to create drama where there was none, and Anna had been confident that a quick phone call to her husband would clear things up. But a dozen attempts later Anna was none the wiser. Was it possible that the mobile networks had crashed, like they had in London during

7/7? The thought made her shiver. Surely they weren't dealing with something like *that*?

But the presence of a police helicopter wasn't reassuring. It seemed to be fanning out from central Portswood, flying in ever larger circles, moving away from her, then returning towards her once more. Though she hated flying, part of her wished she was up there with them, rather than stuck down here. At least then she would know what was going on. She had fiddled with the radio, dragging the frequency away from Alan's jazz staple to the local news, but there was scant detail in any of the reports. The police had not given a press conference, provided no tangible information, though the gist of things seemed to be that shots had been fired in a Portswood shop and that there had been casualties. Everything else was speculation.

Perhaps Alan was helping out, tending to the injured – that would be just like him. He had always had a sense of vocation – while also having a commercial head on his shoulders – and would have wanted to use his training to good effect. Yes, that was probably it. She hoped he wouldn't be too shaken up by it – he was far more sensitive than he ever let on.

Anna had her eyes glued to the returning helicopter and jumped out of her skin when her phone suddenly rang. She snatched it up, answering it swiftly, but was surprised to find a female caller on the other end.

'Mrs Sansom?'

'Who is this?'

'My name is Emilia Garanita. I'm –'

'Whatever it is, it'll have to wait. I'm trying to keep this line free in case my husband calls.'

Invoking her husband's name generally did the trick, but the woman on the other end seemed undeterred.

'I'm assuming you've heard about the incident in Portswood?'

'What of it?' Anna said busily, suddenly keen to be rid of this woman.

'Look, Mrs Sansom, I'm a journalist with the *News* and it's my duty to pass on what information I have.'

Suddenly Anna Sansom felt a chill run down her spine.

'What are you talking about? I've told you that I'm waiting on –'

'I'm really sorry to have to tell you this, but your husband was involved in the incident earlier this morning . . . The shooting, I mean.'

'I'm not having this conversation.'

'I'm not after a comment,' the voice on the other end continued, somewhat unconvincingly, 'but I thought you ought to know. The police are terrible about getting in touch with the next of ki—'

'It's not true.'

'Believe me, I wish it wasn't, but –'

Anna ended the call. Moments later, her phone rang again, but she ignored it. 'Number withheld'. Who were these people, who'd ring you up out of the blue, suggesting all kinds of things . . . ?

Anna gripped the steering wheel hard, staring straight ahead. The traffic was beginning to move now, uniformed officers diverting the vehicles away from Portswood. Away from what? Horrible images flooded Anna's head, but she pushed them away. Alan was fine. She would know if he wasn't. Somehow she would know.

Wouldn't she?

35

11.15

They were walking fast along the corridor, marching towards the incident room. Charlie had been debating how best to broach the subject – or indeed whether to mention it at all – but had not hit on a subtle or clever approach yet. She felt she had to say *something*, however, so, as the incident room came into view, Charlie took the plunge.

'Before we start the briefing, can I have a word with you about DS Sanderson?' Charlie said, keeping her voice low.

'What about her?' Helen responded, barely breaking stride.

'I think she's feeling a bit exposed at the moment, a bit isolated . . .'

'From whom?'

'You,' Charlie said quickly, keen to get it out in the open before they entered the office.

'And why would she be feeling that?' Helen replied tersely, finally slowing her pace and turning towards Charlie.

'Because of all that's gone on, the Robert Stonehill investigation, her part in your arrest –'

'We've been through this. I sat her down and we talked about it –'

'But you haven't forgiven her,' Charlie interrupted, surprising herself by her bluntness.

Helen said nothing, staring at her. Charlie knew that her boss disliked being reminded of her arrest and her time behind bars – understandably she wanted to move on, start a new chapter in her life – but Charlie had the distinct sense that Helen was punishing Sanderson.

'I know it must be difficult for you to feel you can trust her again – I get that, I really do – but she's a good police officer and she's been a good friend to me this past year,' Charlie went on.

'Is that where this is coming from?'

'No, of course not. I just think we could be using her more –'

'And that's your call, is it? How I deploy my team?'

'You should talk to her. If there is a problem between you, then you should deal with it. For everyone's sake.'

Charlie had hoped to present it as a process that would benefit everyone. And it was true – she was thinking about Sanderson, but also of Helen. She didn't want her old friend and ally to become bitter, to be permanently damaged by her traumatic experiences.

'Look, Charlie,' Helen responded carefully, struggling to control her emotions, 'I know you're trying to be helpful, but this is neither the time nor the place. Maybe there's a grain of truth in what you're saying, maybe I do lean too heavily on you, but we are in the middle of a *major* investigation –'

'Which is why we need our best people.'

'I'll decide who I use and who I –'

'Don't freeze her out, Helen. That's all I'm say—'

‘A woman died in my arms this morning,’ Helen interjected bluntly, raising her voice. ‘I tried to save her, but there was nothing I could do. I had to watch her die in front of me . . .’

Charlie stared at Helen, silenced by this sudden outburst.

‘My first responsibility now – my *only* responsibility – is to catch those who killed her. Until we do, all matters relating to . . . personnel are going to have to wait. Is that clear?’

Cowed by Helen’s harsh tone, Charlie said nothing.

‘Is that clear?’ she repeated, louder this time.

Helen was staring directly at her, challenging Charlie to defy her. But she didn’t, nodding mutely instead.

‘Then let’s get on with it,’ Helen concluded, opening the door to the incident room and marching inside.

Charlie watched her go, feeling angry and annoyed, then followed suit.

36

11.21

'Our first task is to work out who this "J" is.'

The incident room was busier than usual, officers on leave having been recalled to duty. Charlie joined DC Edwards and DC Reid at the front of the group, casting an eye over the officers' faces, as Helen began her briefing. The vibe in the Major Incident Team had been odd of late, but today everybody was paying attention.

'Where are we at with Sonia Smalling's list of probationers?'

'Well, there are thirty-four men or boys whose first name begins with the letter "J",' DC Reid replied, pulling the names up on to the big screen.

'That's too many,' Helen told him. 'Let's narrow it down to men in their early twenties, who've had contact with her in the last eighteen months.'

Reid typed some more and the list swiftly shrank.

'That leaves us with eight names.'

'Now pull up those who have a history of drug abuse.'

'Ok,' Reid replied, typing.

'And let's prioritize those who have been accused or convicted of assault, aggravated burglary or possession of a weapon.'

'Three names,' Reid concluded. 'John MacDonald, Jason Swift and James Bennett.'

'Thank you.' Helen turned to McAndrew. 'DC McAndrew, I want you to take their mugshots to Melissa Hill. Ask her if she recognizes any of these men.'

'Straight away,' McAndrew acknowledged, gathering up her things.

'The rest of you are going to check out these three suspects,' Helen continued, turning back to the wider group. 'Medical history, charge sheets, family background, known haunts and of course any connection to Sonia Smalling or Alan Sansom. Let's climb inside their lives and see if we can work out what's caused this sudden explosion of violence.'

The room was silent now. The officers present could tell Helen wasn't finished yet.

'There will have been signs that this was coming. The robbery element of these crimes seems like a means to an end – stealing a car to get them to Portswood, amphetamines to keep them going. These murders are about something else. Our perpetrators are *angry* – with their families, their employers, the community they live in, because of slights or injustices they've endured . . .'

'Does this mean they're not going to stop?' DC Edwards asked.

'Probably not,' Helen continued. 'These guys are on a roll now – they've gone too far to pull back, so they'll probably keep going until they are arrested or killed, or run out of ammunition. They seem to be well-armed and resourced, so the key is to find them and neutralize them as swiftly as possible.'

A sombre atmosphere filled the room, so Helen pressed on.

'When you're checking their medical records, look for a history of self-harm or suicide attempts. We may be looking at a pair of spree killers here – people who want to create as much carnage in as short a time as possible. If so, then it's likely their worlds have recently caved in for some reason. They are probably depressed, they may be on medication and it's likely they have attempted to take their own lives in the past. They have no hope and their crimes could be a case of suicide morphing into homicide. There will be a medical footprint pointing us in their direction. If anyone is flagged up, dive into their recent personal history. Visit the family home, talk to neighbours and friends. Nine times out of ten there will be a specific trigger incident – a crime committed, a family row, a death in the family, something that means there is no way back. Find out what it is. Find out who they are angry with and maybe –'

'We can work out where they will strike next,' DC Osbourne offered.

'Exactly. Obviously we have uniform out on the streets, but it's our job to predict their movements and try to get ahead of them. If we can, we have a fair chance of bringing them in safely. They may well have committed acts of vandalism against people or institutions they dislike – building up to something bigger – so run the rule over their recent charge sheets. Typically, killers of this kind exhibit a hostility to all forms of authority. So who have they targeted and why? Will they go back to finish the job?'

'What if their targets are random? What if they have no real plan?' Edwards asked, looking genuinely concerned.

'Then our job will be a whole lot harder. But if they are killing at random, why are they moving around? In those cases, the killings tend to be localized – in one building, one village – but these guys are moving to different areas of the city and they are being *careful*. Forensics haven't lifted a single fingerprint or DNA trace off the Audi, so our perpetrators are wearing gloves, they are not dropping hairs. I think they have a plan which they want to see through.'

'And are we sure that Sonia Smalling is an important connection? That we can definitely link our killers back to her?' DC Osbourne bravely piped up once more.

'No, but have you got any better ideas?' Helen replied, raising a couple of wry grins. 'The first murder might be random, but they lay in wait for her and ambushed her, and my gut tells me she wasn't selected by chance. On the face of it our two victims are very different – Sonia was married with kids, lived in the countryside, whereas Alan Sansom was childless, lived near the city centre. Their social lives don't overlap, they don't share the same hobbies, he was born in the UK, she wasn't, but . . . I believe their killings are linked. So let's get out there and find the connection.'

Helen had said enough and the team now got to work. Charlie organized them, dividing the officers into three separate groups and directing their energies and enquiries as best she could. Helen meanwhile walked back to her office, her mind turning on the morning's events. As she did so, she saw DC Reid approaching fast. She could tell by his manner that he had news.

'Just had this in,' he said breathlessly, holding up an

iPad for her to view. 'Sent in by a student in Portswood who heard the news on the radio.'

Helen took the iPad and stared at the image on the screen. It showed two figures – a tall man and a young woman – in the process of stealing an old Fiat. They were dressed in long, khaki coats and Helen's eyes were drawn to the young woman – with her blonde hair, pink cap and aviator shades.

Finally they had an image of their phantom killers.

37

11.59

'These are the two individuals we are looking for.'

Helen's voice rang out loud and clear across the packed media liaison suite. The snatched image of the two figures filled the screen above Helen's head.

'He is over six feet tall, with sandy brown hair. She is five two, five three, with shoulder-length blonde hair. Both are wearing knee-length, khaki-coloured trench coats. They were last seen on Alma Road in Portswood at around 10.30 this morning. We believe they are now in possession of a vehicle – a maroon Fiat Punto, registration number LB05THX. Anyone who thinks they have seen this vehicle or these individuals should contact the police *immediately*. I would like to stress that the suspects should not be approached.'

'Are you linking these two individuals to the incident at Ashurst and the shooting in Portswood?' a local journalist shouted out.

'Yes, we are.'

'And how many casualties are we looking at?'

'I'm not going to go into details on that.'

'Any fatalities?'

'As I said, I'm not going to –'

'Is it terrorist-related? IS or Daesh or whatever they are called now?'

There were a few suppressed chuckles from around the room. Helen was reminded how much she hated these events. Usually she ducked press conferences, but she had no boss to field them for her now, and, besides, this was too important to leave to anyone else.

'No, that's not a major line of enquiry.'

'So this is what? Two crazy kids? Some kind of vendetta?'

'I wouldn't call them kids,' Helen countered quietly. 'The male suspect is in his early twenties, she is late teens. They are young adults who for reasons we don't yet know –'

'What *do* you know for sure?' was the blunt response from the local BBC news reporter.

'We have a number of active lines of enquiry, but our most valuable resource is the eyes and ears of the public, which is why –'

'So you want the people of Southampton to do your job for you?'

'No, I want them to help us –'

'Do you have any idea where the suspects are now?'

'They were last seen in Portswood –'

'Where are they *now*?' a journalist from *The Times* pressed.

'We don't know, but we have dozens of officers combing the city, not to mention several mobile Armed Response Units –'

'So what you're saying is that you've got two shooters at large,' another journalist chipped in, 'and no idea where they are or when they might strike next?'

'It is a developing situation.'

'What are you actually doing to keep the people of Southampton safe?'

'Should you be imposing a curfew? Bringing in the army?'

'In my view, that would be premature,' Helen replied forcefully, raising her voice to be heard above the hubbub. 'Every officer on this force has been recalled to duty. We have two dozen highly trained armed officers who can be scrambled at a moment's notice, not to mention support from the police helicopter and our colleagues in Hampshire Transport Police. We are doing everything in our power and will not rest until the perpetrators are apprehended. *But* our best weapon is the vigilance of the public, which is why I am appealing for your help in sharing this crucial image and raising public awareness of these crimes.'

Helen spotted a journalist about to jump in, but got in first:

'That's all I have for you now. As I'm sure you can imagine, I am needed back in the incident room.'

This didn't stop the questions of course – they poured down on Helen now. But she didn't wait around to hear them, rising and heading for the door instead. She didn't need to be lectured or shamed – she had enough on her plate without a public crucifixion. As she pushed through the throng, her anger levels slowly rose. With her bosses for landing these media duties on her, and with the journalists who came here to point the finger, rather than report the news. Their panicked tone, their indignation, their aggressive accusations – it was so depressingly familiar and predictable. Indeed, the only aspect of this public lynching that had surprised Helen was the absence of one persistent, long-standing critic.

Emilia Garanita.

38

12.04

Her phone was buzzing insistently, but Emilia ignored it. Gardener had tried to get her three times already, but she had let all his calls go to voicemail. He was either going to bollock her for deserting the newsroom or quiz her as to what she was up to. Either way, Emilia had decided to let him stew in his own juice a little while longer. She had always had a flair for the dramatic and she would let him get to fever pitch before delivering her little scoop and silencing him once and for all.

Her replacement on the crime desk was a wet blanket. Simmons was probably at the police briefing now, dutifully taking notes, while she was ahead of the story. She had a positive fix on the number of casualties, plus an eyewitness interview (albeit brief) with the sole survivor and dramatic photos of the young mum and her baby being rushed to safety by armed officers. In the era of 24/7 news, in which everybody with a cameraphone was a journalist, exclusivity mattered. And nobody else had images of Melissa Hill's dramatic rescue.

Would they be on the front page of the *Southampton Evening News* tonight? Emilia still hadn't made up her mind. Her gut instinct was to contact the national papers, as this story was going to be big news. But she had had her fingers burnt before by the London papers and her reputation was still tarnished, following the hatchet job she'd done on Helen Grace. Her instinct for once was to stay local and milk it for all that it was worth. But could she be sure that Gardener would play ball? He had no time for Emilia – indeed she suspected he had little interest in women generally, and he was known to be stubborn and aggressive. Would he ever sanction promoting her over Simmons, or even dismissing her replacement, given that it would inevitably make his decision-making look suspect? Would he ever admit that he'd been *wrong*?

But Emilia was getting ahead of herself. First things first: she had to write her article. She was tucked away in a café that overlooked Portswood's pedestrianized shopping precinct. From her elevated vantage point she could see Meredith Walker and the forensics team plying their trade in and around the pharmacy – she had even taken a few photos of them at work to add colour to her article. Opening up her laptop, she began to compose the first few paragraphs in her head, as she waited for it to boot up. To her surprise, however, her old article sprang up on screen and she realized belatedly that she had forgotten to power down before leaving the newsroom. She cursed herself for her stupidity – the battery was running low now and there wasn't a plug within striking distance in the café – and was about to minimize her article angrily when suddenly she paused.

Her half-finished article was a classic piece of middle-class moralizing, bemoaning a recent spate of graffiti in Southampton. It wasn't particularly interesting or new, but it would get the local mums and dads going. Now, however,

Emilia looked at her article with new eyes, for tucked away by the side of her copy were a few photos of the graffiti in question. One of them, a striking image of a snake devouring its own tail painted on to a drab office building, leapt out at her now.

Because she had just seen exactly the same image spray-painted on the back wall of Sansom's pharmacy.

39

12.37

'I'm going to show you five faces. I want you to study them closely, then tell me if you recognize the man who threatened you this morning.'

Melissa Hill was sitting at her kitchen table, her baby balanced in the crook of her arm. Her husband, Gary, was present, having rushed back from work. He had urged her on several occasions to let him take Isla for a while. But Melissa wouldn't have it, hanging on to her child for dear life, even when faced by DC McAndrew on official police business.

Gary hovered in the background, looking on nervously as McAndrew pulled five mugshots from a slim file and slid them on to the table. McAndrew placed the last one down on the table and lifted his head to find Melissa staring intently at her baby.

'I'm going to need you to look at them, Melissa. I appreciate this may be unnerving for you, but you are safe now, nothing is going to happen to you.'

Melissa raised her eyes, taking in McAndrew, but avoiding the photos on the table. To McAndrew's mind, she was clearly still in shock. She should be resting, possibly even sedated, but she refused to relax, refused to let her guard down.

'Please, Melissa. Our best chance of catching this guy is if we have a positive ID. Without that it's very hard to know where to look. Once we know who he is, we can put his name out in the press, his photo too –'

'Ok, ok, there's no need to bully me,' Melissa cut in quickly, her voice shaking as she spoke.

Slowly she lowered her eyes to the mugshots. As she scanned the five faces, McAndrew ran her own rule over them. Three of them were their 'J's, the other two were control photos plucked from the system. Two of the 'J's had tattoos and Melissa seemed to be scrutinizing them now. McAndrew watched her closely as her eyes flicked back and forth between them.

Finally, Melissa exhaled, long and heartfelt, before reaching out and pointing to one of them.

'That's him.'

McAndrew nodded.

'How sure are you?'

'Hundred per cent.'

'Why so sure?'

'Because of the tattoo on his neck. I remember . . . it kind of bulged as he spoke to me. I'd recognize that disgusting thing anywhere.'

McAndrew thanked Melissa profusely, then hurried from the house, pulling her phone from her pocket.

At last, they had a name.

40

12.48

'Our prime suspect is Jason Swift.'

As soon as Helen had got McAndrew's call, she'd pulled everyone off their tasks, corralling them into the briefing room. McAndrew was the only absentee – everyone else was crushed inside the cramped room, hungry for new information. Helen pulled up Swift's mugshot – unshaven, sandy-coloured hair, with a distinctive skull tattoo on the right side of his neck – and alongside it his charge sheet.

'He's twenty-four years old. Plenty of cautions for vandalism, shoplifting, affray, but only one conviction – for aggravated assault with a weapon. He has, however, been questioned about a number of incidents in which ethnic minorities or foreigners have been threatened or attacked. Southampton's had its fair share of hate crimes recently and Jason Swift seems to be in the vanguard of these attacks. He is unemployed, has links to other troublemakers and has been questioned specifically about three attacks – one on an Asian shopkeeper, one on a young black male and one on a Polish waiter –'

'So this is about racism, about *hatred*?' DC Edwards asked.

'Possibly. Sonia Smalling was born Sonia Wojcik. She's from Poland and came to this country ten years ago.

Despite marrying and having kids here, she never lost her accent and was proud of her heritage. Alan Sansom was born and raised here, after his parents fled to England from Germany during World War Two. He is very prominent in the Jewish community in Southampton and orthodox in his religious views. We all know that attacks on synagogues have been on the rise since the referendum –'

'Because, of course, we all know *they* were responsible for Brexit . . .' Edwards drawled wryly, shaking his head.

'Organizations like Britain First and the English Defence League,' Helen continued, 'have stepped up their rhetoric against Muslims, Jews and others, with fairly predictable consequences.'

'So why hasn't he been charged? If he's been linked to three attacks –'

'Because the victims wouldn't press charges. They were scared, didn't want any trouble . . .'

This silenced the room – Helen's answer was as depressing as it was predictable. Sensing the energy levels in the room dropping, she pressed on:

'Three months ago, Swift threatened his social worker with a nailgun. He lives with his mum and survives on benefits, and his case worker obviously caught him on a bad day. He should have done jail time for it, but his lawyer managed to wangle a Community Payback sentence – which is where he came into contact with Sonia Smalling. True to form, Jason stopped turning up after the first couple of days.'

'And – let me guess – nobody followed it up?' Edwards chipped in.

'Doesn't look like it. He's registered as living at an address in Woolston. I've sent McAndrew there with an armed unit, though I doubt he'd choose such an obvious bolt-hole. We've tried to contact his mother, but she's not picking up.'

'Could she be a victim too? The *trigger* for all this?' Osbourne asked.

Helen ignored the uncomfortable gnawing feeling in her stomach: 'Let's hope not. We'll keep trying her, but so far we've had no joy. I have, however, asked media liaison to pass on Jason Swift's name to the press, so hopefully his mother will get wind of it and be in touch. I have drafted in extra operators for the comms room – be prepared to field a lot of leads in the next few hours. Some will be cranks, some will be mistaken, but some may prove useful, so we'll have to chase them all down.'

Helen rose now, handing photocopied files on Swift to the individual officers, who opened them and greedily read the contents.

'Any particular areas we should concentrate on?' DC Bentham asked.

'We've no addresses other than his mum's, so check out friends, family, but also the girl. Is she a girlfriend? A school friend? Could she be shielding him? Jason Swift has no place of work, only claims benefits once a week, so it's ground up on this one.'

Helen paused briefly, before concluding:

'We have to find Jason Swift.'

41

13.01

He sat on the cheap plastic seat, his eyes glued to the screen in the corner of the room. The TV was tuned to Sky News, which was majoring on the murders in Southampton. In days gone by, a breathless reporter would have filled the screen, rattling out the details, but nowadays viewers wanted pictures, not people. So a montage of shots played out, of the quiet country lane, of the suburban pharmacy, while a rolling ticker tape of headlines jogged along the bottom of the screen. There were images of harassed police officers, tearful members of the public and then the money shot – snatched footage of a body bag being wheeled out of the pharmacy towards the awaiting ambulance.

The images were meat and drink to him. They were everything he'd been hoping for. He loved the fear, the distress, the sheer *chaos*. Nothing like this had ever been visited on Southampton before.

'Fucking hell . . .'

His companion had looked up from her burger and Jason heard her swear quietly as she took in a new image on the TV. A close-up of his police mugshot filled the screen, leering out at the other customers in the down-at-heel café. He looked drawn, a bit demented . . . but kind of cool. Jesus Christ, he had made the news . . .

As he stared at the screen, Jason thought about the things that had brought him to this point. The sneering, the accusations, the harassment. He remembered all the people who'd said he would never amount to anything – the teachers, the kids, his own fucking mother. What would they think now? Still, at least his mother had been *present*, which was more than he could say for his dad. What would that little prick think? What would *he* say when he found out that he had spawned a devil? He suddenly wished that he could visit all his tormentors in turn, ramming their insults back down their throats, rubbing their noses in his deeds. He had done more in a few hours than they would do in a lifetime.

'We should go, Jason.'

'Shut up, will you?' he replied, distracted and irritable. 'I'm trying to listen to what they're saying –'

'We need to go. We shouldn't have come here,' she persisted, rising suddenly and abandoning her burger.

He turned to her, ready to continue the argument. But her anxious expression silenced him. She was right. However much fun he was having, it wouldn't do to linger. So, reluctantly, he rose, following her to the door, allowing himself just enough time for one last look at the screen. He saw his own face staring back at him and swallowed a smile. No question about it, this was the happiest day of his life.

And he intended to enjoy it to the full.

42

13.16

McAndrew stood in the small room, breathing in the scent of failure.

Jason Swift lived with his mother in a two-bedroom flat in Woolston. They were on the top floor of a tower block which showed all the signs of the recent cutbacks. This was austerity Britain writ large – peeling paint, cracked windows and wall-to-wall graffiti. No one even pretended to maintain the property any more. The one small mercy was that the lift was working, saving McAndrew eight flights of stairs.

Predictably the lift had stunk to high heaven and the flat wasn't much better. It wasn't that the place was a bombsite – the washing-up was done, clean clothes were drying on a clothes horse – it just had a deep, lingering odour that was hard to place, but unpleasant to experience. Ingrained dirt? Dodgy sanitation? Whatever it was, it had a profoundly depressing effect on McAndrew and she thanked the Lord that she had managed to rise above her own humble beginnings.

Armed police had barrel-charged the door to the flat, but emerged empty-handed shortly afterwards, having checked the flat from top to bottom. They were packing up now in the car park below, leaving McAndrew behind to sift the evidence. She wasn't by nature a fearful or superstitious person, but she wished they had remained a little longer. It wasn't that she felt in danger, just that there was an atmosphere in the place that got to her. She sensed that there had been a lot of unhappiness within these four walls.

Pulling herself together, McAndrew continued her examination of the flat. She had explored the lounge and kitchen but had found little of interest, nothing out of place, so had moved on to the master bedroom. There appeared to be nothing out of the ordinary here either – a double bed with a tired old duvet, a wardrobe full of discount jeans and fleeces, a few bits of make-up, headache pills, a well-thumbed library book. This was presumably the mother's room and McAndrew was struck by how bare it was. A testament perhaps to a life barely lived, to a woman scraping by.

Jason's bedroom was of more immediate interest and McAndrew hurried there now. The aroma of cannabis was strong, but other than that it could have been any young man's bedroom – dirty washing on the floor, the bed unmade, an ashtray with cigarette butts. By the side of the bed, however, was a small bookcase that was loaded with books, both old and new. McAndrew took in the titles, growing ever more depressed as she read the spines. There were books on white supremacy, fat tomes by well-known Holocaust-deniers, as well as biographies of Hitler and Anders Brevik, and even a former SS officer's book on race theory and mate selection. Nestled in among all of these were various homespun pamphlets and booklets, advertising demonstrations and marches and in one case outlining the threat posed by militant Islam.

Moving away from the bookshelves, McAndrew approached the small desk by the window. A battered laptop lay on top of it and, having slipped on some latex gloves, she flicked it open. To her surprise, it was not password-locked and in fact a video was running. Sitting down at the desk, she took in the images – it was a clip that had been uploaded to YouTube and was on a loop. McAndrew instantly recognized Swift, who was playing to the camera. He was framed by trees and fields and was wielding a sawn-off shotgun, pressing it to his shoulder and firing it once, twice, before turning it directly on his unseen companion, pointing the barrels directly down the lens. Turning up the volume, McAndrew could hear a young woman protesting, telling him not to point the gun at her.

Swift seemed to find this amusing, eventually turning the gun away from her and reloading it quickly, before firing at some passing birds.

'Piece of piss,' Swift laughed as he pretended to stumble backwards with the recoil, before turning once more to the camera. 'Oh yeah. Someone's gonna get it . . .'

His tinny voice filled the room, sending shivers down McAndrew's spine. The video then looped back to the beginning, so she closed the laptop, took an evidence bag from her pocket and placed it inside. Sealing it, she pulled out her phone to call for the forensics team, but, even as she did so, she hesitated, struck by the scene in front of her. This had once been an ordinary young man's bedroom, but somewhere along the line it had become corrupted.

Now it was a shrine to hatred.

43

13.22

'Joanne!'

No sooner had Sanderson entered the incident room than her name rang out. Her heart sank. She had had a thoroughly dispiriting couple of hours, chasing up non-existent witnesses in the environs of the pharmacy. She had turned up precisely nothing and her efforts had then been superseded by a student's mobile footage, providing the police with the details *she* had been tasked with unearthing. She had missed the briefing and was behind the beat, and now Helen was summoning her to her office. Sanderson crossed the room like a condemned woman – she desperately wanted to contribute, but the fates seemed to be conspiring against her today.

As soon as she walked into Helen's office, she spotted it. Her transfer request had been opened and lay face up on Helen's desk.

'What the hell is this?' Helen demanded.

'It's a transfer request,' Sanderson replied flatly, hoping she didn't sound like she was taking the piss.

'I can read, Joanne. What's it doing in my in-tray?'

'I put it there this morning, because I think it would be best for everyone if I move on. I had thought about moving to another department, but I now feel that a new force, a new start, would be better –'

'Seriously?'

'Well, I don't seem to be doing much good here and –'

'You seriously want to do this *now*? Today of all days . . .'

'No, I mean, I put it there this morning, before all this kicked off. I wasn't going to bring it up obviously, but –'

'You're a piece of work, you know that? People are dying out there and you want to discuss your career?'

'No, no, it's just that I've felt excluded for a while now and –'

'Well, I'm sorry if I've hurt your feelings, DS Sanderson, but allow me to let you into a little secret. The world does *not* revolve around you.'

'I know that –'

'You are part of a team. A team that can only function if every member is pulling his or her weight. And you haven't been, not for a long time.'

Sanderson said nothing, shamed by the accusation.

'Now I've put up with that because of everything that's gone on, but I won't excuse it today. We have two killers at large who are likely to strike again, so suck it up and *do your job*.'

She thrust the transfer request back at Sanderson, who accepted it reluctantly. Helen was shocked to see that her own hand was shaking – such was her anger – and she was about to dismiss Sanderson, when Charlie knocked and entered.

'For God's sake, Charlie, can't you see I'm in the middle of –'

'You'll want to see this,' Charlie fired back, unrepentant.

Charlie handed a copy of Swift's full file to her. Helen was aware that Sanderson was hovering, unsure whether to stay or go, but opened it without delay.

'Page seventeen, at the back,' Charlie continued.

Helen flipped through the file, anxiously searching for the relevant page, but her junior beat her to the punch.

'He's tagged.'

Helen paused and looked up at Charlie.

'Jason Swift was sentenced to Community Payback a few weeks back, but given his previous bad record of attendance . . .'

Charlie looked flustered, pointing excitedly to the small paragraph on the final sheet.

'. . . they tagged him.'

44

13.28

'Familiarize yourself with your weapons – make sure you are ready to use them if required – but *remember* that the ARUs have overall control of any incident requiring armed response. These weapons are for your protection and that of the public: leave the heroics to the guys in helmets.'

Helen, Charlie and a handful of experienced DCs were in Southampton Central's armoury, signing out their Heckler and Koch pistols. Sanderson was notable by her absence – she had been detailed to some mundane follow-up work – but none of her junior colleagues seemed to miss her. It was extremely rare for the team to be issued with firearms and the levels of excitement and adrenaline in the room were palpable.

Following Charlie's revelation, Helen had raced to the station's communications unit, her deputy in tow. Every offender tag contains a GPS device with a range of several miles and they had soon picked up a signal. As expected, the signal was not emanating from Woolston – near the Swift family home – but instead was coming from Southampton city centre, a mile or so south of Portswood.

'Surely he'd have got rid of it?' Charlie had suggested, as they hurried to the armoury.

'Maybe, but they're buggers to get off and, besides, maybe this is part of his plan.'

'You think he actually *wants* us to find him?'

'Ninety per cent of these incidents end with the death of the perpetrator. Either at their own hand or through suicide by cop. So, yes, I'd say that that's a distinct possibility.'

Charlie shivered, unnerved by this idea.

'My first thought was that he would have just dumped it in the nearest bin,' Helen carried on. 'But the signal shows that he is moving. The question is, where is he heading and why?'

'You don't think he'll go to ground?'

'He doesn't show any sign of slowing up. I imagine he's drunk on the power, excited about where he will strike next. I want us to be waiting for him when he does. Everyone clear on protocol?'

There was a flurry of nodding.

'Good, then let's go.'

The team descended the rear steps to the car pool. Helen would take point on her bike, guided in by the comms room, while Charlie and the rest would follow in unmarked cars. There would be no lights, no sirens, as Helen was keen to preserve their advantage.

Helen climbed on to her Kawasaki and fired up the engine. As she did so, the hard bulk of her holstered weapon jabbed uncomfortably into her ribs, reminding her of the last time she'd fired a gun in anger. Suddenly her mind was full of hideous images – Marianne screaming, her own finger pulling the trigger, the awful aftermath . . .

Helen could feel her heart racing, her breath becoming short, so she pushed these thoughts away quickly, roaring out of the station car park. There was no time for morbid introspection, no room for weakness, despite her jangling nerves. She had been shaken by her argument with Charlie *and* her confrontation with Sanderson – shocked by her own levels of emotion – but she had to get a grip.

She had a pair of killers to catch.

45

13.31

He stared at the people walking past, seeking eye contact, but each face was as blank as its predecessor. Most of the passers-by had headphones on and were totally cut off from the world. Those who didn't were scarcely more engaged, staring dully ahead as they scuttled along the pavement, unaware of their fleeting brush with celebrity. It was lunchtime and they were keen to get to Pret, Boots, whatever, swerving from their intended route whenever someone had the temerity to cross their path. It would have been funny, if it wasn't so tragic.

He seemed to be travelling against the tide. Maybe he was imagining it, exaggerating his own importance, but everyone seemed to be going in the opposite direction today. It felt good. He was able to see things more clearly now – these passers-by were just following the herd, doing what the person in front of them was doing. Maybe that's how these shops made their money – selling mediocre sandwiches to people who couldn't think of anywhere better to go.

He was different. They were different. Why? Because they weren't scared. This hadn't always been the case – they had endured endless humiliations and rejections, which had cut deep. But that was all behind them. Once you stop caring, everything gets better.

A woman tutted as he brushed past her, forcing her off course. She was one of those classic tight-arsed young professionals who'd convinced herself that every second of her time was precious. At first, she looked as though she was going to say something to him. But then she clocked him – the unshaven chin, the unkempt hair, the sheer size of him – and chickened out, hurrying on past. He grinned at her as she went. She would recognize him later, when she read the papers, watched the news, but for now she would occupy herself by debating whether to have a tuna and mayo or cheese and pickle sandwich . . .

The whole world is in chains, scared and impotent. The ordinary people – the little people – exist in a state of . . . what was that word she'd used? Torpor. They exist in a state of torpor, terrified to act, to do anything because they are fearful of the consequences. Maybe they'll get told off? Arrested? Lose their job? Perhaps their friends will disapprove, give them a thumbs-down on Facebook? They are frozen, incapacitated by thoughts of the judgement that might follow.

But what if there *were* no consequences? What if there was no comeback? They were past worrying about the consequences of their actions now, for them only the present was real. And it was thrilling. They could do exactly as they pleased, treating people as they deserved to be treated. There was an honesty in their actions, an element of mercy too. Those bastards killed people slowly, over many years, but they were putting them out of their misery quickly. It was the one good thing he had ever done in his life and still it was more than they deserved.

He felt his blood rising once more and slipped his hand inside his coat, gripping the handle of his gun. It felt good. He had been let down so many times, but a gun doesn't let you down. A gun is your friend. And it was time to use it again.

It was time to release the beast.

46

13.33

Emilia Garanita pulled out her camera, as she took in the run-down building in front of her. There was little point trying to grab some pictures at Sansom's pharmacy – she would have to wait until the police circus died down first – so instead she'd jumped in her car and hurried down to Totton.

This wasn't the most glamorous part of Southampton, but it was home to the local probation service. Many a young offender – and even a few who were older and should have known better – had made the trek out here to begin their Community Payback. Many used the no. 38 bus – it was a running joke that few local bus drivers wanted to drive that route – while others were dropped off by anxious parents, hoping against hope that their progeny would suddenly turn over a new leaf. Few actually did and as a result many were repeat visitors. Emilia could count herself among their number now – she had recently visited their office to check out the graffiti that defiled its walls.

The place was in dire need of renovation and the social workers she saw trudging through its doors looked beaten and downcast. Perhaps this was their usual demeanour or maybe they'd heard the news about their fallen colleague. As she stood outside, Emilia had asked a couple of passing faces about Sonia Smalling – what they thought of her, was she well liked – but nobody would talk to her and, besides, that wasn't what she was here for, so, abandoning her position before security got wind of her, she began her circuit of the building. It had once been painted a dull, grey colour, which local psychologists had felt would least 'excite' the young offenders. In fact, all these well-meaning fools had managed to create was a pleasingly blank canvas for the innumerable young graffiti artists who passed through its doors each day. As a result, almost every surface was now decorated with the repeated tags of its unrepentant visitors. It made Emilia chuckle, such was the idiocy of the headshrinkers and their politically correct paymasters. They deserved everything they got.

Sonia Smalling had not deserved her fate, however, and snapping herself out of it Emilia had continued her tour, carefully inspecting the numerous designs on the brickwork. And it was as she reached the back of the building that she found what she was looking for. A large, emerald serpent which appeared to be devouring its own tail.

She had seen it before, when she'd been researching the article, but hadn't paid it much heed then, beyond noting that it was better executed than most of the others. Now Emilia paid it close attention, taking numerous pictures of it, before stepping back to survey the scene. A lone CCTV camera hung, limp and broken, on a fence post nearby. Judging by the cobwebs that covered it, it had been out of action for some time. The fence itself was a decrepit, chain link affair, with plenty of gaps in it. Emilia could see why the perpetrators had chosen this spot to paint their tag – they weren't overlooked and there was pretty much zero chance of them being detected. They could add their signature and be away before those inside were any the wiser.

Lowering her camera, Emilia stared at the emerald snake. No one entering or leaving the building would have spotted it but perhaps that was the point. Was this a little in-joke, meant for others to discover after today's events? Sonia Smalling's workplace had been defiled, as had Alan Sansom's. Was it possible that the killers were marking out the territory? Signalling in advance who they intended to target?

It was a thought that made Emilia shudder. It left her wondering how organized this rampage actually was. And, more importantly, where it would end.

47

13.35

Helen sped through the city streets, darting in and out of the traffic. She had made a decision to dispense with the blues and twos, but was already regretting it. The traffic was particularly bad today and the rest of their team were struggling to keep pace with her. She would be in the vanguard of the action – she just hoped that the Armed Response Units coming up from the south of the city would join her in time.

One person who would not be joining them was Joanne. She was back at base, fulfilling duties scarcely commensurate with her rank or experience. Now that her emotions had cooled a little, Helen knew that Charlie had been right to take her to task. She *was* punishing Joanne, calling her out on every minor failing, taking grim delight in humiliating her. To what end? She hadn't meant to drive her out of Southampton Central – in fact she hadn't really *meant* to do anything. Her unpleasant behaviour towards her DS was instinctive and unthinking and said more about Helen's state of mind than Sanderson's. In damning a colleague who had just been doing her job, Helen had broken her spirit and deprived the team of a valuable and talented officer. Hardly an ideal situation given the operation they were now involved in.

'Any update on location?' Helen barked, angry and frustrated.

'Give me a minute,' a disembodied voice replied.

Helen's helmet had built-in Bluetooth, hooking up effortlessly to the police radio strapped to her chest. She had been communicating with Southampton Central from the minute she left the bike park, demanding updates.

'He seems to have paused on or near Walton Road,' the operator was saying.

Immediately Helen started mentally scrolling through possible destinations.

'Now he's on the move again, heading west, seems to be picking up speed.'

Already alarm bells were ringing for Helen. Was this because Swift had speeded up again, as if geeing himself up for another attack? No, it was something else, something she remembered reading earlier . . . Helen pictured his charge sheet in her mind, running down his misdemeanours one by one. Cautions for affray, threatening and abusive behaviour, shoplifting . . .

And then she got it.

'I think he's heading for the WestQuay.'

There was a silence at the other end. The WestQuay centre was Southampton's premier shopping destination – three floors of shops, boutiques and restaurants. It was always heaving, especially so at lunchtime.

'He was picked up for shoplifting at the WestQuay. H&M, I think,' Helen continued.

Helen could hear the operator typing furiously at the other end.

'Yes, he was arrested there, but the store decided not to

pursue it. It says here that Swift had tussled with the security guard, wanted to charge him with assault.'

'Where was the guard from?'

'Let me check . . .'

Helen held her breath, as the operator searched for the details.

'Somalia, I think . . . Yes, he's a Somalian student here on a work visa. His name's Yusuf Muhamud.'

Now Helen remembered the details. Having been spotted shoplifting, Swift had attempted to flee the store and had been thrown to the ground, bruising his face in the process. The store had clearly decided the matter was best brushed under the carpet. Jason Swift clearly didn't agree.

'Alert all units,' Helen said breathlessly. 'Tell them I want all entrances and exits covered. I'll coordinate from the main atrium.'

'Will do.'

The operator clicked off and Helen wrenched back the throttle, roaring away from the traffic. The perpetrators had been one step ahead of her so far, but finally Helen had them in her sights and she was determined to make it count.

48

13.37

The shops were particularly busy this lunchtime. Margaret was pressed for time – her lunch break was a break only in name – and the volume of people in the WestQuay had frustrated her at every turn. The queue in Boots was so bad that she'd abandoned her purchases and nipped into Superdrug instead. She'd grabbed a sandwich while she was in there – BLT, she thought, but she hadn't really looked – then hurried into H&M.

She calculated that she had ten minutes at most, before she started to exhaust her supervisor's patience. He could be very ratty if he felt you were taking the mickey and Margaret couldn't face an afternoon of his snippy comments, so she hurried down the aisle of clothes. She had a couple of things to pick up for her boy and she might even chance her arm on something for herself – if there was anything her size on the sale rail.

She picked her way to the menswear section, which was towards the rear of the store. As ever there was a bewildering display of styles, and even when she did find one she liked, it was still an ordeal to get it in the right size. Why did they have to make these things so darned difficult? Wasn't life tough enough? Sneaking a look at her watch, Margaret realized there would be no time for herself today, she would be lucky if she made this purchase soon enough, having singularly failed to find a 'large' in light grey.

Changing tack, she rootled out a 'large' in charcoal instead. It wasn't quite what she was after but it would have to do. Turning away from the groaning racks, she hurried towards the tills, only to find that they were deserted.

'What the hell . . . ?' she muttered under her breath, surprised that the staff would abandon the tills in this fashion.

She cast around for the manager, but there was no one. She had never seen it like this – it was like the *Mary Celeste.* What was going on?

Then she spotted them. There was some commotion at the entrance to the shop, where the staff were gathered together. They seemed to be agitated, wound up, ushering shoppers from the store, while talking fast at the security guard, who now hurried out on to the concourse. In their excitement they seemed not to have noticed her and for a moment Margaret was tempted to shout at them, to remind them that she did actually exist. But then she had another idea.

Checking that the staff were still occupied, she leant over the counter and slipped the security tag into the little plastic slot by the tills. It came off effortlessly and in one fluid movement a very satisfied Margaret had pushed her 'purchase' into her Superdrug bag.

Today had been a pretty depressing day so far, but suddenly things were starting to look a whole lot brighter.

49

13.40

Helen stalked the level three concourse, scanning the floors below. Having dumped her bike and linked up with an Armed Response Unit, she had hurried into the West-Quay. The rest of her team had fired up their sirens and were arriving outside, but Helen hadn't wanted to wait. Something told her every second counted.

Dressed in her biking leathers, Helen had cut a striking figure, flanked by a quartet of men in body armour, all of whom were clutching carbines. They had moved forward quickly, alive to any danger, homing in fast on the central information desk. Assuming control, Helen had presented her credentials to the bemused WestQuay manager, informing him that they would be evacuating the shopping centre. She had asked him to start ringing round the stores to inform them, then, making sure the main entrance was covered, moved forward, heading straight up the escalators, as the armed officers went store to store, searching for Jason Swift and his accomplice.

Her team were starting to appear now – two at the far exit, two at the main entrance – and Helen hurried along the third-floor concourse. A sudden flurry of activity on the ground floor might alert the suspects positioned higher up and Helen wanted to avoid that at all costs. The possibility of hostage-taking in such a crowded environment was extremely high, so it was vital that she maintain the element of surprise for as long as possible. Besides, H&M was on the top floor and Helen had a feeling that their suspects would be heading straight there.

As her walk became a run, she eased her weapon from its holster and carefully released the safety catch. She prayed she wouldn't have to use it today, though her gut told her she would. She couldn't see Swift coming quietly.

She was making good progress along the concourse and the store's gaudy red letters now came into view. There was a crowd of confused shoppers outside, who seemed reluctant to move on, despite the entreaties of the teenage staff. There was no sign of the security guard yet, nor of anyone wearing a long trench coat. Helen immediately clicked on her radio, connecting herself to Southampton Central's operations room once more.

'Where are they?'

'They've stopped moving,' the panicky operator came back quickly.

'Where?'

'They are in the WestQuay somewhere, your position pretty much matches theirs, I'm surprised you can't see them.'

Helen looked about the concourse, searching for khaki trench coats, for Swift's tall form, for anything out of the ordinary, but there was nothing.

Where the hell were they?

50

13.42

Charlie paced back and forth, trying to dispel her nerves. She was positioned at the rear of the WestQuay, gun discreetly concealed in her hand, watching and waiting. She was in radio contact with the rest of the team and knew that the evacuation of the shopping centre had begun. Most of those within would head out of the main entrance on to the pedestrianized precinct, but others who wanted to cut down to the docks or the south side of the city would emerge from the rear of the building. It was Charlie's job to hurry them away, keeping a sharp eye out for Jason Swift and his accomplice as she did so.

Charlie hopped from foot to foot, trying to keep warm now that the sun had disappeared. DC Osbourne had been detailed to keep her company, but he had spotted a fire escape nearby that nobody was covering and, having sought Charlie's permission, had headed off to investigate. Charlie couldn't fault his courage or his thinking – their suspects might well try and conceal themselves in the flood of shoppers if they intended to escape, but they might also attempt to go it alone. Their well-executed attack at the pharmacy suggested that they had recce'd the shop in advance and had always had an escape route in mind. How much easier to find a way to slip away here, given the size and complexity of the WestQuay. Had the pair been stalking the concourses in the days, even weeks, preceding this? The thought made Charlie shudder and she now regretted sending Osbourne away – a single armed officer against two pitiless killers didn't seem a very fair fight.

She was about to radio her colleague, when a loud noise made her look up. The rear-exit doors had swung open and shoppers were emerging. They looked confused and concerned, the sight of so many officers in body armour unnerving them. They had seen this kind of thing on the news, in Paris and London, but not in Southampton. They obviously wanted to put some distance between themselves and danger, hurrying away from the centre.

A trickle became a steady flow, then eventually a flood. The shoppers were four deep, jostling with each other, exchanging heated words as all semblance of calm evaporated. And they were moving fast, making it hard for Charlie to take them all in as they scurried past her. Gunmetal-grey clouds now hid the sun. It was trying to rain, spitting malevolently on the shoppers below. Umbrellas were being deployed, hoods being pulled up – it was virtually impossible to keep track of who was who.

Jason Swift was tall, so Charlie kept her gaze high, dismissing anyone under a certain height. Her nerves were rattling, she was wound tight, but as yet there was no sign of their suspects and she suddenly wondered how Osbourne was getting on. She had been so wrapped up in her own situation, she had failed to notice that he had gone rather quiet. She had given him strict instructions to stay in touch and his radio silence bothered her.

She pulled her radio from her pocket, but as she raised

it to her mouth, she suddenly stopped dead. Amid the undulating sea of humanity in front of her, she glimpsed a flash of khaki, the swish of a coat tail. Lowering her radio, she moved forward, craning her neck for a better view. Someone had just left the shopping centre at speed – they were still forty feet from her or so, boxed in by shoppers so she couldn't see them properly – but now she realized that there were two of them, a man and a woman. Concealing her gun by her side, she moved forward, keeping herself low along the edge of the human stream to hide her approach. As she moved silently ahead, she pressed her radio to her lips, ready to call for assistance.

They were only twenty feet from her now. Heads flashed in front of her, obscuring her view. The pair seemed to be keeping their eyes down, but were talking to each other, keeping up a constant dialogue. Both were wearing long coats, both had tattoos, both seemed intent on getting away as fast as possible.

They were nearly level with her now, so Charlie made her move, arrowing across the line of shoppers. She waited until the last minute to raise her gun, then, stepping forward, shouted:

'Armed police! On your knees.'

The effect was instant. Shoppers fled, a woman screamed and two terrified Goths in trench coats sunk to their knees. Instantly, Charlie saw her mistake. They were the right height, the right sex, but they were far too young – fifteen at the very most. Cursing, Charlie holstered her weapon.

The killers were still at large.

51

13.43

Helen pushed through the store. Her eyes darted to each corner in turn, searching for signs of life. The main display area was large, but crammed with heavily laden clothes rails – perfect cover for an ambush. Helen hadn't heard any shots and no one else had reported any incidents, but she felt sure that something was about to give.

Helen took point, while the other armed officers spread out, probing the rails nearest the walls. Helen had always disregarded her own safety, but even she exercised caution now, the memory of Sonia Smalling's corpse still fresh in her mind. At any moment she expected to hear the roar of a shotgun and moved forward slowly, ready to dive for cover at the first sign of trouble.

She was nearing the back of the store now. There were only a couple of clothes rails left to check, and, crouching down, Helen stole a glance around them. They were clear, and she quickly straightened up. The changing booths were all empty, which just left the till area. The counter was wide and tall, so Helen moved towards it cautiously, her gun raised. And now she noticed that one of the till drawers lay open and empty.

She gestured to her colleagues and they moved towards the area, their feet padding quietly but purposefully on the polished wood floor. Helen cried out:

'Armed police!'

Silence.

'Armed police!' she repeated, louder this time. 'Come out slowly, with your hands on –'

Now there was movement. Helen's trigger finger tensed, but to her surprise a middle-aged woman in a tatty raincoat emerged from underneath the till counter. Her hands were shaking, as she held them in the air, and her face was flushed pink.

'Is there anyone with you?' Helen barked, immediately concerned she might be looking at a hostage.

'No, no . . . it's just me,' the woman stammered in response.

'Are you *sure*?' Helen's eyes swept the area behind the tills.

'Of course. Come round here if you don't believe me.'

Helen crept around the edge of the counter, while the rest of the team trained their guns on it, alive to any possible threat. To Helen's surprise, the woman appeared to be telling the truth.

'Have you seen a man and a woman? He's early twenties, she's late teens.'

'No . . .'

'They are in the store, we're sure they are in the store . . .'

But even Helen was starting to doubt this now.

'It's just me, I told you, everyone else has gone. I got scared, so I hid.'

Helen rather doubted it – a brand-new hoodie was stuffed into her carrier bag and she seemed to be shielding her handbag, which Helen suspected held the contents of the till – but she let it go.

'Have you seen this man?' she said, offering the woman her phone. On the screen was a close-up of Jason Swift's mugshot.

The woman looked at it blankly.

'Have you seen him?'

The woman stared at the image and then her face slowly began to crumple. Helen had an inkling of what was coming, but was still surprised when the woman finally gasped:

'Why are you looking for my Jason?'

52

13.46

Helen marched away from the WestQuay, furious with herself, furious with Margaret Swift. Charlie was waiting for her, looking almost as downcast as she did. Helen tossed her an evidence bag, which Charlie just about managed to catch.

'He took it off,' Helen said bleakly.

Charlie stared down at the GPS tag, now sealed in the plastic bag.

'Somehow he managed to get it off,' Helen continued. 'Then he stuffed it into his mother's bag, underneath a bloody treasure trove of receipts, make-up, tights, the works . . .'

Charlie stared at the tag, bitterly disappointed to have been proved right.

'I scrambled pretty much our entire team here . . . to pick up a middle-aged woman.'

'You did the right thing, we had to chase it up.'

In the background, Charlie saw an ashen-faced Margaret Swift being escorted to a squad car by DC Edwards.

'What happens now?' she asked.

'We'll have to take a statement, but she doesn't know anything. She and Jason hardly speak from what I can make out.'

'Does she know where he might be? Where he's heading?'

Helen shook her head.

'Apparently he moved out two weeks ago. Threw a few things in a bag and went. She didn't think too much of it, he's done that before. He returned to the flat briefly last night, but only stayed for an hour or so –'

'To put the tag in her bag . . .'

'Clearly.'

'So he's staying with the girl? Squatting? Sleeping rough?'

'She says she was aware her son was running around with some girl, but she never saw her. Jason wouldn't bring her to the flat, apparently, was ashamed of it, of her . . .'

Helen glanced at the squad car, which now pulled away from the kerb. It was impossible not to feel *some* sympathy for Margaret Swift – she had been dealt a pretty rough hand and certainly hadn't been expecting *this* – but, even so, she had unwittingly set their investigation back significantly, which made Helen's blood boil.

'He wanted us to come here,' she said ruefully, turning to Charlie once more.

'You think he knew we'd work out who he was, put a trace on him . . .'

'Judging by his performance with the traffic camera, he's not bothered about having his picture taken. He must've known we'd eventually discover a link to him.'

'So why hide the tag in her bag? If he doesn't plan to get away with it, why would he worry about us tracing –'

'To buy himself time to execute another attack,' Helen

said quietly, silencing her colleague. 'He deliberately wanted to drag us over here . . .'

Helen looked up, fixing Charlie with an anguished stare.

'. . . and we fell for it, hook, line and sinker.'

53

13.47

Sanderson stared at the screen, scarcely able to breathe.

She had been locked away in the stuffy office for over an hour now, pointedly ignoring the knowing looks from the data operators. News of her dressing down had clearly spread around the station. There had been a few whispered comments, some suppressed chuckles and worst of all a charity cup of tea, brought to her by one of the greener members of staff. This act of pity had cut the deepest – Sanderson had never felt so dejected in her whole life – and the cup of tea remained untouched on the desk in front of her.

She had been given the job of tracing the perpetrator's car. While Charlie, Osbourne, Bentham and the rest had raced across town in pursuit of the suspects, she had been landed with a mundane investigative task. Had she been in better odour, she would have objected, or at the very least tried to offload such drudgery on to a lower-ranked officer. But as Helen had specifically given her the chore, there was no question of doing that. This was her penance and she had to suck it up.

The Automatic Number Plate Recognition system had pinged the stolen Fiat approaching Itchen, but after that it had dropped off the radar. Maybe the perpetrators had hidden it, maybe the traffic cameras hadn't got a decent look at the number plate since, but it had vanished. Which had left Sanderson with little choice but to trawl through the recorded footage from the various traffic cameras in the area, hoping against hope for a glimpse of the missing vehicle.

It had seemed a pointless and depressing task, but just as Sanderson's eyes were beginning to glaze over, she spotted it. Seizing the controls, she whizzed the footage forwards and backwards repeatedly, watching the car disappear into an alleyway off a quiet, suburban street. She couldn't make out the whole number plate – just the last four digits – but that proved enough. Running her index finger down the list in front of her, she quickly discovered that there were no other cars of that make and colour, with those four digits on the plate, registered in Southampton. It had to be the missing Punto, didn't it?

Exhaling slowly, Sanderson pondered her next move. She should call it in straight away. After all, if she was right, then the whole team had been scrambled to the *wrong* side of town. But if she was mistaken and she hampered the investigation in any way . . .

Given the perilous nature of her position, there was nothing for it but to check it out herself first. So, rising quickly, Sanderson snatched up her jacket and hurried from the room.

54

13.58

Helen tore off her jacket and tossed it on to the floor. Turning the cold tap on, she cupped her hands underneath the gushing water and threw the contents on to her face.

She had raced back to Southampton Central, summoning the rest of the MIT to join her for an emergency briefing. But on arriving back at base Helen had headed first to the armoury to return her firearm, then to the ladies' loos on the tenth floor. She needed to calm herself before the others arrived and few people visited this out-of-the-way facility. Helen often fled here when she wanted to be alone.

Her throat felt dry, her face was burning. The water seemed to make little difference, which only angered her further. What was wrong with her? Why did everything she touch turn to shit? Turning the tap off, she kicked the basin hard and raised her eyes to look at herself in the mirror. A bedraggled, beaten woman stared back. Without hesitation, Helen slammed her fist into the glass. Once, twice, three times . . .

Pain flared through her and suddenly Helen relented. Looking down she saw that her hand was ravaged, her knuckles torn and angry. Cursing herself, Helen grabbed a paper towel and started aggressively dabbing at her cuts. As she did so, she looked back up at the mirror. A thick crack ran across the middle of it, distorting Helen's reflection, turning her into a malformed freak.

The mirror didn't lie. Helen *was* a gross parody of the successful officer she had once been. She was out of control – suspicious, vengeful and isolated – leading the team stutteringly from one disaster to the next, while two deranged killers struck at will. Was this it then? Had she lost it for good? She was supposed to be the team leader, but who in their right minds would follow her now? Her anger – her keen sense of personal betrayal – was clouding her vision at a time when she needed a clear head, but she could see no way of ridding herself of these stupid self-destructive thoughts. She had never doubted herself like this and staring at herself in the mirror she wondered if *she* was the problem. For the last few months, she had been wondering if she could trust her colleagues.

Now she was wondering if she could trust herself.

55

14.00

Jason Swift wielded his gun, laughing as he fired it into the air.

His YouTube video was playing silently on the big screen in the incident room, but as the team had watched it twice already, it was muted, now merely an unpleasant backdrop to their discussions. It was framed by a gruesome selection of images on the murder board – photos of the corpses and crime scenes – as well as maps outlining the murder sites, Swift's flat, the addresses of local racist organizations and the locations of his past assaults.

'What have we got on his previous targets?' Charlie demanded, keen to make some progress. 'The Polish waiter, the young black male.'

'We've been in contact with those who are still in Southampton,' McAndrew replied. 'They are all fine and have been advised to stay away from the city until Swift is apprehended.'

'What about his prior arrests and cautions?' Charlie continued. 'I'm thinking particularly of vandalism and anti-social behaviour.'

'He's handy with an aerosol and not averse to smashing things up either.'

'What has he targeted?'

'Mostly residential properties near his home, a couple of cars, phone boxes . . .'

'Any institutions?' Charlie pursued her line. 'Probation offices? Council buildings?'

'Nothing on file.' Reid sounded a little deflated.

'How many cautions does he have for possession?'

'Several. He's a bit of a stoner . . .'

'Has he ever exhibited signs of paranoia?' Osbourne queried. 'That can be one of the effects of long-term cannabis abuse. He might have started to believe that people or agencies were against him.'

Charlie flicked a look at Helen to see if she wanted to field this one, as she was far more knowledgeable on these matters than she was. But Helen seemed oddly distracted, staring mutely at the crime scene photos, barely following the discussion. Normally, she would have led the briefing, but she was withdrawn and distant, cradling her right hand, which she appeared to have injured. Charlie wondered if she was angry with herself, or perhaps angry with *her* following their argument, but she knew better than to ask, quietly assuming control of the briefing instead.

'His medical history is pretty thin,' Charlie explained. 'I don't think he believed in doctors. His mum said she took him a few times, trying to get him treatment for depression, but he never stuck with it.'

'But it's possible,' Osbourne persisted. 'Perhaps he had mental health issues that had gone untreated. He came to believe that he was right, that certain people had wronged him. I know for a fact that Sonia Smalling made offenders apologize to their victims. Perhaps she made him do that and he felt belittled, humiliated . . .'

'It's a decent theory,' Charlie acknowledged. 'But what about Alan Sansom?'

'I don't know, maybe they just needed some uppers. By the sounds of it, they stole enough amphetamines to keep them going for a whole year. Now they've got cash, drugs –'

'But why the extreme violence?' McAndrew pitched in.

'Maybe they're high? Maybe they're getting off on it?'

'I don't buy it,' Charlie said, asserting her authority. 'It's a long drive from Ashurst to Portswood, they abandoned their car, they had a preplanned escape route –'

'We *think* they had a preplanned escape route,' Osbourne corrected her.

'Ok, we *think* they'd scoped the place beforehand, but it feels too deliberate to me. If they were interested in taking potshots at random punters, they would have done so on the way into Southampton.'

'Maybe they don't want to blow their wad too early. They want to make life as hard as possible for us.'

'Well, we can agree on that at least . . .' Charlie said ruefully.

Silence filled the room. Charlie was about to continue, conscious of the need to rally the troops, when Helen suddenly spoke.

'What's the trigger?'

Osbourne was about to say something facetious, then thought better of it. Fortunately, as Helen now turned to look directly at him.

'We're saying Jason Swift is the instigator, but, if so, what's set him off?' Helen went on. 'Sure he's an unreconstructed racist, an apologist for white supremacy. But this isn't a one-off attack. Or a political statement. This is an . . . explosion of violence. Why's he so angry? These things are nearly always caused by some crisis in the perpetrator's life, so what is it?'

The officers watched Helen closely, unsure if she wanted them to respond or not.

'McAndrew, you went round to his flat. Was anything out of place?'

'No, nothing. The place was neat and tidy, no signs of an argument –'

'And Margaret Swift swears blind that there was no bust-up,' Helen continued. 'Jason just left one day . . .'

'What about the gun?' Charlie countered. 'The tech team are still sifting his online activity, but it looks like Swift was trying to buy guns on the dark web, plus he had downloaded numerous video clips from the US showing white supremacists training with firearms –'

'He hasn't got any previous convictions for possessing or acquiring firearms,' Helen cut in. 'In fact his crimes seldom if ever involved violence and when he *did* threaten his social worker, he used something close at hand, a domestic nailgun –'

'Not exactly Don Corleone, is he?' Reid chimed in.

'In fact, if you look at the key traits of these murders, they exhibit a very definite step up for Jason. He may be a thug and a racist, but murder, possession of a firearm, robbery . . . they're not very *him*, are they?'

'I'm not sure what we're saying here,' Charlie interrupted. 'He remains our best suspect –'

'Look at the crime scene photos.'

Helen moved quickly past Charlie towards the murder

board and the graphic photographs. Instinctively the team moved forward, watching as Helen ran her finger over their glossy surfaces, tracing the outlines of the horrific injuries.

'The angles are all wrong.'

She was speaking quietly, but there was a weird energy in her voice.

'I don't follow,' Reid queried.

'Both Sonia Smalling and Alan Sansom were on their knees when they were killed. Now, this guy clearly knows what he's doing . . .'

She gestured at the big screen, where Swift had jammed the butt of the shotgun into his right shoulder and was firing with measured accuracy.

'. . . he's a practised shot.'

'No question.'

'And he's tall. Very tall in fact. Both victims were blasted at close range and the impact was only angled slightly. It's almost a head-on shot. If a guy who is six foot two, holding the gun to his shoulder, had shot them, then the angle of impact would have been much more extreme, much more on the diagonal. But if you were shorter, significantly shorter in fact . . .'

'So we're saying he *didn't* kill these people?'

Helen nodded, walking over to the big screen and turning the volume back up. Swift's Southampton drawl came over loud and clear.

'Into my shoulder, hold and . . . boom.'

The gun erupted, the sound echoing round the room.

'Piece of piss . . .' Swift laughed.

And now Charlie got it.

'He was teaching her how to shoot.'

'Exactly,' Helen exclaimed. 'I think *she* shot Sonia Smalling and Alan Sansom.'

Helen turned, fixing her eyes on her startled team.

'I think she's the key.'

56

14.05

'You want some more?'

Jason looked up from the open boot of the car and directed his gaze towards his companion. She stood close by, but her face was turned to the ground. She had been distant and distracted since the café – pissed off no doubt that he was getting all the glory – and he wanted to wrench her back on track. Grabbing a fistful of cartridges from the boot, he shoved them into his coat pocket.

'You don't want to go into this one undercooked. There's going to be a lot of people around. And if we have to fight our way out –'

'I'm fine.'

'That's a matter of opinion,' he mumbled to himself, as he grabbed another handful of shells.

She was beginning to irritate him now. Things were going precisely as planned – better than planned in fact – but still she refused to crack a smile. Fuck it, *he* was having fun. Would it kill her to enjoy it a little too? He was tempted to shout at her, to rant and rave, but he knew that wouldn't work. She never responded to *that*. He needed her in a calm frame of mind, so there was nothing for it but to try and coax her into better spirits. Swallowing his irritation, he turned to face her again.

'Come on, sweetheart, don't lose heart now.'

'I'm not losing heart.'

'Ok, so they know my name, but the cops . . . the cops don't have a clue what we're planning, what this *is*.'

Still she didn't look at him, so he reached towards her, raising her chin.

'They can't touch us,' he continued. 'They can't *stop* us. We're going to put the world to rights today, you and me, just like we planned.'

She looked into his eyes, as if seeking reassurance. To his surprise, she looked uncertain, even a little fearful.

'So put a smile on your face and let's do this thing . . .'

He leant down and kissed her gently on the lips, provoking a small, snatched smile.

'That's better,' he said, turning back to the boot to scoop up one last handful of shells. 'Bonnie and Clyde had fun, so why shouldn't w—'

A savage blast ripped through him, slamming his body against the car. He half collapsed, half stumbled into the boot, as he was instantly assailed by the most incredible pain. His eyes were suddenly full of tears, he was having problems breathing, but even in the midst of his agony, he tried to right himself. Somehow, he managed to gain purchase on the frame of the car and, using all his strength, levered himself around to face his attacker.

Daisy was standing five feet away from him, her shotgun raised and smoking. A lop-sided frown disfigured her face.

'What the fuck?' Jason gasped, but even as he did so, a thin trickle of blood escaped from his mouth.

'I'm really sorry, babes . . .'

She muttered the words and Jason was surprised to see tears pricking *her* eyes.

'Please,' he begged. 'You know I love you. That I'd do anything fo—'

She squeezed the trigger again and the gun roared. Jason's body jerked wildly, before slumping backwards into the boot. She had hit him in the chest this time and now he lay still, even as the gun blast reverberated off the nearby brickwork. Daisy didn't linger, shoving his still warm body into the boot and slamming it shut, before hurrying away from the scene, her eyes searching the alleyway for witnesses or, worse still, the police.

But there was no one.

57

14.07

Anna Sansom sat alone in the visitors' room, casting anxious glances at the door. She had been here for the last twenty minutes, despite the promises of the Family Liaison Officer.

She had battled her way through the traffic, eventually making it to the shopping precinct. The place was crawling with police officers, journalists and shoppers and she'd had to fight her way to the shop, only to find it was taped off and completely inaccessible. One of the uniformed officers present had tried to get her to move back and she had shrieked at him, really shrieked at him. He'd eventually worked out who she was and had hurriedly called his superior over. After that, she'd been passed from pillar to post, with no one giving her any concrete information, despite her desperate enquiries, before eventually being driven to Southampton Central.

There, in the tatty visitors' room, they had broken the news to her. She didn't even take in the officers' names and could barely comprehend what they were saying. Alan had been shot and killed. She had known it was something bad, but she had never expected that. Shot? Killed? Alan was a good man, a kind man . . . She'd asked them if it was a robbery – as if that would make it any better – and after that they had clammed up, promising to find her a senior officer to inform her about the investigation. They had clearly failed to find one, hence their continued absence. She presumed they were trying their best, but it wasn't right to leave her like this, alone and in shock . . .

The door opened and immediately Anna looked up. Two female officers hurried towards her, seating themselves quickly in front of her.

'About time too. I have been waiting for ages for someone to tell me what the hell is –'

'I'm very sorry about that,' the taller officer said. 'And we're very sorry for your loss. I can't imagine what you're going through.'

Her obvious sincerity affected Anna. All her anger suddenly dissipated, as tears came to her eyes.

'My name's Detective Inspector Helen Grace,' the officer continued, 'and this is DS Brooks. We are running the investigation into your husband's murder.'

Anna nodded mutely, not trusting herself to speak.

'Things are moving pretty fast, but we do have an image of the two individuals we think are responsible for this. I know it's tough, but I'm going to have to ask you to look at this photo and tell me if you recognize them, particularly the young woman.'

'A woman?' Anna asked quietly, disbelieving.

Helen took a print-out of the student's grabbed mobile-phone image and put it in Anna's hand. The ashen-faced widow continued to stare directly at Helen, struggling to understand events.

'Please, Mrs Sansom. We really do need your help on this . . .'

Now Anna lowered her eyes to the image. The officers were watching intently, so she tried to focus on the two figures in front of her. The man she didn't recognize, but there *was* something familiar about the young woman's face.

'It looks . . .'

'Yes?'

Anna scrutinized the image. She knew she had to be sure.

'It looks a little bit like . . . Daisy.'

Anna looked up to find both officers staring at her.

'Did she work at the pharmacy with your husband?'

'No,' Anna replied absently, her mind clearly turning on the possibilities. 'No, we looked after her for a bit. Alan and I . . . we couldn't have children, so we fostered. Daisy had a pretty bad home life, her mother walked out years ago and her dad is a waste of space, so we had her for a couple of months, but . . .'

Now she paused, the horror of the situation dawning on her.

'. . . she was very unpredictable. Quick to take offence, abusive on occasions. I would have kept faith with her, but Alan . . . Alan said we had to draw the line somewhere, we had our *other* foster kids to consider . . .'

Anna stared at Helen, incredulity writ large on her face.

'Did she . . . did *she* do this?'

The police officers said nothing. And in that moment, Anna Sansom had her answer.

58

14.09

Sanderson slammed the door shut and hurried away from her car. She had raced across town to Itchen, locating a parking space near the mouth of the alleyway. She knew Southampton like the back of her hand and had switched off her sat nav, instead using the many short cuts that she'd discovered during her years patrolling the city.

On the ride over, she'd questioned the wisdom of pursuing this lead alone. What if the perpetrators were still by the car? Lying low until the dust had settled? She'd told herself that as soon as she found the car – as soon as she had a concrete lead to offer – she would radio the station for back-up. But now, as she caught sight of the maroon Punto ahead, she hesitated. There was no movement in or near the car – it appeared to have been abandoned. Waiting for back-up would waste valuable time, so . . .

Double-checking that there were no civilians nearby, Sanderson hurried down the alleyway. Her eyes roved over the narrow passage, looking for any signs of ambush, but there was little cover and no obvious danger, so she pressed on. Now she just wanted to get this over and done with. In less than a minute, she was beside the car. To her enormous relief, it *was* empty. More than that, it was unlocked.

Teasing open the driver's door, she looked inside. She

had been hoping to find a sat nav, something that might tell her which targets the killers had scoped in advance of today's bloodbath, but the interior was empty, save for a crumpled magazine on the backseat and an empty Diet Coke bottle. She would have to ask forensics to take a look at them of course, but there was no telling whether these items had been left by the suspects or the car's owner.

Pushing the door to, Sanderson straightened up, stretching her aching back – too much time spent hunched over computer terminals of late. As she did so, she pulled her mobile from her pocket. She punched in the number for the incident room and was about to press 'Call' when suddenly she paused. She hadn't investigated the boot yet and now she had spotted something. A piece of fabric peaking out from under the lip.

It was a dull khaki colour. The hem of a trench coat perhaps, caught after having been discarded by their suspects? It seemed an odd decision to dump their coats, given how useful they were in concealing bulky weapons. Suddenly Sanderson's head was full of questions. What were this pair planning next? Were they changing their MO? Were they ridding themselves of their clothes, before attempting to flee undetected?

And she noticed something else. Fresh blood on the ground. A spatter of it, just beneath the rear of the car. Was this a new victim or . . . ?

Sanderson could feel her courage failing her as her anxiety steadily rose, so, stepping forward decisively, she grabbed the handle of the boot and yanked it open.

59

14.10

Daisy strode along the pavement, casting nervous glances at her watch. Her whole body was shaking and she felt cold, despite the heavy coat she was wearing. She was behind schedule now, in danger of missing her opportunity, so she upped her pace, half stumbling as she hurried down the street.

She hadn't wanted to do it. But what choice had she had? They were only a few hours into their operation and already one of their identities had been blown. She had no idea how the police had worked out who Jason was. Was it something they'd left behind at one of the scenes? Something they'd said? Had someone recognized them and contacted the police? No, that was impossible . . .

Once they'd realized that the police were looking for Jason, they'd faced a stark choice. Continue regardless or pull the plug on the operation? Daisy had dismissed the latter option instantly. So much planning had gone into this – and it felt so *right* – there could be no question of backing out now. They had to keep going, but she could see that Jason was getting distracted, seduced by his sudden celebrity, trying to catch the eye of passers-by. It was unforgivable – they had a plan, a plan they'd *both* agreed on . . .

She refused to cry for him, despite the tears that now threatened. Had she loved him? No, but she had been very fond of him. He had been her rock, the only person who ever stood up for her, and he was *loyal*. Loyal as a dog and just as enthusiastic. She hadn't needed to sell her scheme to him, he'd wanted to hurt people as much as she did. Her feelings for him had grown during their brief relationship, though she suspected he'd always felt more for her than she had for him. They were shipwreck victims, clinging to each other amid the wreckage . . . but nothing more. Once he had jeopardized all they'd worked towards – strutting down the street like he was seven feet tall – he'd effectively made the decision for her.

That hadn't made it any easier and she breathed in and out slowly now, trying to calm her jangling nerves. She cast another look at her watch – 14.10. She would just make it. She could see the crowd ahead now and hurried towards them, buttoning up her coat to hide the large bulge in the inside pocket, before once more checking that she had the additional shells. She fingered them nervously in her side pocket, praying for luck.

This was it then. She hadn't planned to do this solo, but she had no choice. Discarding her cap and shades, she pulled off her blonde wig and tossed it into a nearby bin. Opening her backpack, she then pulled out a bobbed black wig and slipped it on to her head, securing it carefully. Caution was the name of the game now. She could already see a few familiar faces and she had no intention of announcing her presence just yet. The crowd started to move, so, keeping her head down, Daisy slipped in among the bodies, shadowing their progress towards the building. As they reached the door, she waited patiently, then slid her ID into the card reader. The light pinged green, as it had on their recce, and the door sprang open.

Gratefully, she slipped inside.

60

14.12

'Our suspect's name is Daisy Anderson.'

Helen's voice rang out loud and clear. She was feeling a little calmer now, though she was still reeling from the speed of the developments in this exceedingly complex case. She handed out photocopies of Daisy's charge sheets and social services reports, as she continued:

'She's eighteen years old, a young offender with a string of convictions and cautions for shoplifting, drunk and disorderly, vandalism, affray. We think she met Swift during her last stint of Community Payback.'

'And do we think she's responsible for . . . ?'

DC Bentham didn't need to spell it out. An agitated Sanderson had called moments earlier with news of her grim discovery – Swift's bloody corpse, wrapped in his coat and stuffed into the boot of the Punto, which she'd located in an alleyway in Itchen. Helen had spoken to her personally, thanking her for her good work, before despatching a forensics team to the scene. Sanderson would remain there until they arrived and Helen had been tempted to join her, before deciding to pull the team together instead, to process the latest developments.

'Meredith Walker will tell us more, once she's examined

the body, but it seems highly likely. According to DS Sanderson, Swift had been shot at point-blank range with a shotgun.'

'But why would she do something like that? She and Swift have obviously been together for some time, he was helping to facilitate these murders . . .'

'We'll have to ask Daisy that, when we *catch* her,' Helen replied forcefully. 'Maybe they fell out, had a disagreement about what to do next –'

'Or maybe she was rattled?' Charlie interjected. 'Jason Swift's name is all over the TV, the radio . . .'

'Whatever the reason, Swift can't tell us much now. DS Sanderson undertook a brief search of the body – he doesn't have anything on him other than ammunition and there's nothing of significance in the car.'

'How long *had* they known each other?' Reid queried.

'Six months or so,' Helen answered. 'I think his role was as an enabler. He probably sourced the guns from the dark web, helped her plan the attacks –'

'But *she* decided the targets?' Osbourne asked.

Helen turned to look at Charlie. Was it his age, his height or his gender that had led them to assume that Jason Swift was the leader? Whatever the answer, they had got it badly wrong, wasting valuable time.

'That's our working theory,' she went on. 'Daisy Anderson probably harboured feelings of bitterness and resentment towards Alan Sansom, and Sonia Smalling's colleagues have confirmed that the probation officer recently "failed" Daisy, because of her frequent absences from her Community Payback programme. Daisy was potentially looking at a custodial sentence –'

'And in her anger she turned to Swift. Who was already pretty angry himself . . .'

Helen nodded – it was a pretty toxic combination. A young disenfranchised man, with a simmering anger towards society and a clear interest in guns, and Daisy, a young woman who clearly felt she'd been *wronged*. Had she used him to cover her tracks, getting him to source the guns while she remained off grid? Or had she genuinely felt something for her accomplice?

'Daisy's the product of a broken home, she lives with her dad on a farm in Hedge End. The Punto was dumped a few miles from there, but I don't think she's heading home – it's too far to attempt on foot. We'll despatch units to the farm, but I want us to focus on her past convictions, places of work, schooling, friends, relatives. Does anyone she might have a grudge against live or work in Itchen?'

'She was picked up in Topshop, but that's more central,' DC Osbourne said, flicking through Anderson's charge sheet.

'There is an affray charge in Woolston,' DC Bentham suggested. 'That's pretty close. An assault on another teenager . . .'

'Someone known to her?' Helen asked.

'Doesn't look like it . . .'

The officers desperately looked through their documents. Helen did likewise, poring over the pages, until she suddenly stopped and looked up.

'Meadow Hall Secondary School. Where is it?'

The surprised officers raced to google it.

'Itchen,' Osbourne said quickly, handing her his phone.

Helen took it, looking at the school's location on the

map. It was only a few hundred yards from where the car had been dumped.

'What do we know about it? Does she still go there? Were there any proble—'

'She was kicked out,' Charlie said solemnly, consulting her file. 'She was excluded.'

'When?' Helen demanded.

Charlie paused momentarily, before replying:

'Six weeks ago.'

61

14.14

Squeak, squeak, squeak.

Her trainers made an enjoyably unpleasant noise as Daisy marched across the polished wood floor. Moments earlier the corridor had been full of students, laughing and joking as they made their way to their afternoon classes. Now it was all but deserted, the sound of her shoes echoing around the empty space.

She walked slowly, firing glances left and right to see if anyone had seen her arrival. Nobody had taken much notice so far and her progress had been smooth and unimpeded. The occasional student looked up as she passed, mildly curious, before returning their attention to the whiteboard. No wonder the results from this place were so good.

'Can I help you?'

Daisy stopped in her tracks, turning quickly to find a portly man in overalls hurrying towards her.

'Excuse me?' she replied.

'This is a school. You can't just come wandering in off the street –'

'I'm a pupil here.'

'No, you're not. I know everyone who comes in and out of those gates and I don't recognize you . . .'

The man came to a halt just in front of her. Now he scrutinized her more closely – Daisy thought she began to see the tiniest flicker of recognition there.

'What's your name?' he demanded.

Smiling, Daisy stepped forward, ramming her left knee into the man's groin. The shocked caretaker gasped in pain, but his agony was short-lived. The butt of her shotgun now crashed into his face. The impact was brutal and her victim crumpled to the floor, his legs giving out beneath him.

Slipping her gun back into her coat, Daisy spotted a clutch of students moving to the window of a nearby classroom. They looked down at the prone caretaker, then back up at her. But she was already on the move. Ruining the fat man's day had not been part of the plan and it wouldn't pay to get distracted.

She had work to do.

62

14.15

The school campus was impressively large. Emilia marvelled at the size of it – her secondary school had been far smaller and much less well resourced. From where she was standing she could see an astroturf pitch, a swimming pool, a tennis court, not to mention a swanky science block. Emilia hadn't attended school much, thanks to her father's misdemeanours, but she would have killed to have gone somewhere like this.

Having investigated the graffiti at the probation offices in Totton, Emilia had gone back over her research, flicking through the numerous photos on her laptop, casting an eye over the various institutions which had suffered during the latest spree of graffiti. It had been tedious and irritating, but eventually it had paid dividends. Emilia had felt sure there was at least one other place she'd visited that had been marked with the distinctive serpent and, after half an hour of patient research, she'd remembered which.

It had taken her a while to locate the graffiti from memory but on the back wall of the school, out of sight near the municipal waste tip, she discovered the freshly painted serpent devouring itself. It was sufficiently recent for Emilia to be able to breathe in the paint fumes – a smell she had always loved. A shiver of excitement ran through her as she inhaled the rich, chemical odour.

Ahead of her, the playing fields and recreation areas were largely empty, the students having returned to their classrooms. After scaling the chain link fence at the back of the school, standing comically on top of her Vauxhall Corsa in order to do so, Emilia had a pretty clear run towards the main buildings. There didn't seem to be much security to speak of and the gardener had just headed off to dispose of his grass cuttings, so she emerged from the shadows.

Was she doing the right thing? Should she call the police? The coincidence of the graffiti was striking, but it was possible that it was just that – a coincidence. Besides, would anyone take her seriously, now that her stock had fallen so low? No, she needed more, before she revealed her hand. So, keeping a watchful eye out for the gardener, she padded across the grass towards the school buildings.

63

14.21

Helen tore up the steps and hurried into the school atrium. An armed unit flanked her and the rest of her team weren't far behind. It would be their job to secure the site, until they knew for sure whether or not Daisy intended to come here.

No sooner had Helen set foot in the cavernous reception area than she saw them – a small crowd of startled students huddled around a prone figure. Raising her warrant card, Helen ran towards them. The crowd parted to reveal a stocky, middle-aged man lying on the floor. His face and overalls were sticky with blood, but Helen was relieved to see that his injuries were relatively minor, a sodden handkerchief being clamped to a nasty gash on his temple.

'Has anyone called an ambulance?' Helen demanded.

One of the students nodded dumbly, so Helen turned to the injured man.

'Can you tell me where she is?'

The man looked up at her, but he seemed to be having trouble focusing.

'I *need* to find Daisy Anderson. Can you tell me which direction she went in?'

Now the man seemed to stir. Grimacing in pain, he

raised a finger and pointed down the main corridor. It gave on to several classrooms and led to a large stairwell. Thanking him, Helen rose and gestured to the armed unit to proceed. Carbines readied, they moved carefully, but purposefully, down the corridor. The shocked students watched them go, clearly alarmed by the heavy-duty weaponry that was on display. Some looked like they were on the verge of tears – their school had always been a safe, fun environment, but terror had breached its walls today.

Gesturing to Charlie to join her, Helen hurried away down the corridor. The armed officers were making good progress, moving in and out of the ground floor classrooms. Finding nothing, they hurried to the stairwell. Helen nodded to them to proceed, so they pushed on, moving cautiously up the stairs. Helen gave them a tiny head start, then followed suit, keen to be in on the action.

They were only minutes behind Daisy Anderson now.

64

14.22

The door burst open and Daisy marched into the classroom.

Sarah Grant looked up, faltering slightly in her delivery. Despite holding the position of deputy head, Grant still taught a full roster of lessons, taking great pride in the school's French and German results. She was slightly in love with the sound of her own voice and was often to be found reading aloud to her students. That was the case now, but she stumbled, then halted altogether as the intruder marched up to her desk.

'Can I help you?' she said, trying to sound calm.

'You guys can help me . . .' Daisy replied, turning to the class, '. . . by getting the fuck out of here.'

As she spoke, she pulled the sawn-off shotgun from her coat. There was an audible intake of breath from the students.

'Now!' she roared.

Chairs scraped back as the young men and women rose from their desks and hurried towards the doorway. Daisy watched them go. When the last one was free and clear, she slammed the door shut, before ramming a desk up against it, barricading them in.

'Just you and me now,' she said, turning back to the startled teacher.

'Look, if you want money, my pho—'

'On your knees.'

'What are you . . . what are you *talking* about?' the teacher blustered.

'Do it now,' Daisy replied, raising her shotgun to eye-level.

Grant suddenly obliged, her legs buckling beneath her.

'Why are you doing this? I haven't done anything to you . . .'

'Don't you recognize me, Sarah?'

The teacher stared up at her attacker, taking in her features properly for the first time.

'Daisy? Is that you . . . ?'

'Go to the top of the class.'

'Look, I don't know what this is about but . . . please . . .'

She was fumbling for words, terrified by the twin barrels pointing directly at her.

'I have a family,' she continued, falteringly.

'You should have thought of that before . . .'

'Before what? What have I done?'

'You're a bitch and bitches need to be put down.'

'No, Daisy, no . . . I'm not an animal, I'm a human being . . .'

But her captor just shook her head, dismissing these pleas for mercy.

'Look, if you run now, they might not catch you. My students will be calling the police, you must know that, so don't hang around to get caught . . .'

But even as she said it, Sarah suddenly thought that perhaps Daisy didn't want to get away. She had read about school shootings in the US and knew how they usually ended.

'Just tell me what I can do to make things right,' she said, changing tack abruptly once more.

'I'm not here to explain,' Daisy retorted, readying her weapon.

Grant looked at her former pupil. Daisy was clearly enjoying wielding the power of life or death over her.

'I don't want to die,' she pleaded. 'I know I can be . . . a bitch. And if I've done something to upset you, then I am truly, truly sorry . . .'

Tears were pricking her eyes now, her voice choked.

'I'll do whatever you want me to do, say whatever you want me to, but please don't kill me. My family won't cope without me – I know they won't, so please . . .'

She looked Daisy directly in the eye, even as she fought back tears.

'. . . please don't kill me.'

But even as she spoke, a wicked smile lit up the young woman's face.

65

14.24

They thundered down the stairs, sweeping past her as if she wasn't there.

Helen had reached the first-floor landing and had deployed the armed units to sweep the classrooms. She and Charlie had remained in the stairwell, radioing around the team, desperately searching for pointers as to Daisy's whereabouts in the vast school complex.

Bang! The loud noise had made Helen and Charlie jump. But it was just the stairwell door crashing into the wall, on one of the floors above. Moments later, thirty terrified students had appeared, running for their lives. The cacophony was frightening. They bowled past, oblivious to any obstacle, but Helen reached out an arm, tugging one of the petrified students towards her.

'Where is she?'

The student struggled in her arms, desperate to get away.

'*Where is she?*' Helen repeated, louder this time.

'Language labs, third floor,' the anguished student replied.

Now he wrenched himself free and Helen let him go. Gesturing to Charlie, she mounted the stairs to the next floor, clicking her radio on as she went.

'All armed units to the third floor. Repeat, all units to the third floor.'

Clicking off, she continued her ascent, taking the steps three at a time. Within moments she and Charlie had reached the third-floor landing. Taking a deep breath, Helen swung open the door and pushed out into the corridor.

66

14.25

It was full of people. Students and teachers had emerged from their classrooms, unnerved by the noise. They looked at each other, bemused and concerned.

'You should leave,' Helen said, as she marched towards them.

'Why? What's going on?' the nearest teacher asked.

'If you've heard any of the reports on the radio today . . . I would just go.'

Now the shocked teachers seemed to catch her drift, hurriedly ushering their charges towards the stairs. Seconds earlier they had been disoriented and confused, but now they came alive, knocking on doors, alerting others, clearing the floor. Helen was surprised and impressed by how calm and assertive they were and found herself pitching in, urging the students not to dawdle, as she chivvied them towards the fire escape at the opposite end of the corridor.

Cutting against the crowds, the armed officers now approached. A sign on the wall directed them towards the language labs, so they hurried in that direction. There were four classrooms towards the end of the corridor, comprising the languages department. Three of the doors were open, but the fourth was closed, with the blind pulled down over the window.

Dropping back, Helen watched on as the armed officers took each of the open doors in turn. Using mirrors, they checked the classrooms, before quietly heading inside. Helen waited tensely, but moments later all three emerged, silently shaking their heads.

They moved forward again, keeping tight to the wall, Helen now just behind them. She was expecting the glass with the blind to erupt at any moment, but they made it to the final door safely. Carefully, quietly, one of the officers reached out to the door handle, using the wall as cover. Grasping it, he turned. The handle moved, but as he tried to shoulder the door open, he met solid resistance. The door gave a couple of centimetres, but no more.

This is what Helen had been scared of. She had no idea how many people were in there with Daisy, nor what she was planning to do next.

'Daisy, this is Detective Inspector Grace. I'd like to talk to you,' she called out in a crisp, clear voice.

But there was no response from inside.

'Daisy, I can't help you if you won't talk to me.'

Helen strained to hear, hoping for a reply. None was forthcoming, but she *could* hear something else. A pitiful, low moaning, like an animal in pain . . . She gave the unit's leader a questioning look.

'Stun grenade?' he whispered.

Helen had to make a split-second decision – whether to try to engage in dialogue or take action. She didn't believe Daisy was the type to come quietly, and if there were already people injured, she didn't have much choice.

She held up two fingers. Immediately, two officers prepared their grenades, while two more readied themselves for the charge. Counting down silently from three, they launched themselves at the door. It moved slightly, allowing them just enough room to toss in their grenades. A second later, there was a deafening noise and a blast of white light. Now the officers didn't hesitate, ramming the door hard once more, before pushing into the room, weapons raised.

'Armed police!'

Helen waited until the last officer had hared inside, then she followed suit. She was breaking protocol and hoped Charlie wouldn't follow her, but she had to know what they were dealing with. Keeping low to the ground, she moved swiftly into the classroom, desperately casting around for their quarry. But no sooner had she stepped inside than she realized they were too late. Daisy had fled and the barricade blocking the door was not a barricade at all.

It was a middle-aged woman lying in a pool of blood.

67

14.32

Emilia Garanita was braver than most. It was something she prided herself on, happily going where angels fear to tread. During her time as a journalist on the South Coast, she had constantly put her life on the line in search of a good story, but today she was prepared to make an exception. She wasn't ashamed to admit that she'd been alarmed by the streams of students pouring from the school. She'd had to make an instant decision and on this occasion had decided to retreat.

Acting on impulse, she had cut against the crowds, heading down the fire escape that brought her out at the rear of the school. This was partly because she didn't want to get caught in the crush, but mostly because her first instinct was to retrace her steps back to her car. It had felt good sprinting down the stairs, away from the danger, and better still to push out into the sunlight.

She had continued to run, her heeled boots clicking over the tarmac of the recreation area, before eventually ducking out of sight behind a shed which lay some distance from the main building. It was a small shed – Emilia could see that it contained a ride-on lawnmower and a few gardening tools – but it provided good cover. Hidden from view, Emilia had paused to catch her breath, wiping the sweat from her face with her sleeve. She wasn't keen on exercise as a rule and suddenly felt utterly spent.

As she rested against the warm wood of the shed, she began to calm down a little. Had she been foolish to turn and run? It would have been risky to stay, given the obvious panic on the faces of the students, but hadn't she come here to get a story? So far all she had was a theory – a theory that had been proved right admittedly – but precious little actual material. Could she really go back to Gardener empty-handed?

Summoning her courage, she moved back around the shed, sneaking a look back towards the school. Immediately, she recoiled. A young woman in a khaki trench coat was hurrying across the playing fields. She wasn't heading in her direction exactly, but she *would* pass quite close to the shed. Where her companion was, Emilia had no idea. Was he fleeing the school via a different escape route? Or had something *happened* to him?

Emilia moved round to the other side of the shed, away from the approaching figure. As she did so, her camera bag bumped up and down on her hip, gently goading her into action. Quietly she unzipped the bag and pulled out her trusty Nikon. Reaching the far corner of the shed, she peeked round it. The woman was sixty, perhaps seventy, yards from her and moving fast. In a few seconds, she would pass by the shed and the moment would be lost, so Emilia now raised her camera and zoomed in on the fleeing figure. She was young and female, that's all that could be said for sure, but now was not a time for details. She pressed the button down, shooting rapidly. As she did so, she felt a surge of excitement, of pride even, happy once more to be ahead of the pack.

Emilia fired off ten, eleven, twelve shots. Then suddenly the woman looked up. In the viewfinder, Emilia saw her glance in her direction. Immediately she ducked back behind the shed. Had she heard something? No, that was unlikely at this distance. Had she seen something then? Had Emilia's lens caught the glare of the sun, revealing her presence? Or was she just imagining it? Was the woman simply taking stock as she fled the school?

Getting a grip on herself, Emilia slowly craned her neck round the corner of the shed once more. To her surprise, there was no sign of the woman. She had disappeared.

Now Emilia started to panic. Stuffing her camera back in her bag, she hurried round the shed, determined to make a run for it. Only to find the woman blocking her way, pointing a gun directly at her.

68

14.35

'Does anyone have eyes on them?'

Helen had left Charlie in the third-floor classroom, tending to the grievously injured woman, and headed outside on to the fire escape. Daisy clearly hadn't fled down the main stairwell – as they would have encountered her – so she must have used this as her means of escape. Instead of descending, however, Helen had climbed, vaulting the barrier at the top of the staircase to land gently on the asphalt roof. Marching to the roof's edge, she had clambered up on to the ledge and radioed DC Edwards, who was coordinating the campus search.

'Nothing yet,' came his squawked response.

'Nothing at all?' Helen returned, scarcely believing that they had lost her again.

'It's chaos down here. We've got parents turning up, the press, not to mention seven hundred students. We're trying to secure the perimeter, but –'

'Where's the helicopter?'

'On its way. You should be able to see it any minute now.'

'Ok. Keep in touch. In the meantime, I want us to issue Daisy's mugshot to the press. We need to put out an all-ports warning and I want roadblocks on *every* road out of Itchen. '

'Yes, boss.'

Edwards clicked off and Helen now heard it. She turned to see the dark dot in the sky heading towards her, growing bigger with each passing second. Moments later, the police helicopter roared overhead, arcing up in the sky, before circling round to sweep the campus from the air.

Helen should have felt reassured by its presence, but she didn't. She had never worked on a case like this – their killer was striking fast and hard, moving on without hindrance. Four victims in a matter of hours and still she didn't seem to be sated. Helen was hot on her trail, but so far their best efforts had come to nothing and Daisy Anderson remained at large.

They had been close, but not close enough.

69

14.36

The young woman looked anxiously up at the sky. Emilia was slightly ahead of her, but using her peripheral vision as best she could, fearful that at any moment she might raise her gun and pull the trigger. And she saw it – a flash of concern on the woman's face – as they both heard the sound of the helicopter.

She was scouring the heavens for signs of danger. Emilia did likewise, chancing a quick look while her captor was distracted. Frustratingly the helicopter, which had sounded like it was heading straight for them, had changed direction to hover directly over the school buildings.

The woman turned back and Emilia snapped her head forward again. They had reached the perimeter fence, the border of the school grounds, though they were some distance from where Emilia had gained access. She slowed to a halt, wondering what was coming next.

To her surprise, the woman snatched her camera and, tossing it aside, barked at her:

'Over the fence.'

Emilia did as she was told, grabbing at the chain link fence and scrambling up and over it. She landed clumsily on the other side, falling backwards on to her bum, to the amusement of her captor, who landed deftly beside her moments later.

Smiling, the woman offered her a hand up. Surprised, Emilia accepted, hoping that this considerate treatment might be the prelude to her release, now they were clear of the school premises.

But her relief was short-lived, as the woman turned to her and said:

'You got a car?'

70

14.52

Sanderson eyed the line of cars in front of her. A huge network of roadblocks was being established around central Itchen, in an effort to cut off any possible escape routes. There were dozens of traffic and police officers involved in the operation, but it had fallen to Sanderson and DC Reid to coordinate their efforts. Sanderson was not ungrateful – it was good to be tasked with something important – but it was still a major undertaking. To her relief, the uniformed officers under her temporary command had been responsive and her roadblock had been set up in record time.

The residents of Itchen were not thanking her of course – all of the major arteries in and out of the area were now clogged with traffic – but Sanderson wasn't worried about that. The latest updates from Meadow Hall School suggested that Daisy Anderson was still at large – nobody had seen hide nor hair of her as yet. She was sailing close to the wind – Helen must have missed her by a matter of minutes – but so far her luck had held.

Daisy had not rested on her laurels. It was still only early afternoon, but already she had struck four times. Tellingly, she had moved on swiftly after each attack, travelling considerable distances before striking again. On at least two occasions, she had stolen a vehicle in order to travel undetected, hence the importance of a thorough, well-manned roadblock.

DC Reid was stationed at the western edge of the suburb, monitoring the road to the Itchen Bridge. If Daisy wanted to head back into central Southampton, she would have to go that way. Sanderson was positioned towards the east, where Portsmouth Road met Spring Road. This was a likely route if Daisy wanted to make for her home in Hedge End or make a break for the M27. From there she could head north-east towards London or south-east towards Portsmouth. Either way would be useful, if she wanted to disappear.

Was this what she was planning? The frequency and brutality of her attacks suggested that she had no qualms about being captured – perhaps even that she wanted to be. But the robbery she'd committed at the pharmacy suggested that she was stockpiling cash and goods. To what end? To pay for her escape? Or live off while she laid low?

Whatever her intentions, she would have to escape first. Hampshire's police helicopter was circling the neighbourhood, scouring the streets from above, and another had been requested from West Sussex police. All the roads in the area were now subject to police checks and, given the probable timing of the most recent shooting, it was clear that Daisy was *somewhere* nearby.

Was it possible she was sitting in the queue of traffic in front of her? Cradling her shotgun? Sizing up her options? Sanderson paced back and forth, trying to dispel her nerves. In days gone by, when she was a little younger, she would have been exhilarated by a situation like this. Now, however, she just felt a little scared.

71

14.54

The traffic was horrendous, so Nick Dean pulled over to the side of the road. He had battled across Itchen to get this far, but had been stationary for nearly ten minutes now, so, abandoning his car in a parking bay, he hared off down the street. He didn't bother to lock the car, couldn't even tell if he'd shut the driver's door properly, but he didn't bother looking back, twisting in and out of the bodies that blocked his route on the congested pavement.

He had been in a meeting when the call came through. He wasn't supposed to take calls during the weekly team briefing and he had let it ring out at first. When it started ringing a second time – another school mum calling him – he had snatched it up and hurried from the room, ignoring the black looks from his boss.

'There's been an incident at the school, Nick. On the radio they're . . . they're saying it's a shooting.'

Her words had left him reeling. It seemed impossible. That was something that happened in America, not here. Ringing off, Nick hurried to the car park, pulling up the local news website on his phone as he did so. Nausea crept over him as he read the brief reports of the ongoing incident at Meadow Hall School, of the rolling roadblocks around Itchen. It was happening, all right . . .

He was in his car in less than a minute. He knew he should follow Mandy's good example and ring round the other parents, making sure they understood what was happening. But such generosity of spirit seemed beyond him right now, so instead he burned away from the office, heading towards the school. Dozens of awful scenarios filled his head as he sped towards Meadow Lane. He had heard that there had been a shooting near Ashurst this morning, but paid it little heed as he got caught up in the working day. Now the radio was saying that the shooting at the school was the third such attack that day.

'Please, God, not Jeannie. Not my little girl . . .'

He muttered the words, but they did little good. He felt so powerless, so clueless. Wouldn't someone have called him by now if there was a problem? Presumably not, as the incident was apparently ongoing, the perpetrators still at large. Nick had hammered the horn in frustration – at the slow-moving traffic, at his lack of information – before giving up on his car. The going was slow, there appeared to be as many people heading towards the school as there were trying to get away from it. Nick recognized a few faces – other parents from the school run – and suddenly realized that he must look as anguished as they did. They were ashen, drawn, bewildered – cheery folk that he often said hello to at the school gates all at once looked as if they had aged ten years in a day.

He picked up the pace, barging past a couple of protesting parents. It wasn't nice, it wasn't *right*, but suddenly he just had to know. They only had one child, she meant everything to them . . .

'Jeannie?'

He bellowed her name as he approached the massed ranks of people who hung by the police cordon outside the school. The crowd was ten deep or more and seemed to be composed almost entirely of tearful students holding on to their parents, their friends and in some cases police officers and paramedics. It was a deeply distressing sight, which only served to alarm him further.

'JEANNIE?'

His cry seemed to die on the wind, so, giving up, he grabbed a student who was hurrying away from the fray. Nick half recognized her, he thought she might be in Jeannie's class.

'Have you seen my daughter?'

The student looked at him blankly.

'Have you seen Jeannie?' he persisted, louder this time.

'No, no,' the student replied finally. 'I haven't seen anyone, I just ran . . .'

Abandoning her, Nick moved forward, running along the edge of the crowd.

'Jeannie?'

He was screaming her name at the top of his voice, but it was so hard to be heard above the crying and moaning.

'Jeann—'

'Dad?'

He stopped in his tracks, spun round. It certainly sounded like her, but he couldn't be sure.

'Jeannie?'

Then suddenly there she was, bounding towards him,

throwing herself in his arms. She was in floods of tears, as was he, but she appeared to be ok. She was clearly very shaken, however, and he let her cry for a good few minutes, holding her close, before he eventually eased her away from him. Wiping her tears, he kissed her several times and when at last she seemed calmer, he asked:

'Have you seen Mum anywhere?'

72

14.56

Helen looked down at the woman's body. The paramedics had worked tirelessly to save her life, but her injuries had been too severe. Daisy's fourth victim had been shot at point-blank range – once in the chest, once in the lower part of the face. The blood that still clung to the wall in the far corner of the room revealed the precise location of the shooting – Daisy had backed Sarah Grant into a corner and then fired. The amount of blood was significant, as was the fact that part of her jaw and cheek had been cut clean off by the impact.

Amazingly the grievously injured woman had managed to propel herself across the room. Perhaps Daisy had left, believing that her job was done. Whatever the case, Sarah Grant had wanted to live and had dragged herself to the door. The long bloody smear on the floor showed she had made it all the way, as did the bloody fingerprints on the door handle. But the poor woman had only succeeded in shutting the door on herself, before presumably collapsing just inside. It sickened Helen to think that Sarah Grant's body had been the blockage – the barricade – that they had struggled against as they laboured to gain entry to the classroom.

Sarah Grant was a wife and mother – Helen had

managed to gauge that much already – but she had bled out on the cold wooden floor. Why? Because Helen had allowed herself to be conned, tricked into racing to the WestQuay, while Daisy Anderson was heading here. Heading to school with murder in mind.

Helen had failed Sarah, just as she'd failed the other victims. Hers was another death on Helen's conscience, another ghost to parade before her tortured conscience. She knew she had to stay strong, if she was to catch this remorseless killer, but Helen felt that familiar darkness creeping over her now – and with it a burning anger that she was struggling to control.

73

15.02

'Shit.'

Emilia had caught sight of the roadblock thirty seconds ago, but her companion had only just spotted it. She had been distracted, fiddling nervously with the buttons on her coat, lost in thought. But as the car ground to a halt behind a long line of traffic, she'd looked up. The flashing blue lights and the sheer number of uniformed bodies in the road ahead clearly alarmed her and she squinted towards the rear of the car. But they were boxed in from behind by queueing traffic – there was no way back now.

The cordon was fifty feet away. The officers manning it seemed to be taking their time, quizzing each driver at length. Emilia didn't have a cover story – she and her captor had hardly said a word to each other since they climbed in the car – and she wondered what she would say. Where had she been? Who was her companion? Had she seen anything? It was probably best to stick as close to the truth as possible. She would present the police with her press pass and say that the woman was helping her with a story about graffiti artists. Emilia was by nature a good liar, but suddenly she felt nervous, as if the police would see right through her fiction.

There was always a chance they would make it through

the cordon, but then what? Emilia suddenly felt a cold stab of fear. Was she doing the right thing? The car was moving forward and they were now only twenty yards from the cordon. Should she take her chances? Say something to the police? What if she just opened the door and made a break for it? It might result in a shootout, but she would be free . . .

Emilia felt a sharp jab in her thigh. Looking down she realized that the woman had pushed the barrels of her gun into her leg.

'Just act natural. Answer their questions and no one gets hurt, right?'

Had she sensed what Emilia was thinking? There was steel in the woman's voice which she hadn't heard before and a coolness in her actions, as she slipped off her coat and laid it over her arm, concealing the gun from view. It was obvious to Emilia that she didn't intend her adventure to end here. Unless Emilia wanted her head blown off, it would probably be wise to obey.

Calming her breathing and fixing a smile on her face, Emilia drove slowly towards the awaiting police officers.

74

15.16

'Are you sure? Are you absolutely *sure* it's her?'

Charlie was huddled with Nick and Jeannie Dean in a police support vehicle parked up by the school entrance, the now deserted buildings visible through the small, square windows. Sarah Grant had not taken her husband's name when they got married, but once it had been established that she *was* Nick's wife and Jeannie's mother, Charlie had given them the terrible news. She had suggested that his teenage daughter might be better off with friends or relatives, but Nick Dean had insisted that she stay. He clearly didn't want to let her out of his sight, even when it became clear that Charlie had some very bad news to impart.

'I'm afraid we are. One of her colleagues has already identified her, though of course we will be asking you to formally –'

'How did she die?' Nick Dean said quickly. 'Did they . . .'

He seemed to run out of words, so Charlie stepped in.

'She died of a gunshot wound.'

'Was anyone else hurt? Any of her students . . . ?'

'No, it was just her.'

Nick Dean looked utterly mystified by Charlie's responses.

'But why? Why would anyone do something like that?'

He was staring straight at her, while his daughter's brimming eyes were fixed on the floor. In their different ways they both looked pole-axed by this sudden tragedy and Charlie sincerely wished she could tell them something that would ease their burden. But her head was still clouded by visions of Sarah's brutal murder and it was hard to think of any consoling words.

'We don't know yet,' Charlie conceded. 'As you may know, there have been a number of shootings today and we think that it may be part of a pattern –'

'You know who's responsible then?'

'We have an idea of who might be resp—'

'So why haven't you caught them? You know who's doing this, they've already done it twice before, why haven't you caught them?'

'Believe me, we're trying our best. We're throwing everything we can at this –'

'That's what you people always say,' he responded bitterly.

He turned, pulling his daughter to him. She was weeping now, quietly but persistently, pushing her face into her father's chest.

'I just hope you can sleep at night,' he continued, aiming his barbs at Charlie once more. 'Because it's people like us that have to deal with the consequences.'

He pulled his daughter closer to him, burying his face in her hair, whispering words of comfort. In spite of his anger and bitterness, he was showing admirable strength, refusing to break down in front of his daughter. His words stung, but Charlie hoped that his defiance, his resolve, would help Jeannie make it through this terrible ordeal. Father and daughter were cleaving to each other – propping each other up – and Charlie knew from experience that their fierce, defiant love was the only thing that would keep them going in the dark days ahead.

75

15.18

'Tell me about Daisy Anderson.'

Helen's time was limited, so she came straight to the point. An exhausted Simon Henshaw, the school's headmaster, sat opposite her in the abandoned classroom, casting occasional glances at the crowds outside. He clearly wanted to be out there with his students, providing whatever support he could, but Helen needed information.

'Daisy was . . . difficult,' Henshaw replied hesitantly, clearly still struggling to believe that a former student could have been responsible for murdering a member of his staff. 'I think she was basically a good kid who'd had a very rough time.'

'In what way?'

Henshaw looked slightly surprised by Helen's brusque tone.

'Her mother isn't on the scene,' the headmaster resumed falteringly, 'so she lives with her dad. He's a loving parent, but erratic. He never turns up for parents' evenings, has no interest in her school work. I think he likes to protect her from us, which obviously makes life difficult. He's a drinker too.'

'Did Daisy drink?'

Henshaw nodded.

'We caught her with bottles in her locker on a couple of occasions.'

'Drugs?'

'Yes. She took them, but also used them as currency, I think.'

'To impress people, make friends?'

'Yup, not that it really worked.'

'Because?'

'Because she was different. Her dad . . . her dad offered her a kind of . . . benign neglect. Never bought her clothes or make-up. She always came to school with her books in a plastic bag. Staff members thought she didn't wash much either, was often visibly dirty –'

'And the other kids mocked her for it?'

'We tried to police it, but you know what teenagers are like. She looked . . . she looked like a farmer's daughter and a poor one at that.'

'She was bullied?'

'Yes,' Henshaw confirmed, now looking a little shame-faced. 'She gave as good as she got, believe me, but then her grades started going south. We tried to remedy this, but Daisy felt that her teachers were singling her out, trying to humiliate her, so she stopped attending school. We gave her a number of chances to re-engage, but if a child refuses to come we have to exclude them. We have a long waiting list and –'

'And Sarah Grant was the one who expelled her?'

'Excluded, yes. My role is more pastoral, Sarah is the disciplinarian, so she dealt with it. But she was only ever trying to help Daisy, she had gone out of her way to ensure that she made progress, that she had the support she needed –'

'But Daisy felt Sarah Grant was picking on her?'

'Possibly,' Henshaw conceded, looking like a man who wished he could turn back the clock.

Helen stared out of the window at the students below. A picture was starting to emerge of a young woman who'd been dealt a bad set of cards and was now revenging herself on those whom she felt had rejected or humiliated her. All of her victims – Smalling, Sansom and now Sarah Grant – had tried to help her in different ways, but all had unwittingly enraged her.

'Did she have any pals at school?' Helen said, snapping out of it.

'Friends?'

'She only left school a few weeks ago, so is there anyone she might call on, lie low with? Someone perhaps who didn't show up for school today?'

Henshaw thought long and hard, before replying:

'We had pretty much full attendance today and, no, there's no one who'd *willingly* go out on a limb for her. It shames me to say it, but the truth is . . .'

The headmaster paused, before concluding:

'. . . Daisy didn't have a friend in the world.'

76

15.23

'What's the nature of your business in Itchen today?'

The police officer was curt and to the point, as he ran his eye over the interior of the car, taking in the two women.

'Working on a story,' Emilia said brightly, offering him her credentials.

The police officer, a tall, terse character, looked at her press pass, then at her scarred face, before handing back her documents. Emilia thought she saw a flicker of recognition in his jaundiced expression.

'What sort of a story?' he said witheringly.

'Teen graffiti. There's been a spate of tagging recently and the good folk of Southampton are not happy about it . . .'

She was trying to sound jolly, but knew it was coming out forced.

'Who are you?' He turned his attention to Daisy.

'Alice Baines,' she replied sullenly. 'I'm showing her the ropes.'

'You're a tagger?'

'One of the best,' she spat back defiantly.

In spite of herself, Emilia couldn't help but be impressed. The young woman showed no sign of nerves and her cocky manner was a good front. The police officer studied her closely, taking in her eyes, her features, her hair colour. Emilia had worked out some time ago that her black bob was a wig, but it suited her and was pretty convincing.

The officer stared at her for a long time, then returned his gaze to Emilia.

'Either of you seen anything? A young woman acting suspiciously? Aggressively even? She's got blonde hair, is about five foot two –'

The two women shook their heads. The officer looked down the long line of cars backing up behind them, before continuing:

'Has anyone asked you to assist them? Help them in some way?'

They shook their heads.

'And would you be willing to submit to a vehicle search, if required to do so?'

Emilia hadn't been expecting this question and was unsure how to respond, so Daisy stepped in.

'Of course. We've got nothing to hide.'

It was said confidently, with a smile, and now the police officer relented, turning to shout to one of his colleagues, as he gestured them to move forward.

They had passed the test.

77

15.26

Helen had barely made it across the school atrium, when DC McAndrew came bustling towards her.

'Boss, you need to see this . . .'

She was wearing latex gloves and holding a Nikon SLR camera. Helen pulled a fresh set of gloves out and, snapping them on, took the camera from her.

'We were doing a sweep of the grounds and found this near the perimeter fence.'

Helen examined the back of the camera and pressed the 'Play' button. Immediately a photo sprang up – it was of a young woman wearing a long, khaki trench coat, walking across the playing fields. Her heart pounding, Helen skipped through the sequence of photos, which were obviously taken very recently.

'I thought you'd want to see them straight away because –'

'She's got black hair,' Helen interrupted.

'Right, our guys are looking for a blonde and –'

Helen didn't wait for her to finish, sprinting towards the exit instead.

78

15.27

Sanderson's eyes were glued to the car. She was at the rear of the cordon, running a final rule over the vehicles as they passed by, and she had spotted Emilia Garanita immediately. Hers was a face that was hard to miss.

There were two things that struck Sanderson as odd, as the car moved slowly past. Firstly, Garanita was staring straight ahead of her, turning occasionally to speak to her passenger. Sanderson was only a few feet from them and normally Garanita wouldn't have missed the opportunity to engage with *her* – a tart look, a few choice words. This time, however, she had pointedly ignored her, seemingly more interested in her dark-haired companion.

The second strange thing was that Emilia was deliberately driving away from a major story. The car was fifty yards away now, signalling to turn the corner, heading even further from Meadow Hall School. Emilia Garanita lived and breathed the news – there was no way she wouldn't have heard about the latest shooting. Sanderson would have bet her house on the experienced crime reporter heading straight to Meadow Hall to pursue the students and harass the police officers – all in the interests of resurrecting her flagging career. But in fact she had chosen to drive in the opposite direction, her car now rounding the corner, heading *away* from the scene of Southampton's first school shooting. This troubled Sanderson – the rest of the nation's press corps were hurrying to Meadow Hall School, so why wasn't she?

Turning back to the cordon, Sanderson continued to ponder this, as a green hatchback passed by. But suddenly her reverie was broken, her radio sparking into life.

'Please advise all officers . . .'

The voice was Helen's and Sanderson was immediately alarmed by her anxious tone.

'. . . that our female suspect now has short, black hair. She is no longer *blonde*, she has a glossy, black bob . . .'

Sanderson froze. Helen had perfectly described Emilia's mystery companion.

79

15.33

'Turn right.'

Emilia obliged, steering the car carefully around another corner, then away down the road. Since clearing the police cordon, they had been turning constantly – right, then left, then right again, in a series of evasive moves, designed to confuse anyone who might be following them. Emilia was sure that nobody was shadowing them, but she nevertheless kept shooting hopeful glances at her rear-view mirror.

'Now left.'

Emilia had no idea where they were heading, only that they were driving away from the residential parts of the city towards its more remote fringes, the dead land between Southampton and Eastleigh. As her anxiety steadily rose, Emilia knew she had to try and engage the young woman, if she was to survive this ordeal.

'Can I ask you something?' she said, trying to sound as unthreatening as possible.

The woman's eyes remained glued to the road ahead of her, barely acknowledging the question.

'I know it's none of my business . . .' Emilia continued, gamely, '. . . but why are you doing this?'

Still she didn't respond.

'Look, I know you've got your reasons. I'm sure a lot of these people have done you wrong . . . but you can't run for ever. They'll catch up with you in the end.'

They were now passing Westwood Woodland Park – there was not a house or person in sight and Emilia's suggestion that the net was closing in on them was ringing rather hollow, but she had to persist nevertheless.

'You're an intelligent woman, you obviously know what you're doing. And there's no need for this to end in a bloodbath. You've already made your mark, you'll go down in history, folklore even . . . *especially* if you choose the manner of your ending. If you show the world that *they* couldn't catch you, that it was you who was in control all along.'

Emilia could tell she was listening, so pressed home her advantage.

'I can tell the world what you did. That you had the police chasing their tails, that you were the author of this story, handing out just retribution to the bad guys, how it was all *designed and run by you.* Think about it. This is your chance to be a star. Let me help you . . .'

The woman thought for a moment, then slowly raised her gun, pointing it at the woodland up ahead.

'Pull over there.'

80

15.46

'Tell me what you can see.'

Helen climbed on to her bike, her radio clamped to her ear. There was a long burst of static, then the helicopter pilot responded.

'No eyes on the Corsa yet.'

'They are heading east, perhaps towards the M27. Widen your range and let me know what you see.'

There was another burst of static, then the pilot confirmed her orders. Helen sat astride her bike feeling powerless and frustrated. She wanted to head east herself, but couldn't communicate with the chopper via her Bluetooth, so would have to stay put. Once more she cursed the fact that she had no boss to coordinate proceedings for her – more than ever the day's events were beginning to feel like a perfect storm.

'Anything?' she said impatiently.

'We're over the Portsmouth Road now . . . nothing significant, it's pretty free of traffic. We'll double back once we hit Netley . . .'

It was clear now that Daisy had commandeered Emilia Garanita's car, but where were the pair heading for? The M27 would be a fast getaway, but would make it easier for the police to trace them, because of the multitude of traffic cameras on the major road. Somehow Helen doubted that was their destination – Daisy had spent her whole life in and around Southampton, so where else could she go? She had no other family, no friends – surely she would use her local knowledge to survive for as long as she could? She was heading in the right direction for her family farm, but would she really take that risk? If she did, there would be officers waiting for her, but Helen suddenly wondered if she had left the neighbourhood at all. Heading east from Itchen took you out along an exposed A-road, perfectly visible from the air. Much better to hide out on the outskirts of Itchen or head south-east to Butlocks Heath, with its mixture of woodland and residential areas.

'Where are you now?' she demanded of the pilot once more.

'Coming back up the Woolston Road. Nothing yet . . .'

Now Helen lost her patience. Seeing DC McAndrew approaching, she tossed the radio towards her, the startled officer grasping it as it sailed through the air.

'Let me know if they spot anything interesting.'

Before McAndrew could respond, Helen started the engine. Sitting idle was killing her, so opening up her throttle, she roared away down the road, determined to play her part.

81

15.58

She gripped the wheel, scanning the road in front of her. The lights were flashing, the siren was blaring, but she barely registered them. Her eyes were fixed on the horizon, searching for a flash of red, something, *anything*. She had let Daisy drive right past her and now she was praying for a little bit of luck, so that she could make amends.

Sanderson cursed herself. She had been out in the cold for so long, dead to Helen, yet only a couple of hours ago she had detected the first signs of a thawing in their relationship, following her discovery of the missing Punto. 'Good work, Joanne' – that's what she'd said. It wasn't much, but it had momentarily sent her spirits soaring. For, much as she privately censured Helen for her actions, she'd also spent a lot of time reflecting on *her own*, questioning as never before her ability and aptitude to be a police officer. The small break she'd engineered in today's investigation had been a real fillip for her, yet now she was back in the role of team fuck-up again. How they must be cursing her, picturing her waving the red Corsa through, with a stupid smile on her face . . .

A car pulled out in front of her and Sanderson had to react sharply, swinging her car to the left, before sliding back into lane. Chiding herself for getting distracted, she concentrated once more on the task in hand. There had been no sightings of Daisy or Emilia since they made it through the cordon, but something told Sanderson that they were close by. She had passed Sholing and was now on her way through Newton. Tickleford Gully was to her left and beyond that the waste transfer station – there were plenty of places to hide out here if need be.

Was that Daisy's plan? She had come pretty close to getting caught, having to bluff her way through a roadblock. Would this make her think twice before continuing her rampage? Or was that just wishful thinking?

Sanderson found her thoughts returning to Emilia once more. Why had Daisy taken her hostage? Was it simply to guarantee that she'd get through the cordon or did she have something else in mind? Was she going to use her to try and engineer an escape? Sanderson shuddered at the thought of what the young journalist must be going through. Was that why she looked so grim as she drove past, barely registering anything or anyone around her? It was an image that Sanderson was trying to push from her mind, but it kept returning to her. She had never seen the journalist look so pale. Truth be told, she had looked like a condemned woman.

82

16.08

They were marching through woodland, crunching the leaves as they went. The young woman had ordered Emilia to park up on a rough track by Priors Hill Copse, abandoning the car and tossing the car keys into the dense undergrowth. Then she'd told Emilia to walk.

They were moving in single file, Emilia taking point while the woman with the gun followed just behind. Emilia had no idea where they were going and occasionally the woman barked at her to change direction, to veer off a path, cut up a hill. Did she know where they were heading or did she just want to get somewhere remote and isolated? Emilia fervently hoped it was the former.

Emilia had desperately wanted to break this story, but now she was increasingly worried she was going to become part of it. She had tried her best to engage her captor, to get her to talk, but her efforts had been rejected. So Emilia had kept her counsel, obeying the woman's orders and keeping her head down. But the silence was chilling – she had no idea what she was doing behind her, what she was planning – and her nerves were shredded.

'This'll do.'

They were right in the heart of the woodland now, shielded on all sides by trees.

'Get down on your knees.'

'Please, you don't have to do this . . .'

'On your knees!'

Emilia felt the cold barrels of the gun ram into the back of her head and stumbling forward she fell to her knees.

'Look at the floor.'

'I won't say anything to the police, I promise. I'll pretend this never happened . . .'

'I think we're a little beyond that, don't you?'

Emilia hung her head and sobbed. All the anxiety that been building up in her now burst forth and she cried without restraint, tears streaming down her face.

'Please . . . I'm begging you,' she spluttered. 'I have brothers . . . sisters . . .'

She couldn't find the words. She had always been confident, gobby, eloquent, but at this crisis point in her life, she simply couldn't find the words. Her head was filled with images of her siblings, the way they fussed around her when she came back into the house, demanding cash, relaying their grievances, teasing and cajoling her. They were infuriating, but having been mum and dad to them for so long, she loved them deeply. But how could she put that love into words? It was too much, it was overwhelming.

'Please . . . my father's in jail, my mum's long gone, I'm . . . I'm everything to those kids . . .'

Emilia knew she wasn't making much sense, but she seemed to have lost the power to speak intelligibly. She was gabbling wildly, all the while expecting to be flung forward as the gunshot ripped through her.

'I don't want to die . . .' she mumbled pathetically, though she knew it was hopeless. 'I don't want to die . . .'

She closed her eyes and wept. She could feel the damp grass beneath her knees, could hear the birds twittering overhead. Her senses suddenly seemed so heightened, like she was getting drunk on the world for the last time, sucking in the last few seconds of life before the inevitable, violent end.

83

16.13

Helen sped along Grange Road, roaring past the dawdling cars as she cut north. She had checked out Woolston and was now leaving Netley. There were an old vicarage and a lake house there that she'd wanted to investigate, but finding them both secure and deserted she had abandoned her search and was now heading for Butlocks Heath. There were a couple of schools there with large playing fields, plus a sizeable cemetery, all of which had potential for a fugitive wishing to vanish for a while.

Hitting the junction by Abbey Fruit Park, Helen dropped her speed and swung right on to the Woolston Road. The road opened up in front of her now and she ramped up her speed, flying across the tarmac. The ride was smooth, the handling precise – in any other circumstances Helen would have thrilled to the sensation of roaring along this quiet country road. But the pride she'd felt in her new ride at first light seemed a very long time ago. A lot of blood had flowed under the bridge since then.

Sanderson was tearing around old Netley, the chopper had circled back over Weston Common and McAndrew was coordinating the rest of the team's efforts to trace their fugitive. But still she eluded them. What was her secret? Was she just lucky or was this some kind of military-style operation? It seemed unlikely – she was so young – and yet what other possible explanation was there for her ability to evade capture consistently in this way?

Helen was moving away from the more residential areas of Butlocks Heath, woodland now flanking the road. And as the road turned south towards the coast, Helen suddenly saw movement ahead. Dropping her speed quickly, she registered that two cars were parked there. Neither was the red Corsa they were looking for, but something was going on and Helen's instincts told her that it was significant.

As she got closer to the obstruction, she realized that the drivers had abandoned their cars and were huddled over something. Firing up her siren to alert them to her presence, Helen pulled up sharply, climbing off her bike. As the elderly motorists looked up, Helen ran towards them, pulling off her helmet and raising her warrant card. She prayed to God there hadn't been yet more bloodshed, but, whatever it was, she had to know.

As she approached, the small crowd seemed to part for her and Helen was surprised to see a bedraggled Emilia Garanita sitting in the middle of the road. Her clothes were muddy, her whole body was shaking and she had foliage in her tangled hair – but she was alive.

'Are you ok?'

Helen walked up to her, offering a supportive hand.

'Emilia, are you ok?'

But the journalist said nothing, simply turning to Helen before bursting into tears.

84

16.31

'Did she say anything? Anything at all?'

Emilia was now sitting in the back of an ambulance, a blanket wrapped around her. She was still in shock, unable to hold the cigarette that she clearly craved. Whether this was as a result of her abduction or the impact she'd felt as she crashed down on to the road was unclear. The concerned motorists told Helen she'd come from nowhere, tearing down the bank at the roadside and into their path. On another day they might have run her over, but at the end of her ordeal, the journalist's luck had held.

Paramedics had given her the once over, and while they were keen to get her to hospital, Helen needed to speak to her first. Understandably she was unusually taciturn, staring at her feet as she tapped her toes on the ambulance floor.

'Emilia, did Daisy say anything about where she was heading?'

Charlie joined in now, as Helen's words seemed not to have cut through Emilia's self-absorption. Charlie had rushed to the scene as soon as she'd got Helen's call and the trio were holed up together in the cramped ambulance.

'No, she hardly spoke to me.'

'How long were you with her for?' Charlie persisted.

'An hour and a half or so, no more,' Emilia replied. 'Like I said, I went to the school to check out the graffiti, but she found me on the playing fields, forced me to go with her, told me that she needed a car.'

'What else did she say?' Helen persisted.

'Nothing, she told me which direction to head in, shouted at me when I was going wrong.'

'And why do you think she spared you?'

Emilia paused, seemingly confused by Charlie's question.

'I don't know . . . she told me to get down on to my knees, I thought . . . I thought she was going to do it . . . then nothing happened. I turned round and she'd gone.'

'Do you think she bottled it?' Helen asked, keen to get some – any – insight into the young woman's mind.

'Maybe . . .'

'Or was she toying with you? Enjoying scaring you?'

'Probably . . . I don't know.'

'And you didn't hear anything as she left? You've no sense which direction she may have fled in?'

But Emilia wasn't listening any more. Her whole body was shaking again – she was back in the midst of her trauma – and when she looked up, she was fearful and upset.

'Please . . . can I go home now? Can I just . . . go home?'

She stared directly at Helen, her red-ringed eyes appealing for mercy. And, in that moment, Helen felt something for her erstwhile nemesis that she'd never felt before.

Pity.

85

16.35

'Did they find anything in the car?'

Helen and Charlie were marching away from the ambulance towards Helen's bike. Emilia's car had been spotted by the chopper on a track near Priors Hill Copse and McAndrew had headed straight there, while Helen and Charlie had conducted their interview.

'Nothing yet,' Charlie told her. 'The forensics guys are crawling over it now, but there's nothing obvious. They'll find Daisy's DNA, I presume.'

'That won't get us anywhere. Kidnapping charges are the least of Daisy's worries.'

'Why dump the car?'

Helen paused. Charlie's question was a good one and had been worrying her too.

'Did she think she'd been clocked, that we were looking for the Corsa?' Charlie suggested.

'There's no way she could have known that,' Helen replied. 'She must have assumed we had no idea who her hostage was or even that she had one at all.'

'Perhaps she was just being cautious, changing vehicles as often as possible. She left it somewhere pretty remote after all.'

'But then what? She'd have to walk a fair way to find

another. Cars don't pass that often round here and when they do they are travelling at speed.'

'She's making life difficult for herself, that's for sure.'

'So why do it?'

There was a moment's silence, before Charlie eventually responded.

'Maybe she's just winging it now, making it up as she goes along . . . ?'

'I don't buy it. You heard what Garanita said – she's been marking her territory in advance with the serpent graffiti, she's worked out entry points and escape routes for the places she wanted to target . . . I think she's planned every stage of her journey, so it plays out exactly how she wants it to.'

'But she couldn't have *known* she would run into Garanita, that she would take a hostage . . .'

Charlie petered out once more. Helen stood, hands on hips, scanning the road as if it could somehow provide the answers they were groping for.

'She loses mobility by dumping the car,' Helen continued, 'so what does she *gain*?'

'Well, once it becomes known she's taken a hostage, then obviously we'll be looking for her car.'

'But she makes herself very visible by proceeding on foot, unless she can find some other way . . .'

Helen tailed off, looking down the road in the direction of Netley.

'How long would it take to walk from Priors Hill Copse to Netley?'

'Five minutes or so.'

'And if you wanted to make tracks without running into

roadblocks *and* without your moves being seen from the air –'

'Then you'd take the train.'

'Netley train station is a five-minute walk away. From there she can head to Portsmouth or back into Southampton virtually undetected . . .'

Charlie was already pulling her radio from her pocket.

'Alert the transport police,' Helen said. 'Make sure they have access to the photos Emilia took and up-to-date descriptions of Daisy's hair colour, clothes and appearance. I want officers despatched to every station on that line. If Daisy's been there, let's find out what direction she headed in, then track her on station CCTV. Also, make sure all news outlets have an image of the serpent graffiti tag. If anyone has spotted something similar on a building near them, we need to know asap.'

Helen had been walking and talking, but had now reached her bike. She climbed on to it, picking up her helmet.

'Where are you going?' Charlie asked, her radio hovering by her mouth.

Helen paused a moment, before responding:

'To have a chat with Dad.'

86

16.44

Daisy watched the world go by. The train had passed through Sholing and was rattling towards Itchen station. In the middle distance, she could glimpse the blue lights flashing, though she couldn't see Meadow Hall School itself. She wondered what it was like there now, what was going on. She could imagine the scenes – the sobbing students, the bunches of flowers, the blank shock, but she suddenly had a desire to *see* it. She might get to watch it on the news later, but it wouldn't be the same.

She was the only person in the carriage, so she pulled out her cigarettes. She had bought them yesterday and, as superstition required, immediately threw away the first one. She looked down at the packet in her hand – it was crushed and slightly bent. She didn't like to think too much what that signified, so she pulled one out and lit it. She inhaled deeply, then blew the smoke out into the deserted carriage.

As she did so, she noticed that her hand was shaking. The five minutes she'd spent waiting on the platform for the suburban train had seemed like an eternity. She had discarded her trench coat, so as not to draw attention to herself, her shotgun now safely stowed in her backpack, but still she knew she looked odd, wearing just a thin cotton T-shirt on what was now becoming a cold autumn evening. She had expected people to point the finger at her, to recognize her, to alert the police to her presence . . .

She took another long drag on her cigarette, letting the smoke swirl around in her mouth. She had to keep calm, keep focused. She had had a very close shave, had had to think on her feet, but it was done now and there was no point getting hysterical. She was ashamed now to think of how rattled she'd felt moments before. As the train *had* finally roared into the station, for a brief moment she'd been tempted to jump, to land on the tracks, to *feel* the impact of metal on bone . . . She'd contemplated this many times before of course – ever since she was old enough to be out alone really – and it would have been quick and easy. A simple end to a difficult day, especially now things had become complicated . . .

She angrily stubbed the cigarette out on her hand, gritting her teeth as the skin sizzled and a thick blister rose. She had to be strong, she wouldn't let those bastards win. Throwing the cigarette butt into the bin, she reached into her trouser pocket and pulled out a small bottle of amphetamines. She had been living off these for as long as she could remember. It was one of the reasons why she was so pleasingly thin. Unscrewing the lid, she tipped three small pills into her hand, then tossed them into her mouth, before slipping the bottle back into her pocket.

She let the pills dissolve slowly, enjoying the feeling as they fizzed and dissipated. Slowly she felt her mood begin to lift, her optimism and energy start to return, as the pills took effect. There was no room for weakness here. She *would* soldier on, she would see this through to the bitter end . . .

She sat back in her seat and looked out of the window once more. She felt oddly calm, the last vestiges of autumn sunshine playing over her face, as the train rattled back towards the city centre. She was still alive, she was well armed and suddenly she felt sure that everything would be fine. The train was speeding up, propelling her towards her destiny. As she stared out of the window, a smile crept across her face.

The sun was beginning to drop now and soon darkness would descend.

87

17.01

They pulled up at the side of the road and sat in silence for a moment. Sanderson killed the engine and looked up at the terraced house. It was Victorian and shabby chic at best – the windowsills needed painting and the pathway was covered in weeds – but it was a house that was full of life. The lights were on and, flicking her gaze from window to window, Sanderson could see the inhabitants moving around inside – laughing, joking. It was a touching scene at the end of a very tough day.

'Would you like me to come in with you?'

As she spoke, she turned to Emilia, who was sitting beside her in the car.

'If you need to rest, I can talk to your brothers and sisters, tell them what's happened . . .'

'I'll do it.'

'It's no trouble –'

'They're my family. I'll do it.'

Emilia's tone was firm, but not unfriendly. Sanderson decided not to push it, nodding her assent, while pulling out her card.

'This has got my numbers on it,' she said, handing it to the journalist. 'If you remember anything useful . . . or if you need my help at all . . . don't hesitate to ring.'

Sanderson half expected Emilia to reject the overture, but she took the card, even as she leant over to open the door. But her hand lingered on the handle and the journalist turned back to Sanderson.

'Thank you . . . for bringing me home.'

'It was the least I could –'

'I know you didn't have to do it and I appreciate it, Joanne.'

Climbing out of the car, she walked up to the house. Sanderson watched her go, impressed by her bearing and dignity. Emilia had been in a state earlier, shaking with shock, but only half an hour later she had gathered herself, regained her composure. Sanderson could see Emilia steeling herself for the onslaught of her family, preparing to answer their questions and alleviate their concerns. She looked purposeful, resolved, but above all strong.

Sanderson had always been suspicious of and occasionally even downright hostile towards Emilia Garanita. But tonight she had new-found respect for her. Would she have shown similar strength if the roles were reversed? Who could say, but she would bear the journalist's example in mind. From now on, she would never be paranoid or weak again.

88

17.08

The mud squelched beneath her tyres as Helen's bike came to an abrupt halt in the yard. Two squad cars were parked up by the ramshackle farmhouse and the attending officers now hurried over to meet her. They had been despatched to intercept Daisy, should she try to return home, but they had found the old farmstead deserted.

'We're already inside, ma'am,' one of the breathless officers said, struggling through the mud towards her. 'I think you'd better take a look . . .'

Alarmed by his sombre tone, Helen nodded her thanks and moved on towards the house. It had once been a fine building, but was now in an advanced state of disrepair. Paint was peeling, tiles were missing and one of the shutters hung lazily off a single hinge. The whole place looked lonely and unloved.

As she moved purposefully forward, Helen took in the rest of the site. There were outbuildings, filled with rusting farm equipment, and beyond them open fields. The plots weren't huge round here, thanks to the natural boundary of the River Hamble on one side and the M27 on the other, but they had been prosperous back in the day, providing milk and livestock for Southampton, Portsmouth and other South Coast markets. But the fields on this farm were empty now. The lonely farmstead reeked of defeat. Whether this was due to economic forces or more personal troubles Helen wasn't yet sure.

The house was framed by ruddy brown fields and tall oak trees, which looked ominous and foreboding in the half-light of dusk. Taking them in, Helen had a sudden jolt of recognition. The rural background, the empty fields, the birds circling in the sky . . . she felt sure that this was the vista she had seen on Jason Swift's home movies. This was where he had taught Daisy to shoot, where they had planned and trained for their killing spree. It was a pleasingly isolated location, with no busybody neighbours to interfere or ask awkward questions. But why hadn't Daisy's dad intervened? Neglectful he might have been, a drunk even. But he had no criminal record and surely must have sensed that something was badly wrong here?

Helen continued towards the front door. As she mounted the porch, the boards creaked warningly beneath her feet. Looking down, Helen realized that she would have to pick her way to the door carefully – the woodworm had been having fun on this farm even if no one else had. The door itself swung back and forth in the rising breeze, having been barrel-charged by the attending officers.

The interior looked gloomy, so Helen pulled a torch from her jacket pocket. The way now lay open for her, so sliding sterile covers over her muddy boots, she quietly slipped inside.

89

17.10

Helen proceeded cautiously, testing each floorboard as she went, keeping her eyes open and her senses alert. Stepping into the hallway, she was surprised to find that everything looked pretty normal. A chair had been knocked over, but otherwise there was nothing alarming about the scene that greeted her. Moving on quickly, she toured the kitchen, where a carton of milk sat on the table, before heading across the hall to a small study.

This room had clearly been the administrative centre of the farm – Helen could see a long line of box files on the shelf marked 'Accounts', 'Admin', 'Statements' and so on. But it was now little more than a glorified storeroom, crammed full of broken furniture, empty food boxes and piles of unopened letters. Keeping half an eye on the corridor, Helen leafed through the letters quickly. She wasn't surprised to see that several had a bank's logo on them, while others had been sent from Meadow Hall School. All of them had been discarded, deemed unworthy of interest.

Dropping the letters, Helen now noticed the framed photos on the desk. There were three of them – all of Daisy at various ages. A baby grinning while lying on her back, a gappy-toothed seven- or eight-year-old smiling warmly at the photographer and a surly teenager, looking unhappy and self-conscious in a pretty summer dress. The effect of the trio of photos on Helen was surprising and strong. This was love – there was no other word for it. Love of a father towards his little girl. Helen immediately thought of her own father, who'd had only a perverted interest in his children. Whatever had happened in this family over the last few weeks and months, one could be in no doubt that Michael Anderson had loved his daughter deeply. Was this why he had ignored the letters from school? Why he had overlooked her criminal offences? He was not on record as having remarried and there were no pictures of a girlfriend or partner – perhaps Daisy was the only meaningful thing in his life.

Leaving the study, Helen mounted the stairs to the first floor. More framed pictures of a young, smiling Daisy graced the wall and at the top of the staircase, Helen discovered the teenager's bedroom. This was in a state of some disarray – the wardrobe was open, clothes were scattered – but it was no worse than many a teenager's and you could still tell the room had been done out nicely, if cheaply. The bed was unmade and next to it was a pile of magazines. It would be an illuminating place to explore, but not yet.

Helen walked down the corridor to another bedroom. Slowly she teased open the door. It groaned as it rolled back on its hinges. Inside, the furniture was broken, the curtains were torn from the rails and lying in the middle of the double bed was a corpse.

Taking care not to disturb the scene, Helen crept towards the body. It was pale and looked to be in an advanced stage of rigor mortis. The blood that covered the victim and most of the bedspread was dry, but the body had not yet started to decompose. He had been dead for two days or so therefore, but no more than that. The victim had been shot in the chest and neck repeatedly. The skin on his face was lacerated and covered in blood as a result, but Helen was pretty sure that she was looking at Michael Anderson, Daisy's father. He had been murdered in his own bed, gunned down at point-blank range.

Was this the trigger then? Was this what had precipitated this terrible killing spree? Helen suspected it was, not just because it preceded the other murders, but because of what it meant. This man had looked after Daisy in his own way, had perhaps been the teenager's only link to real life – to family, to love, to compassion. And she had killed him – no, she had destroyed him. Helen could count at least five impact wounds – this was not a cold, calculated attack, but an explosion of rage. She had butchered a man who loved her, had severed her last link to normality and after that there was no way back. Nothing to stop her from launching her terrible vengeance upon the world.

Had she and Swift sat downstairs afterwards, making their final preparations, as Michael Anderson lay dead upstairs? It was a chilling thought and should have served as a warning to Jason Swift, the junior partner in this killing spree. He thought he was Daisy's lover, her right-hand man, destined to go down in history as the co-architect of this infamous spate of killings. But he was deluded if he felt Daisy owed him anything, for, as the body on the bed proved, Daisy was utterly ruthless. Forces bigger than herself were driving her – though she was not deranged, she was psychotic, single-minded and totally bent on destruction. If her earlier actions had not already proved it, the discovery of Michael Anderson's corpse confirmed that Daisy would not stop now until something – or someone – halted her in her tracks.

90

17.16

Suddenly she felt as if the eyes of the world were upon her.

The station was heaving with commuters and Daisy hadn't found it difficult to slip in behind one of them as he passed through the ticket barriers. She had been in good spirits – feeling carefree, even a little high – as she'd hurried towards the exit, but then suddenly she'd spotted something that had pulled her up short.

The *Southampton Evening News* was on sale and the vendor was doing a brisk trade today. Predictably the paper was majoring on the day's shocking events, promising its readers the very latest on the murders. What Daisy hadn't been expecting was the confident headline: 'Schoolgirl named as suspect'. She wasn't close enough to read the text beneath it, but even from this safe distance she could make out her face. It was splashed across the front page – an unflattering school photo taken last year, which her dad had predictably shown no interest in buying.

How had they worked out who she was? Was it the caretaker? Her hostage? She'd assumed they would discover her identity eventually, but had never thought that her name would be front-page news *tonight*. Now, as she stood stock still, taking in the line of commuters queueing up to buy the paper, Daisy became aware of something else.

Police, lots of police. Some were regular beat coppers, others were Hampshire Transport Police, instantly recognizable in their fluorescent jackets, but all were engaged in the same task, scrutinizing the commuters' faces on the platforms, searching, searching, searching for their quarry . . .

So far Daisy had escaped their attention, boxed in among the suits, but feeling suddenly exposed, she made a break for it, keeping her head low as she weaved through the crowds towards the exit. There were officers there too of course, earnestly examining the passing faces, so Daisy didn't hesitate, ripping off her black wig and tossing it aside.

Running her hand over her shaved head, she walked quickly and confidently forward. She had cut off her blonde locks three days ago in preparation for battle and she was very glad of it now. Her buzz cut made her look older, more aggressive – a far cry from the gawky blonde in her school photo or the dishevelled teenager in her police mugshots.

She was close to the exit now and an officer was looking directly at her. She hoped that her smooth head and dark eye make-up would do the job, but just to be sure she gave the officer a saucy wink and ran her studded tongue over her lips suggestively. Embarrassed, he looked away, and with her head held high Daisy strutted past him, giving him one more wink for good measure.

Once out of the station, she hurried away from the main drag, dodging locals who seemed absorbed in their newspapers. Everywhere she turned, people were either drinking in the news or deep in earnest conversation about it. *Was* the whole world looking for her? It felt that way, so, turning down a side street, she moved away fast from the clamour of the station.

Now she slowed. Her heart was beating nineteen to the dozen and, though she was lightly dressed, she was sweating. Wiping her face with her arm, she caught her breath and considered her options. She had made it past one police officer but would her luck continue to hold when they were scouring the city for her? She had a fair way to go and suddenly she didn't fancy it – walking along the wide thoroughfares, constantly looking over her shoulder . . .

Surveying the street, she was pleased to see that she was alone. Walking up the line of parked cars, she examined the locks, but all she saw was little red lights flashing at her, proudly announcing their alarm systems. Then, just as she was about to give up hope, she found what she was looking for. An aged Peugeot 205 with no alarm. This was Jason's domain really – nobody could pop a lock like he could – but Daisy had neither the time nor the inclination to muck about, so using the butt of her shotgun she stoved the window in instead. It broke easily and, lifting the lock, she opened the door and, sweeping the glass off the seat, climbed inside.

Flinging her backpack on the passenger seat, she got to work. Reaching under the steering column, she slipped her hands beneath the cheap plastic surround and wrenched it away to reveal the wiring underneath. Her delicate fingers quickly located the wiring harness connector and from there she pulled aside the battery, ignition and starter wire bundle. She was now at the most sensitive stage of the process and she took her time, gently stripping away an inch or two of the insulation, before twisting the battery wires together.

The ignition kicked in, and as she pumped the accelerator the engine roared. Reducing the gas, she listened to it purr, smiling contentedly to herself. She had had a short, fiery and ultimately ill-starred relationship with Jason, but he had taught her a few things. Not least how to hot-wire a car. This was his gift to her, his legacy.

And it just might see her home.

91

17.29

'You've no right to do this, no right at all. You're no better than the rest of them . . .'

Charlie stood alone in the cramped study, the mobile phone resting in her gloved hand. She had arrived at the farm shortly after the forensics team and, as they were now at work in the main bedroom, she'd commenced her search downstairs. She'd found Michael Anderson's mobile phone in his coat, which hung on a chair in the study, and had immediately investigated his call history. A few were withheld numbers, but the vast majority of the calls were from a number labelled Daisy in his Contacts, all made in the last few days. It would take a while to get any info from the phone company, so she'd proceeded straight to his Voicemail. It was an ancient model without a password prompt or any security, so moments later Charlie was playing his messages on speakerphone.

'You say you love me, but then you land *this* on me? Look in the fucking dictionary, see what love actually means . . .'

Daisy's words rang out in the small room. She was angry but also upset, her voice shaking occasionally as she ranted at her father. There was clearly love still there, some affection for her father, her tone softening occasionally even in the midst of her outbursts. But her blood was up and another explosion of righteous indignation was never far off.

'I have always looked out for you, always had your back . . . and this is how you treat me?'

Charlie was on to her third message, but each had the same tenor, the same central accusation.

'Jason is a decent guy. You have to give him a chance, Dad . . .'

Other members of the search team had uncovered evidence of Jason Swift's presence in the house – a bank card in Daisy's bedroom, used condoms in her bin – and these phone messages made it clear that this was the reason for the breakdown in relations between father and daughter. Although they would need to access Daisy's messages to get the whole picture, it was clear that Michael Anderson had told Jason Swift to move out. Or put another way, he had asked his daughter to choose between them.

Charlie could picture the fallout and it depressed her. Michael Anderson had clearly been a negligent, indulgent parent, allowing his daughter to slip into bad habits. The evidence all around suggested he had given up on life, be it the dilapidated state of the farm, the unpaid bills or the numerous empty whisky bottles in the bins, but he had clearly never relinquished his love for his daughter. And up until the last moment, neither had she given up on him, imploring him in her fourth and final message to see reason.

'It doesn't have to be like this . . . you're *making* it into something worse than it is. Jason is sound, please believe me, don't make me choose . . .'

They were seemingly couched in conciliatory terms, but these messages had a dark undertone, laced with threat, steeped in bitterness. The man she thought she could rely on had turned on her. Perhaps he hoped to shock her into changing her ways, into getting her life back on track, into renouncing her thuggish, violent boyfriend. If that had been Michael Anderson's intention, it had backfired spectacularly.

Boxed into a corner, Daisy had made her choice.

92

17.42

The room was full of hatred. Most of Helen's officers were concentrating on the crime scene, but she was exploring the teenager's bedroom. In her experience, teenage girls guarded their secrets carefully and she had little doubt that if she wanted to climb inside Daisy Anderson's brain, this was the place to start.

She had rifled through the stack of magazines by the bed – *Guns and Ammo*, *The Modern Solider* – before delving into the drawer in her cheap bedside table. It was full of make-up, lighters, hunting knives and trinkets of teen rebellion, but underneath all the junk Helen had found a small diary. Opening it up, she was not surprised to find on the first page a carefully drawn sketch of a large serpent devouring itself. More evidence, if it were needed, of Daisy's connection to the day's atrocities.

Flicking past the sketch, Helen investigated the contents of the diary. Daisy was not a regular writer – the entries were intermittent at best – but the brief, angry testimonials contained within the journal gave a clear picture of a young woman who was too bitter, too alienated for her tender years. She hated her school, both the pupils and the teachers, railed against those who had picked on her, but reserved special hatred for those whom she perceived to have rejected or belittled her. Helen wasn't surprised to discover that several entries mentioned Sonia Smalling, Alan Sansom and Sarah Grant by name.

There was a clear theme throughout the entries – a patent mistrust of institutions, of the motives of individuals who were presumably trying to *help* her. She had failed to finish her Community Payback and regularly skipped school, often retreating to the farm that had been her home for as long as she could remember. Judging by some of the framed photos in her room, she had enjoyed her time here when she was young – hunting, fishing and messing about with her dad. But recently two had become three with disastrous consequences.

Daisy's short diary was littered with incidents and accusations, but certain words kept recurring. *Fake* was used a lot, as was *hypocrites*. But the word that appeared most was *retaliation*. Daisy had become a very angry child, addicted to drink and drugs and fizzing with paranoia and resentment, determined to revenge herself upon her tormentors. These murders *were* hate crimes, as Helen had always suspected, but they were driven by a purely personal rage, not by racism or ideology.

'I can see my heart before my eyes, turning black with hate.'

'They murdered me slow. I'll be kinder, I'll kill them quickly.'

'You forced me into a corner and gave me only one option . . . You just *loved* to crucify me.'

Entry after entry catalogued her murderous rage, her outrage with the world. Leafing past them, Helen hastened to the end of the diary, impatient for clues as to Daisy's thinking or whereabouts. But most of her scribblings focused on her suicidal musings, and the last entry catalogued yet another row with her father. Slipping the slim journal into an evidence bag, Helen resumed her search of the drawer. There were the usual films and books – *Man Bites Dog*, *The Catcher in the Rye*, *Donnie Darko* – that appealed to a teenager's sense of nihilism, but some more specialist items too. Books on the Iraq War, on the subsequent Blair 'cover-up' and, most unusually, a pirated DVD which claimed to contain genuine footage of military action in Afghanistan and Iraq.

Beneath all of these lay a letter. It caught Helen's eye, because the envelope was crisp and brown, suggesting it was a formal letter sent fairly recently. Dipping her gloved hand deep into the drawer, Helen plucked it out. The envelope was addressed to Daisy and had been carefully opened – cut open with a knife perhaps – but the letter had then been stuffed back into it, creasing it considerably. Smoothing it out on the table, Helen read its contents, her sense of anxiety rising with each word.

It was a letter from the British army, in response to Daisy's recent application to join up. More worryingly it was a letter of rejection, citing a problem with Daisy's psychological evaluation. It was artfully worded but the implication was clear – Daisy would never be accepted into the armed forces and was discouraged from reapplying. Given Daisy's obvious interest in guns and warfare, this must have come as a bitter blow.

Worse still, it was a recent blow. The letter had been sent three days ago.

93

17.48

It had been a long and demanding day, but thankfully it was almost over.

Lance Sergeant Geoffrey Clarkson powered down his laptop and headed to the back office to stow it in the safe. It was the first moment of peace he'd had all day. That was the thing about this job – it was totally unpredictable. Sometimes you sat for hour upon hour waiting for the door to open, other times you were utterly overwhelmed, great queues snaking away from your desk, as you took each wannabe soldier through the different options open to them. As team leader, it was his job to organize the staff rotas, but he seldom got it 100 per cent right. Which is why the three of them had had to cope with seventy applicants today.

Autumn was always busy as youngsters who'd failed to make it to the university of their choice considered other options. Even so, normally they would expect to field forty or so enquiries and he wondered what had prompted this sudden surge of interest in the army. Perhaps university clearing had ended, perhaps the recent cinema adverts had had an effect. Either way, something had piqued the public's interest and Geoffrey could reflect on a job well done – there had been several people in today who looked quite promising. Experience had taught him to distinguish between those who were genuinely interested in joining up and those who were just doing it to get their parents off their back. There were loads of *those* – Mum and Dad keen to get Jack or Jill out of the family home – but the majority of those he'd spoken to today looked self-motivated and capable of making the grade.

He never sugarcoated the pill, painting an accurate picture of life in the British Army. He had served in Helmand Province during Operation Panther's Claw and had seen friends and colleagues killed, as they fought alongside him. He himself had narrowly avoided falling victim to an IED and felt it was his duty to outline to potential recruits the dangers – both during and after conflict – that they would face. Pleasingly, the more promising recruits had taken this on board, but had still wanted to hear more. This made him feel good, proud even – despite everything he'd been through he still passionately believed in the British Army and the vital role it played around the world.

Locking his laptop away, Clarkson turned to check tomorrow's staff rotas, which lay on the desk beside him. The radio was still burbling – he'd switched it on this morning but had never had a second to listen to it – and now he became aware of the funereal tone of the newsreader.

'Five people have so far been confirmed dead, at five different locations, and police are urging people in the Southampton area to remain vigilant . . .'

Clarkson stood still for a moment, surprised by what he was hearing. Southampton was a safe place – it barely seemed credible that it had suffered its first mass shooting. Worse still, the perpetrator was still at large. Bloody typical that the police should arrive too late to do anything about it. The army should have been called in the minute they knew what they were dealing with, but he suspected they hadn't been. The armed police guarded their territory closely – probably because most of them were failed soldiers. It was outrageous to think that politics should put lives at risk, but human beings were frail – Clarkson knew that from bitter experience.

He was tempted to listen to more, but he still had to change out of his uniform and the clock was ticking, so, switching the radio off, he placed the staff rotas back in his in-tray. The Saints were playing West Ham tonight and he had promised Sammy they could get a burger before heading to St Mary's. The news had been disquieting, but it always was these days and family considerations came first. Southampton had suffered, several families had been bereaved, but, as his dad always used to say, life goes on.

94

17.50

'All units to proceed to Bray Road, Ocean Village. All units to proceed to Bray Road . . .'

Helen sped down the quiet country lane. She was Bluetoothing on an open channel, communicating with the dozen Armed Response Units that were patrolling Southampton.

'The Army Careers Centre is at number twenty. I want armed officers front and back, but don't announce yourselves unless there is an incident in progress. Have we had any joy contacting Geoffrey Clarkson?'

His was the signature on Daisy's letter – according to his official bio on the armed forces website, he'd run the recruitment office in Southampton for nearly three years now.

'He's not answering his mobile. His wife said he was supposed to be meeting his son to go to the football tonight, but we've not been able to get hold of him either.'

'Keep trying. Let me know as soon as you reach them.'

'Will do.'

Helen clicked off and upped her speed. Her trip to the farm had been useful but had drawn her away from Southampton and now she was keen to be back in the thick of it. Ocean Village was to the south of the city, a smart neighbourhood of trendy apartments overlooking the water. It would take Helen a while to get there even with her lights on, hence her bullish pace. The road ahead was clear and she was keen to make the most of it.

She had no proof that Daisy would head to the Careers Centre – it was instinct that was driving Helen. She had been clutching at straws so far, baffled by these brutal, motiveless crimes, but now she felt she understood what was fuelling this killing spree. Daisy had been rejected one time too many. Abandoned by her mother, neglected by her father, she had never found her place in the world, lacking the confidence, emotional stability or resources to put down real roots. She had been mocked at school, branded a bad apple by the criminal-justice system and generally derided by a world that should have taken better care of her. In the end she had snapped, lashing out at those who had belittled or humiliated her. Which is why Clarkson's rejection letter alarmed Helen so much.

Clarkson's casual crushing of Daisy's dreams must have ignited her fury once more – the latest in a long line of savage setbacks – and Helen wondered whether it was this that been the root cause of her violent quarrel with her father. Whatever the reason, Daisy clearly felt she had crossed a line and would not hesitate to settle a few more scores before she was taken down.

The Army Careers Centre was due to shut at 6.30 p.m. It was not far off that now. Perhaps Daisy had deliberately waited until this hour of the day, when there would be fewer civilians to get in her way. Frustratingly, her team had still not got a proper fix on her – nobody had seen anything of their fugitive for nearly two hours, no mean feat when a manhunt was in full swing.

Helen was hitting the outskirts of the city and immediately joined the ring road heading east. As she did so, the police helicopter roared over her, blasting away towards Ocean Village. Everyone was heading for the same place now and, if Helen was right, she would shortly be coming face to face with Daisy Anderson.

95

17.55

Sanderson rammed the gear stick into reverse. Having dropped Emilia Garanita home, she'd decided to head over to the farm to assist the officers working there. But now the call had gone out to attend an address in Ocean Village, so, executing a hasty three-point turn on a narrow residential street, she spun around and roared back towards the city centre.

She would have been more than happy to assist Charlie and the rest of the search team at the farm – anything to make up for her earlier mistake – but this was a far more exciting mission. She had no idea yet why Daisy Anderson might target the Army Careers Centre, but the conviction in Helen's voice suggested that they were finally *ahead* of their perpetrator, able to predict where she would strike next. If so, then they would now have a chance to bring this thing to an end.

Sanderson had been involved in many complex operations, but few as fast-moving and shocking as this. The sheer number of victims was mindboggling – Sanderson knew that Jim Grieves was struggling to cope with the bodies that were piling up at the mortuary and that many of the junior officers on the MIT had been deeply affected by what they'd seen today. She had found time to comfort a couple of them, in between her bouts of CCTV viewing, and the solace she'd brought them reminded her that she *was* an experienced, accomplished police officer, who had something tangible to offer the team. Having doubted herself for so long, this cheered her and reinforced her desire to prove herself worthy of Helen's trust.

She was only a few minutes away from Ocean Village now. It was not an area she frequented – her tiny flat was in a much less expensive part of town – but she had been driving around Southampton long enough to know her way there. Her siren was off, but her lights were flashing and the traffic seemed to melt away in front of her. Sometimes luck was on your side and she felt sure that she would get there in time to prevent further bloodshed, perhaps even help to bring the perpetrator in herself. She felt energized and excited even.

Having been out in the cold for so long, it felt good to be back in the game.

96

18.21

Daisy gripped the wheel as she drove down the quiet side street. The traffic in the city centre had been terrible and, despite her best endeavours, she was behind schedule once again. She had hoped to be at the Careers Centre half an hour before closing – now she would be lucky if she made it in time. The thought enraged her – this guy deserved his fate just as much as the others, maybe even a little bit more.

She and Jason had scouted out the Careers Centre on the two previous evenings, enjoying the fact that Clarkson was blissfully ignorant of their presence, of what they were planning. They had got to know their target pretty well even in that short time, albeit from a distance, laughing at his ridiculous habits and idiosyncrasies. On both nights he had closed up in exactly the same manner – switching off the house lights in the same pedantic order, checking and double-checking the deadlocks before pulling the shutters down for the night. Last night, she and Jason had defiled those very shutters with their best serpent yet – a huge emerald beast visibly choking, as it tried to devour itself. They had amused themselves later, speculating as to what Clarkson's reaction would be to this 'outrage'.

Why was Clarkson so punctilious about security? The place was a dump and the ancient laptops they used weren't worth stealing. Did these lean pickings really require such heavy security? She guessed it was force of habit and this told you so much about the man. So self-important when there was so little to be self-important *about*. She had disliked him from the moment she'd met him – she could sense his suspicion of her – and those feelings had only grown during their brief acquaintance.

What had he said in his letter to her? That their 'psychological evaluation' had shown that she was unsuited to a career in the armed forces. Why? Because she had a personality? Because she had the ability to think for herself? They obviously wanted lamebrains that they could mould into compliant little boys and girls. Never mind that she was tougher than any of them. A better shot too probably. She could have been a great soldier – she would have run through walls – if she'd been given the chance. But they had ripped up that dream in five short sentences. Or, to be precise, Geoffrey Clarkson had.

She had only been half living on that farm, a zombie stumbling from one disaster to the next. Her dad, her lovely, stupid dad, hadn't given her much, but he had tried to give her her freedom. She'd had her first drink at ten, her first spliff shortly afterwards, and from then on she had spent most of her childhood screwing up her life. Petty crime, violence, cautions and convictions – her dad hardly ever got involved, never tried to direct her life, but even he'd thought that joining the army could be a turning point for her, a last throw of the dice. Perhaps he thought the discipline would do her good. Perhaps he just wanted her off his hands. She wasn't sure which now.

On the drive down to Ocean Village, she had heard

early reports on the radio of another death linked to the day's 'incidents'. A middle-aged man found dead on a farm near the River Hamble. She'd had to turn the radio off at that point. She didn't want to hear it. She'd done what had to be done, but she didn't want them rubbing her nose in it. She had had her fill of that over the last few years.

She turned into Bray Road and swiftly reduced her speed. There would be no time for final checks, for properly scoping the target, as she'd originally planned to do. If he *was* still there – and she was fervently praying he was – she would just have to grab her gun and get it done. If he escaped her tonight, or if she missed him, she might never again get a chance to settle their account.

Pulling up opposite the office, Daisy killed the engine. Reaching across to her rucksack, she slid out the shotgun, but as she looked up at the building, she froze. A motorbike was parked up near the shop – an expensive-looking Kawasaki – and through the large plate glass window Daisy could see that Clarkson was in conversation with a tall woman, clad in biking leathers. It clearly wasn't a careers enquiry – the woman was talking to him earnestly, imploring him to do something, and even from this distance Daisy could see that Clarkson looked shocked by what he was being told. It didn't take a genius to work out what was going on in that cramped office. Cursing bitterly, Daisy realized that she was too late.

97

18.28

Daisy Anderson's room was filled with plastic crates, as her whole world was gathered, bagged and boxed for further inspection. Charlie stood in the midst of them, swathed head to toe in a forensic suit, examining each item as it was handed to her, searching for further clues as to Daisy's intentions.

She had bridled when Helen asked her to remain behind at the farm. Despite the constant complaints of her partner, Steve, Charlie always wanted to be in the thick of things and felt knocked back when Helen asked her to continue the investigation at Michael Anderson's home. She had been tempted to fight her corner, to try to offload her duties on to a DC, but Helen had clearly made her decision and was in a hurry to go, so Charlie had let it slide. The pair of them had been getting on well – too well in some ways – so there was no question of Helen doubting her abilities. Was Helen shielding her then? Keeping her out of harm's way? If that was the case, she wasn't sure whether she should be flattered or annoyed. She was a big girl, even if she did have more to lose than Helen, as her superior often reminded her.

Charlie knew that every part of the investigation was vital and that Helen would expect her to be professional, so pushing her bruised feelings to one side, she'd got on with the task in hand. It had not improved her mood – in fact packing up Daisy's life had been a particularly depressing job. She must be in the midst of some kind of breakdown, Charlie thought, as this girl was not inherently *bad*. She was riven with anger, hostile to authority and full of self-loathing, but none of what had taken place today was inevitable. She could have taken a different path if only somebody had reached out to help her. Because the simple truth was that Daisy wanted to belong. The trinkets, old letters and club badges suggested that she had wanted to find people to be with, a surrogate family perhaps. There were the friendship bracelets, now unravelled and discarded. There was a Brownies outfit, far too small for her and seldom worn. And there were the half-filled applications to join the Young Farmers, the local choir, a paintballing group . . .

All these had had to be excavated – they belonged to a time when Daisy clearly believed that happiness was possible, that the world would give back. They lay several layers down, stuffed in wardrobes under numerous pairs of combat trousers and concealed beneath out-of-date copies of *Guns and Ammo*. But they cast a light on the young Daisy's loneliness and her desire to find emotional succour from somewhere. Whenever Charlie came across things like this, it always made her think how blessed her own little girl was to be so loved and protected. You never found out about these people until it was too late and Charlie dearly wished she could reach back in time to give Daisy the help she needed.

But it was too late for that. Daisy had crossed the line,

murdering her father, then several others. At first they had been convinced Jason Swift was to blame, but now they knew that Daisy had pulled the trigger on the victims, taking personal pleasure in slaughtering those who had made her feel worthless. After years of taking the hits, she was striking back and Charlie felt sure that nothing could contain her.

98

18.29

'Are you *sure* she's coming here?'

Geoffrey Clarkson was struggling to come to grips with Helen's shocking news. Despite her earnest entreaties, he'd made no move yet, knocked back on his heels by the thought that *he* might be next on Daisy Anderson's hit list.

'When did you discover the graffiti on your shutters?'

'This morning.'

'Then she's coming. You need to leave.'

Finally, Clarkson seemed to register the urgency in Helen's voice. Turning, he picked up his keys and phone.

'I'll need to call my son . . . I'm supposed to be meeting him.'

'We can do that from the police station, our first priority now is to see you safe. Everything else can wait.'

'She must be *crazy*,' Clarkson suddenly blurted out, turning once more to Helen. 'Lots of people fail to make the cut, it's perfectly normal –'

'Daisy's in the middle of a breakdown, she's not seeing the world clearly –'

'Jesus Christ, I mean, I had no choice,' he blustered, 'she's completely unsuited to the army. She's volatile, emotional, *plus* she has a string of criminal convictions.

I shouldn't have even bothered processing the application, but I did it anyway, because I'd promised her that I would.'

The Lance Sergeant seemed upset now, as if suddenly worried that *he* had provoked the day's bloodshed.

'She seemed desperate, a bit pathetic even,' he continued. 'If I'd known how angry she was –'

'Save the what ifs for later, Mr Clarkson. Think of your family now and come with me.'

Finally, Clarkson got the message, grabbing his coat from the back of the seat and switching off the desk lamp. Helen watched him impatiently, urging him to hurry up. Daisy was out there somewhere and until they were safely back in Southampton Central, she wouldn't rest easy. Having gathered his things, he turned once more to Helen. To her surprise Clarkson looked lost, as if he had never expected to encounter mortal danger in his own backyard. Helen had seen this before, so she put her arm out to usher him towards the door.

The other patrols would be arriving any minute and Helen's thoughts were already on her next move. Could they set a trap for Daisy? Use a body double of Clarkson as bait for the obsessive teenager? What would be the best – the safest – way to bring Daisy in, so that she could answer for her crimes?

They were nearly at the door, but a strange noise stopped her in her tracks. At first she didn't know what it was – it sounded like a rasping, throaty growl – but then she got it. It was a car being violently revved. All of a sudden the noise stopped, replaced now by a high-pitched squealing, which was growing louder, louder, louder . . .

Too late, Helen realized what was happening. She just had time to shove Clarkson forcefully away from danger, before the car smashed straight through the plate glass window, heading directly towards her.

99

18.31

The car hit something hard and stopped dead, throwing Daisy forward in her seat. She was wearing a seatbelt, but still her head connected sharply with the steering wheel, such was the force of the impact. For a moment, she sat there, dazed and breathless, listening to the tinkling of breaking glass, as the window behind her finally gave up the ghost. Driving through it had been a reckless act, born of fury, but it was not without strategy too. She didn't fancy the odds in a straight fight against two well-trained individuals, even with a gun in play, so she had decided to level the playing field a little.

Shaking off the fuzziness in her head, she retrieved her shotgun from the foot well and opened the driver's door. Immediately she met resistance – an upturned chair was caught underneath it – so Daisy shoulder-barged the door fiercely, shifting it enough to allow her to squeeze out. Her boots crunched noisily over the broken glass and she rounded the front of the car to survey the damage. Chairs had been scattered, desks overturned and a thick haze of dust hung in the air.

Her gun raised, Daisy moved forward. She was expecting a fight, but was heartened to see the woman lying face down in the glass, a good ten feet or so from the car. Daisy was sure she had hit one of them as she crashed through the window and judging by her prone position it was *her*. Crossing to her, Daisy jabbed the gun barrels into her ribs, but the woman didn't move. Daisy turned away – dead or unconscious, it was all the same to her.

Circling back around the car, she made towards the back of the office, picking her way carefully through the wreckage. She could hear something – a dull groaning – and now she crept towards it. It sounded like a man. It sounded like *him*.

Suddenly there he was. He was conscious, having somehow avoided being struck by the car, but he was little better off for it. A desk had catapulted backwards with the force of the impact and the army man was now pinioned beneath it, helpless as a newborn lamb. He was blinking furiously, still trying to understand what was happening, but as he saw Daisy approaching, he started wriggling desperately, trying to free himself. Slowly, deliberately, Daisy placed a boot on top of the slanting desk and pressed down on it. Clarkson cried out in pain and ceased struggling, fixing Daisy with a look that was half anger, half fear.

'Hello, Geoffrey. Remember me?'

'Yes, it's Daisy, isn't it?'

'Very good. Did you remember that all by yourself or did your little friend tell you?'

'I remembered . . . I remember you . . .'

'Course you do . . .'

As she spoke Daisy raised her shotgun to her shoulder, pressing the butt into her flesh.

'Look, I'm . . . I'm . . . sorry about your application,'

Clarkson stuttered, shocked by the sudden appearance of a gun.

'You will be . . .'

'Let's talk about it . . . We can do it agai—'

'While we wait for the cavalry to show up? I don't think so.'

She took another step towards him.

'Please, Daisy . . . don't do anything stupid . . . I know you're in a bad place, but I have a wife, I have a son . . .'

'You should have thought of them, before you did what you did.'

'I was just doing my job.'

'That's what the Nazis said, right?' Daisy replied, smirking. 'But it doesn't change a thing. You destroyed my future and now you're about to learn . . .'

As she spoke, she aimed the gun, so that it was pointing directly at his head.

'. . . that actions have consequences.'

'Please, Daisy,' Clarkson pleaded again, desperate. 'I'm not a monster. I'm just a guy. Nobody special, nobody important. I don't know what you think I am, but, trust me, I'm not worth going to jail for.'

'Oh, I think that ship has sailed,' Daisy answered, laughing. 'I hate to tell you this, Geoffrey, but you're not my first today. But perhaps you already know that?'

'How many . . . how many people have you killed?' Clarkson stammered.

'A handful. But we're not here to talk about me, are we?'

In the distance, Daisy heard sirens, goading her into action. She took aim once more – instinctively her victim raised his hands to protect himself.

'This is it, Geoffrey. Anything you want to say?'

The army man couldn't speak – he gestured hopelessly at her, frantically appealing for mercy he knew would not be forthcoming.

'Not very inspiring. Oh well, have it your wa—'

She didn't get to finish. Suddenly she found herself flying sideways. Too late she realized that the woman had got to her feet and crept towards her, barging into her just as she was about to fire. The pair crashed to the floor, broken glass biting into them, but Daisy scrambled to her feet, still clutching her weapon. She swung it towards her adversary, but the woman was too quick for her, grabbing the barrels and pointing the weapon at the ceiling. Daisy bucked furiously, but to her surprise the woman pressed her hand down on Daisy's trigger finger. The shotgun roared once, twice – harmlessly into the ceiling, sending down a shower of splintered tile.

Daisy felt a knee connect sharply with her stomach, knocking the wind from her. Her adversary tugged hard at the shotgun, trying to wrench it from her grip, but Daisy clung on to it for dear life. They tussled furiously, swaying this way and that, before suddenly Daisy felt herself falling backwards. Her opponent had slipped a foot behind her leg and pushed her over it. Daisy hit the ground hard, still grasping the shotgun, her opponent falling on top of her. But as she did so, Daisy twisted hard, sending the woman over her and riding the turn herself so that *she* was now on top. The woman was winded and, looking down, Daisy could tell she was injured, so she pressed home her advantage, ramming the metal barrels down on to her throat and pushing with all her might. The woman resisted fiercely, but she couldn't breathe and was gasping and gagging. They rocked back and forth but Daisy kept up the pressure, suddenly determined to crush the life out of the stupid bitch. She leant forward, pushing down with all her might. As she did so, her opponent rocked back, then without warning launched herself forward, sending her forehead cracking into Daisy's nose.

There was a horrible snap and Daisy fell backwards. She crashed on to the broken glass, dazed and reeling. She was seeing stars, she wanted to vomit, but clocking that her adversary was on her hands and knees, winded and struggling, she stumbled to her feet. She still had the gun and if she could reload in time . . .

She pulled the shells from her pocket, but they tumbled to the ground, her hands shaking. Her adversary was clambering to her feet, so she scrabbled for the shells amid the glass. She managed to fix on one and ram it in the breech, then she picked up another, moving it awkwardly around until that slid in too. Snapping the shotgun shut, she rose and turned to kill.

But as she did so, she was suddenly blinded. A piercing white light filled the entire shop, even as she heard someone shout:

'Armed police!'

And now Daisy didn't hesitate, turning on the spot and running for her life. Seconds later, she was out of the back door and away.

100

18.37

The air was cool and crisp, ripping over Daisy's sweating face as she sprinted down the alleyway, busting a gut to put as much distance between her and the police as possible. She knew her adversary wasn't finished yet – even as she ran she could hear footsteps behind her. The narrow passageway angled away from the rear of the building after about fifty yards or so, giving her some cover from her pursuers, but would it be enough? She strained every sinew as she raced on, determined not to be taken.

She was aware of noise all around her. Shouts, sirens and the ever present hum of the police helicopter that was sweeping the area with its roving spotlight. Any second she expected it to alight on her. And then what? Daisy had no idea if there were police officers blocking her escape route or not, but while there was an ounce of energy left in her body, she would keep running. She had to finish this thing on her terms.

She was coming to the end of the alleyway now, the brick passageway narrowing to an opening. Caution was called for, but desperation drove her on and she burst out of the alleyway into the quiet street. She had her gun raised, but to her surprise there was no one there to stop her. She paused for a moment to catch her breath, laughing at her sheer good fortune. But her relief was short-lived. Suddenly she sensed danger and whirled round to see a car approaching fast, mounting the pavement to cut off her escape route.

She didn't hesitate, swinging the gun towards the car and pulling the trigger, before sprinting across the road. She expected to feel bullets whizzing past her ears, but her fire was not returned, so on reaching the other side, she darted down another alleyway. Against all the odds, she was still alive.

101

18.39

Helen burst on to the road, just as the fleeing figure disappeared from view down an alleyway. Without hesitating, she lunged across the street in pursuit. Every part of her hurt – she had been winged by the car as she dived out of its path and had been further injured in the fight – but she knew she couldn't let Daisy escape. The teenage girl had proved herself to be an accomplished and merciless killer.

But as Helen bounded across the street, she became aware of a strange, dazzling light. This came not from her own armed units, but from the headlights of a car, which was marooned on the pavement at an unusual angle. Behind the lights, in silhouette, Helen could see movement – a frantic, spasmodic kind of movement that immediately set alarm bells ringing.

Helen had a split second to make her decision, but now altered her course, darting away from the mouth of the alleyway and back towards the car. She knew that it was a pool car and as she neared it she saw to her horror that the windscreen had been shattered, a large hole having been punched through it. The engine was still running, revving slightly as the accelerator was depressed, but oddly the car was going nowhere. Nor was the officer inside.

Rounding the car, Helen seized the driver's door and

wrenched it open. Immediately the interior was illuminated and Helen now saw something that nearly stopped her heart. Joanne Sanderson was slumped in the driver's seat.

Her face was ashen, her eyes moist and her hand was clamped to a huge hole in her chest.

102

18.41

'Officer down!'

Helen's strangulated voice came through loud and clear and Charlie's first instinct was to pick up the radio and respond. But Helen beat her to it.

'Urgent medical assistance required on Garnet Road . . . single shotgun wound . . . considerable loss of blood . . .'

Other officers closer to the scene now answered, before an Armed Response Unit cut in, asking for an update on the whereabouts of the shooter.

'She's moving down an alleyway between Garnet Road and . . . Sandowne Road. Instruct the chopper to follow from the air and cut off all roads around Sandowne Road . . .'

Helen petered out, gasping the last few words. Charlie had to struggle to maintain her focus. She was driving back to base with the evidence from the farm, but the distress in Helen's voice had knocked her sideways, dragging her concentration away from the task in hand. Helen never lost her composure – never – but she was clearly badly shaken. Something had gone very, very wrong.

Charlie's hand hovered over the radio – she was sorely tempted to pick it up and make contact with her superior.

Her heart was beating fast, her mind conjuring up all sorts of dark scenarios. But once more Helen got in first.

'Please hurry. She's one of ours. She's . . .'

Helen petered out once more, anguished and overcome. And in that moment Charlie *knew*.

103

18.43

'Look at me, Joanne.'

Helen meant her voice to be soothing and reassuring, but her words sounded cracked and unnatural.

'It's me. Helen. You're going to be ok, but I need you to focus . . .'

Sanderson was blinking repeatedly, her eyes rolling in their sockets, as if trying and failing to find a fixed point on the roof of the car. She was still in shock, the impact of the shot paralysing her system.

'Joanne, please look at me,' Helen barked, desperately trying to get her attention.

For a moment, the flickering paused. Sanderson's eyes seemed to lock on to Helen's and she tried to say something.

'Pleas—'

A thin trickle of blood spilled from her mouth.

'Don't speak, conserve your strength,' Helen urged. 'The ambulance will be here in two minutes.'

As she spoke, her ears strained for the sound of sirens, but she could hear nothing.

'We'll get you to hospital and you *will* be ok.'

The flickering started again, faster this time. She seemed to be losing consciousness, so Helen gave her a gentle slap to the face.

'Stay with me, Joanne. I need you to . . .'

But she was not responding any more, her body suddenly heavier in Helen's arms.

'Joanne, please . . .'

Her eyes had rolled upwards. Only the whites were visible now. Helen had tears in her own eyes, when she whispered:

'Please . . .'

But it was too late. DS Joanne Sanderson was dead.

104

18.47

Daisy was running for her life.

She had made it away from the Careers Centre, but the hunt was still on. She could hear the sirens all around her, but what really worried her was the dull *thunk*, *thunk* of the police helicopter. Though its harsh spotlight had not yet located her, it seemed to be following her movements, clipping on her heels as she fled north from Ocean Village.

Their original plan had always been to steal another car before moving on. But that was too risky with the helicopter hovering – she would draw too much attention to herself – so she was having to think on her feet. If she went right she would make it to the river, but this was not a part of the city she knew well and she feared running into a dead end, cutting her off from the water. Even if she did make it to the river's edge, was she really going to leap in? She wasn't the world's greatest swimmer and it would ruin her gun, so instead she fled north towards Itchen Bridge.

This would leave her pretty exposed, as cars were constantly crossing this busy thoroughfare, but if she acted calm she might get away with it. Her gun was just about concealed, shoved roughly down the back of her trousers, and though her top was torn and stained, she might get away with it as she looked pretty punkish anyway. The problem was her face. Her nose was swollen and she could feel the caked-on blood that clung to her cheeks. Anybody who encountered her now would probably stop to check that she was ok and that was the last thing she needed.

The whirring of the rotary blades was deafening now and looking up Daisy was shocked to see that the helicopter was directly above her. She was only on Salt Marsh Road, still a few hundred feet from Itchen Bridge. Surely she would be discovered, and then what? She had seen these things before on the TV – joyriders and thieves lit up, tearing about like headless chickens, before eventually running into a trap set by the all-seeing eye above.

The helicopter's beam of light swept past, seeming to catch the back of her heels. She was determined to keep going, but was losing power, exhaustion slowly replacing the adrenaline. On the next sweep, they would see her for sure. And then that would be that.

The helicopter was hovering now and, out of the corner of her eye, Daisy saw the wide circle of light moving steadily, remorselessly back towards her. She had seconds at most in which to react and she suddenly changed course, darting right towards the crash barriers at the side of the slip road that led to the bridge. Still the light moved towards her, getting closer, closer, closer. With one last lunge, she reached the railings and without hesitation vaulted over them.

She felt the air rushing past her, then thump, she landed heavily on the tarmac below. Her ankle rolled over as she did so and she cried out in pain. But even before her scream had ended she was clawing her way across the road. She was almost captured by the light hovering above, but Daisy scrambled into the nice, dark space beneath the flyover. It was strewn with rubbish and stank of urine, but it was perfect for Daisy's intentions. Curling up into a ball, she tried to keep as still and as quiet as possible, ignoring the burning sensation in her ankle. The next few seconds were unbearably tense, but then – unbelievably – the spotlight started to move away, cutting north once more. Leaving Daisy alone.

She wasn't out of the woods yet – the surrounding streets were probably crawling with dozens of officers looking for her. But for now at least she was safe.

105

18.49

Suddenly everybody wanted a piece of her.

Emilia Garanita had almost forgotten what it felt like to be in demand. She had been treading water for months, stuck in a jumped-up graduate's job on a regional newspaper. She knew she had a tendency to be brittle, but throughout her difficult life she had always put on a bold, assertive front. Some of it was bluster, some of it real, but it had worked – generally people thought that she was a force to be reckoned with. But, of late, she had grown used to conceding a point, to backing down. Partly because she knew she had acted selfishly in the past – treating both her colleagues and her own family with disrespect as she chased her career ambitions – but partly, she realized, because her confidence had been knocked by the experience of being embraced then spat out by the national newspapers.

However, now they wanted to talk to her again. She was not only the best eyewitness to today's rampage, but she had also spent time as the killer's hostage, helping her to engineer an elaborate escape from Meadow Hall School and get through the road block. *That* was a story worth telling, so she had ignored the numerous calls from Gardener and instead called a contact at Sky News. They were on their way to her house now. The interview would be brief, but it would pay well. She would make sure of that.

While waiting for them to arrive, she had emailed brief details of her ordeal to her former contacts at *The Times* and the *Telegraph*. She wasn't going to renege on her promise of exclusivity to the TV journalists, but she did want to have other outlets lined up to exploit the minute the interview had aired. Her contacts at the broadsheets had emailed her back immediately, but she had deliberately ignored them, just as she was ignoring her mobile, which buzzed incessantly on the kitchen table. The longer she left them, the more hungry – and generous – they would become.

'You going to answer that thing?'

Her younger sister, Claudia, passed by, grabbing a beer from the fridge.

'Not yet, honey.'

Emilia had already decided to do something nice for the family out of all this. Claudia had had to step into the breach when Emilia hightailed it to London and she knew some resentment still lingered. Emilia was determined to make it up to her – to all of them – and was already dreaming of a holiday they could all take together. Florida perhaps? Los Angeles? They had seldom been anywhere as a family and it was high time they spoiled themselves.

Claudia placed a beer on the table and sat down next to her, laying a supportive hand on hers. Emilia was grateful for it, but she didn't need it. She had been badly shaken earlier but now could see only the positives that would come from the day's unusual events. Good times ahead, a place back at the table and an enjoyable night spent watching her phone buzzing unanswered on the kitchen table.

106

18.52

'Are you ok, Helen?'

It was a stupid thing to ask, but Charlie couldn't think of anything else to say. She had immediately diverted to Ocean Village after hearing Helen's SOS and found her superior standing alone in the middle of the road, as the paramedics attended to Joanne. It seemed awful but once they had pronounced her dead, the forensics team would move in, garnering evidence from the crime scene. Only after another hour had passed would Joanne's body finally be removed from view.

Two paramedics were crammed into the pool car, feeling for a pulse on the cold, pale body. Charlie couldn't bear to look and had turned away, after briefly checking that it definitely *was* Joanne in there. But Helen couldn't take her eyes off the scene playing out in front of her, staring at the paramedics' forlorn efforts to raise the dead. Charlie could imagine what was going through Helen's mind. Her recent issues with her DS of course, but also more distant memories, such as Joanne trying to stop Helen from entering a burning house to save Ruby Sprackling. There were countless other examples of both women looking out for each other, one of them covering her the other's back against dangers both professional and criminal, but now, when it mattered most, Joanne had been alone. Unprotected and undefended, gunned down by a callous killer.

She had died in service, trying to stop the fleeing fugitive in her tracks. That was something. Something for her parents, friends and colleagues to cling on to in their grief.

'This is my fault.'

Charlie looked up, startled by Helen's interjection.

'It's Daisy Anderson's fault, nobody else's,' Charlie responded quickly.

'I was too hard on her. I was angry with her and I pushed her too hard,' Helen continued, seeming not to hear what Charlie had said.

'No, this is absolutely *not* your fault, Helen. Daisy was attempting to murder someone and you asked for units to respond. That was the right call and Joanne was trying to do her job, she was cutting off her escape route –'

'She hadn't even got a gun. She was no threat to –'

'Do you really think Daisy Anderson cares about that? She just wanted to get away. And in her own fucked-up world, she's allowed to do whatever it takes. She is allowed to gun down an innocent person in cold blood . . .'

Charlie's voice wavered now, but she pressed on:

'And it is her responsibility, her fault. Nobody *made* her pull the trigger, that was her deci—'

'But *why* was Joanne here? That's what I'm saying –'

'Because you told all units to atten—'

'She was here because she was trying to impress me. I'd frozen her out and she wanted to get back in my good books.'

'You don't know that,' Charlie countered, despite the fact that there was more than a grain of truth in what Helen was saying.

'An armed unit *has* to take point, Joanne knew that. But she didn't wait for them, she wanted to be the one to bring Daisy in –'

'Don't make this into something it's not, Helen. She was acting instinctively. She saw the suspect escaping and she intervened –'

'You're being kind, Charlie, but you don't need to dress things up. I know how I treated her, I know how she felt, I know what she was trying to do. I drove her to the brink and then I gave her a way back, a shot in the arm, and *this* is the result . . .'

Helen's eyes were still fixed on the car, but Charlie refused to follow suit, turning her attention to the other side of the street. As she did so, she spotted several other MIT officers watching their exchange. They were all too scared to approach their superior, especially when she was so obviously in distress. Charlie was glad that she'd come here to provide support, however difficult this conversation might be.

'She had this on her . . .'

Helen's tone was quieter now, but more hollow. She took a piece of paper from her pocket and handed it to Charlie.

'I saw it in her coat pocket when I was comforting her in the car.'

Charlie took the sheet of paper, which she realized was spattered with blood. Unnerved, she hesitated, then quickly unfolded it. She took in the contents. It was a transfer request, written and signed by Joanne. Charlie digested this, stunned, then turned back to Helen. She wasn't sure what to say, so Helen said it for her:

'This is my fault.'

107

19.18

Daisy stared at herself in the cracked mirror. She had cleaned the blood off her face, watching it colour the water spinning down the plughole, and looked a little bit more human now. Her nose was still swollen and slightly wonky and the bruising around it was starting to spread, but she wouldn't turn heads any more.

She had bought herself some time. They were still out looking for her, but they hadn't got a bead on her yet. She had remained under the flyover for as long as she dared, hoping against hope that the sound of sirens would die down, that the search parties would disperse. It had seemed like an eternity, but was probably no more than ten minutes or so. Eventually she had heard footsteps approaching from the river. She still had no idea if it was a copper, a tramp or a junkie coming to shoot up in peace – she had just fled, sneaking out of the gloom and limping along the road, sticking to the shadows as best she could.

She had heard activity on the road above and fully expected armed police officers to leap out at her, but on and on she went. Ocean Village had its swanky areas – the high-rise blocks looking out to sea – but she was passing underneath these. Through the flood drains, the back alleys and the derelict plots still waiting to be developed.

Slowly she had put a bit of distance between herself and Bray Road and then, as she started to cut back up towards St Mary's, she'd seen it. The Red Lion was a grim, old man's pub that she'd once tried to sell some stolen mobiles in. They'd given her short shrift then, but they could do her a favour now.

It was too cold for anyone to be out in the beer garden, so, hurrying across the road, she'd clambered over the chain link fence. Her ankle had protested, but up she went, dropping safely down on the other side. Then she'd opened the back door and hobbled inside. The toilets were to the rear of the pub and she'd slipped gratefully into the Ladies. It was a risk coming to a public place, but no self-respecting woman would set foot in this pub, so she'd felt confident she would have a few minutes to compose herself.

Progress had been slow and painstaking. She sensed that her nose was broken – it made her feel sick every time she touched it, but she knew she had to if she was to make herself look 'respectable'. So she'd dabbed away with clumps of sodden toilet paper, swallowing down her nausea and wiping away the evidence of her struggle. Her trousers were just about ok, once she had dusted off the last splinters of broken glass, but her dark green top still showed up spatters of blood. Whether they were spots of the police officer's blood or hers she wasn't sure – but either way it wouldn't do to advertise the stains. So she'd ripped her top off, swiftly turning it inside out, before putting it back on again. It wasn't perfect, but it would have to do for now.

Looking at herself, running her hand over her shaved head, she felt a sudden surge of confidence. She actually liked her new look – she'd never had a buzz cut before, but now she felt it suited her better than any other style she'd had in the past. She looked like a warrior. She looked like an Amazon.

She looked like the real Daisy Anderson.

108

19.28

'Am I cursed, Charlie?'

It was such a strange question that, for a moment, Charlie didn't know how to answer. She had eventually persuaded Helen to return to Southampton Central, arguing that she was needed there to coordinate the search teams' efforts and sift the available evidence for clues as to where Daisy might head next. They had travelled back in silence and even as they had passed through the familiar corridors up to the seventh floor, not a word had been spoken. It was only once the pair were safely installed back in Helen's office that her shaken superior had decided to speak.

'You know I don't think that,' Charlie replied, crossing to the door and closing it gently.

'I do sometimes,' Helen continued quietly. 'Sometimes I feel that anyone who gets close to me – anyone I try to help – gets hurt.'

'I'm still here, aren't I?' Charlie contradicted her gamely.

Helen smiled without conviction, then said:

'You've had your moments. Things that shouldn't have happened . . .'

Charlie stared at the floor, shaken by Helen's tacit

reference to the baby she had lost in captivity all those years ago.

'I mean, why isn't it ever me?' Helen wondered. 'I know that sounds morbid and self-indulgent . . . but why does the bullet never hit me? I feel like . . . like I'm indestructible and I bloody hate it.'

'I wouldn't moan about it. Joanne could have done with a bit of that tonight.'

It wasn't meant cuttingly, it was just an observation, but it seemed to land with Helen.

'You're right. I know you're right. I just wish . . . that people didn't have to suffer because of me. I ask too much of them –'

'No more than you ask of yourself.'

'But why? Why do they have to get *hurt*?' Helen demanded, her composure slipping once more.

Charlie considered her response carefully:

'Because you walk towards the fire, Helen. While others look around for someone else to take the lead, you willingly walk *towards* the fire. It's instinctive. Because you want to save lives, because you want to do your job. Yes, you inspire others to follow, and, yes, they sometimes get hurt. But only because they are doing what needs to be done. And you must never stop doing that, Helen. Never. You're the only person who *can* do it . . .'

Helen nodded at the floor, then slowly raised her head to look at Charlie once more. Her eyes were dry, though her face was still ashen.

'And it's what you must do now,' Charlie continued forcefully. 'I will go and talk to Joanne's mum –'

Helen tried to interject, but Charlie was having none of it, talking over her boss.

'*I* will talk to Joanne's mum. It's what I'm good at and I'd like to be the one to break it to her. And you must do what you do best . . .'

Helen was quiet now, her eyes meeting Charlie's.

'Get out there and bring Daisy in.'

109

19.42

'DS Joanne Sanderson . . .'

Helen's voice wavered slightly, but she pressed on.

'. . . and Michael Anderson.'

Helen pulled their photos up on to the screen.

'They are victims five and six.'

Helen turned to face the team. Such was the number of officers now working on the case that they had had to move out of the briefing suite into the main body of the incident room. This was one bonus of not having a boss – Helen had signed off the resources necessary to have this huge team working around the clock. She wanted to throw everything they had at this. From the expression on the faces of those present, the angry, grieving officers were ready to respond to her call to arms.

Helen now saw a unity that had been lacking before. Perhaps she had been imagining the fracture, the lack of cohesion, in the team previously? Whatever the truth of the matter, the whole MIT was ready to follow her. And she was ready to lead.

'The former was killed on Bray Road while attending an incident, the latter was murdered at his farm in Hedge End. His body is being examined by Jim Grieves now, but it's pretty clear that he was Daisy Anderson's first victim.'

'Why did she do it?' Osbourne asked quickly.

'Because he'd asked her to move out. He didn't like Jason Swift, thought he was a thug. And he felt he'd come between him and his daughter –'

'And she was angry that her dad turned against her?' Reed offered.

'Her Voicemail messages make that pretty clear. There *was* evidence of love in that family. In his own haphazard way, Michael Anderson doted on his daughter. Which is why it hurt so much when he forced her to choose. These killings are about rejection –'

'We can't say that for sure. Look at Jason Swift and DS Sanderson –'

'Daisy didn't plan to kill Jason or Joanne,' Helen countered. 'They were necessity killings, so she could keep going. We have to keep our focus on the *root* cause of today's spree. Daisy has no emotional resilience and reacts with fury when she is pushed away or rejected –'

'So the *dad* is the root cause, he loved her, but he turned on her . . .'

'Possibly, but look at her charge sheet. Her behavioural problems go back many years . . .'

Helen turned to the murder board. Daisy's charge sheet revealed a catalogue of misdemeanours starting long before the age of criminal culpability. The formal, black and white evidence of her bad behaviour seemed curiously at odds with the cute photos of the young Daisy that Helen had been staring at only a couple of hours earlier.

'Her first caution was when she was ten years old. Before that she seemed to be a fairly normal kid –'

'Which must have been about the time her mother left,' McAndrew suddenly cut in.

'What do we know about her?'

'We've trawled through the social service reports of the time, the divorce petition –'

'And?' Helen interrupted, impatient for details.

'Well, it appears that Karen Anderson was having an affair. She fell pregnant, the fissure in her marriage was too great, so she left her husband, before her twin boys were born –'

'And Daisy?'

'Daisy continued to attend the same school, was registered at the same address –'

'She left her behind,' Helen said, suddenly getting it. 'Karen Anderson abandoned her daughter and walked away.'

'Looks that way. There's no evidence of Daisy ever having lived with her mother. Her dad got sole custody, the farm. Karen agreed to give it all up for a new life.'

'And Daisy was ten when this happened?'

'Only just. Her mum left two weeks after her birthday.'

There was an audible reaction from several members of the team. Helen felt it too – the image of a ten-year-old girl watching her mother leave the family home, because she chose to prioritize her unborn twins over her own daughter, suddenly forced its way into her mind. What had Daisy felt back then? Confusion, distress, loneliness . . . but later anger and bitterness too? Now Helen thought back to the farmhouse at Hedge End and the total absence of photos of her mother. It was as if Karen Anderson had been obliterated from the collective memory.

'She's not worth it . . .'

'Sorry, boss?'

Helen realized she had been thinking out loud.

'"She's not worth it." That's what Daisy Anderson said about Melissa Hill when she spared the young mother and her baby at the pharmacy. I thought at the time that maybe there was something in the image of a mother protecting her baby that had disturbed Daisy's equilibrium, had provoked some feelings of pity in her . . . but now I think she actually *meant* what she said. To Daisy, the young mother was shit on her shoe, beneath her contempt, certainly not worth a bullet.'

'Karen Anderson *has* to be the next victim. If this is all about rejection,' DC Bentham added, picking up Helen's thread.

'Maybe, though we're not sure Daisy even knows where she lives,' Osbourne replied quickly. 'She hasn't had any contact with her.'

'Plus, all her victims so far have been people who've rejected her *recently*,' DC Edwards added.

'But think about where this all comes from,' Bentham persisted. 'Her mum *chose* not to take her. That would have destroyed a ten-year-old, which is presumably why her dad spoiled her so much, always took her side. But it didn't work – Daisy's problems at school, with the police, started just after her mum left. It's a clear link.'

As her officers continued to debate the issue, Helen stayed silent. Her mind was turning now on Daisy, on the cold rage that was driving her. Abandoned by her mother, she had become insecure, paranoid and hostile, easily enraged by those who hurt or wronged her. Although she loathed Daisy for what she'd done today, Helen suddenly thought she *understood* what was driving her. Daisy had loved her mother, had placed her trust in her, only for her mum to walk away without a second glance. How could a child *ever* get over that? It must have been horrific, bewildering, disorienting, but it was not uncommon. Helen had experienced something similar as a child, when her own mother turned a blind eye to the abuse and the violence being meted out to her offspring. And Helen had felt it more recently too. Sanderson's disloyalty to her had shattered the trust between them, making Helen angry, vengeful and unstable. *This* was what was driving Daisy. A bitter sense of betrayal.

'What address do we have for her?'

The officers suddenly fell silent, turning towards Helen.

'Where does Karen Anderson live?' Helen persisted.

'She moved in with a Bryan Nash after she left her husband,' McAndrew replied quickly, flicking through the file. 'He's the twins' father. Nash has had a few businesses go sideways and it looks like the family moved around a fair bit . . . but this is the latest address we have for them.'

She scribbled it down on a piece of paper and handed it to Helen. It was an address on the outskirts of Portsmouth, less than half an hour's drive from Southampton.

'I'll go there now,' Helen said quickly. 'Try and get hold of them, tell them to stay with friends or neighbours, until I arrive.'

This was said over her shoulder, Helen marching towards, then through, the office doors. She was heading fast to the bike park and thence to Portsmouth. She couldn't be sure she was on the right track but suddenly she couldn't shake the image that was now in her head – of a young family about to be brutally ripped apart.

110

19.48

The icy wind roared past her. Her arms were covered in goose pimples, the thin soft hairs standing to attention to try and preserve some warmth, and she shivered as she limped along the street. She hated the cold, but what else could she do? She had to keep going.

How she regretted discarding her heavy trench coat now. It was proper army surplus, with a bulk that was reassuring and a thick lining that kept her warm. It had been the right thing to do to dump it at the time – it had probably bought her a few valuable minutes and had confused those hunting for her – but the absence of it made her feel vulnerable. She had lost her armour, her protection, and now had only her thin top to insulate her from the cold. Hopefully, if anybody did see her they would dismiss her as a local student without the sense or funds to buy herself a good coat, but this didn't make her feel any better. She was frozen to the bone.

She laid her hand on the butt of her gun, still concealed within her combat trousers, but it didn't afford her any comfort. She was tired, hungry and cold. If Jason were here, he would have given her a cuddle. How she would have liked one. He was a naturally hot person, always kicking the duvet off, complaining that he was overheating. She was not. She felt the cold easily, no more so than now, and she missed him keenly. She and Jason had wanted to see this through together, to be brothers in arms until the end. She had come to rely on his good humour, his black and white optimism, his bullish determination. And yet . . . somehow she always knew there would come a point when she would need to take the lead. To stop relying on his encouragement and resolve and take matters into her own hands.

This had been her idea after all – her fight – so if anyone had to fall during their attempt, then that person had to be Jason. He had been with her throughout, but this had never been about him. This was her story, her revenge, and perhaps it was fitting that, at the very end, she should face her enemies alone.

III

19.52

They sat together in the living room, locked in a terrible silence. Charlie had had to do this many times before – people felt she had the warmth and sensitivity required when breaking the news of a sudden bereavement – but this had been by far the worst. She knew Joanne Sanderson well of course, but more than that she knew her mother. She had met her on a number of occasions in fact, so when Nicola Sanderson opened the door to her, she had initially been unconcerned, even welcoming.

But Charlie's hesitation in entering the house and her subsequent awkward manner had obviously unnerved the sixty-year-old. Charlie wasn't sure how to proceed – Nicola's husband, Eddie, was out playing cards – but when Charlie suggested she summon him home, Nicola took matters into her own hand, demanding to know what was going on. Charlie had had no choice but to tell her, taking pains to say that her daughter had died a heroic death and had not suffered at all. The first part of this, at least, was true.

Nicola had not reacted at first. She had stared at Charlie for a few seconds, before asking her to say it all again. Charlie suspected she hadn't taken in any of the details, her mind fleeing from Charlie's report early on, to avoid facing the awful reality of what she was being told. So Charlie repeated her grim news. Shortly afterwards, a Family Liaison Officer had arrived and while she made Nicola a cup of tea, keeping up a steady stream of comforting words, Charlie had attempted to contact Eddie Sanderson. Her call had gone straight to Voicemail, so she had left a brief message, asking him to return home as soon as possible. It was inadequate and made Charlie feel dreadful – it seemed so cruel that he was out there now, laughing and joking with mates, little knowing the calamity that was about to befall him.

Thirty minutes passed without word from him, so in the end Charlie despatched the FLO to retrieve him, promising to stay with Nicola until their return. In truth, Charlie knew she would stay for a good deal longer than that, despite the pressing need for her presence elsewhere. A major operation was in play, but Joanne was a loyal friend with whom she'd shared much during happy and bad times. Charlie thought of her own mother, who always worried about her, and she knew instinctively that Joanne would have done the same for her had the roles been reversed. Joanne Sanderson had made some mistakes over the years, but she was a good officer with a good heart.

Charlie knew this was just the start. Nicola and Eddie would have to identify their daughter's body, tell family and friends, organize a funeral, deal with the inevitable press interest. Joanne would no doubt get a posthumous commendation and a medal for bravery, but this would mean precious little to her parents. Despite their anxiety about their daughter's choice of career, Charlie knew that they were very proud of her and loved her deeply. The next few hours were going to be some of the bleakest of their lives, which is why Charlie was more than willing to stay where she was, perched on the sofa in Nicola's modest home, holding the hand of a mute mother who was struggling to come to terms with how catastrophically cruel life can be.

112

19.53

The needle was pushing 120 mph, but Helen didn't relent. Every second counted, but the fates were conspiring against her. Portsmouth's archipelago almost touches Hayling Island, but with no bridge connecting them, those wanting to access it are forced to cut north instead. Helen was burning around the A27 towards the crossing at Bridge Lake. It was an unwieldy, roundabout route that was costing her valuable time.

Speed was the name of the game now. Helen was convinced that Karen Anderson would be Daisy's final stop and she was determined to be in at the endgame. Daisy's killing spree had only lasted a day, but to Helen it felt like an eternity. Now, for the first time, they knew what lay at the root of Daisy's rage and they had a chance of intercepting her, before she completed her cycle of revenge.

Her lights were on, her siren was shrieking and Helen cut loose. Her bike weaved in and out of the traffic, which was still plentiful even at this hour. Normally she would have waited patiently for the lorries and cars to move over, but time was of the essence and she dared not hesitate. Daisy Anderson was a woman on a mission, determined to eviscerate the family from which she'd been excluded, to have her revenge on the woman she hated.

Helen had seen this hatred at first hand in her sister, Marianne. Her older sister had endured horrific, sustained abuse from their father. She had suffered in silence, ashamed to speak up, but determined to absorb the pain and humiliation, so that her little sister didn't have to suffer. In the end the burden had proved too much for Marianne and she had snapped, killing their mother and father. Daisy was experiencing something similar, meting out appalling violence to those closest to home. Helen didn't condone it, but she understood it. It's the injuries inflicted by your own flesh and blood that cut the deepest.

Both Marianne and Daisy had been robbed of a proper childhood. They had become world-weary and battle-scarred, unable to countenance the possibility of hope, and instead of growing into normal young adults had transformed into angels of vengeance. The parallels for Helen were all too clear now and she chided herself bitterly for not having seen them earlier.

The road opened up now as Helen hit the top of Hayling Island, and she accelerated once more. Rain was beginning to fall, rendering the surface slick and reducing the visibility. Raindrops streaked across Helen's visor, catching the sodium glow of the lights that illuminated the road, producing strange and fantastical effects as they did so. As she drove down the dark road, Helen thought she saw figures in front of her, faces she recognized. The butchered girls from Holloway, Ella Matthews lying dead on that grimy bed, Ethan Harris spread-eagled on the train tracks, but hovering above all of them was Marianne. Always Marianne staring directly at Helen, with that curious, enigmatic smile.

Helen clamped her eyes shut for a second, desperate to shrug off these ghoulish visions. She had a job to do, a family to save. Reducing her speed, she tried to slow her heart rate, to get a grip. She had to stay focused.

The visions started to recede. The rain continued to pour down, but Helen powered on, energized and alive. It was a race to the finish now.

113

20.22

She shivered and pulled her dressing gown tightly around her. The master bedroom was always cold, because of the ill-fitting windows and dodgy radiators, but tonight it seemed particularly perishing. Was that really the case, she wondered, or was her mind playing tricks on her? Was it the howling wind outside that was sending temperatures plummeting? Or was it the news on the radio that had chilled her to the bone?

Karen Anderson sat on her bed, surrounded by a terrible silence. She always listened to the radio as she got ready for bed – she seldom had time during the day – but tonight she had turned it off in horror, stunned by what she was hearing. She had been aware of her phone buzzing in her bag as the afternoon wore on, but she'd had enough on her plate finishing work, picking up the twins and trying to get them to do their homework before bed, so hadn't bothered picking up. It was only as she was eating her own dinner that she fished out her phone and realized that the calls were actually from a number of different friends. Their slightly awkward phone messages made it clear why they were trying to get hold of her so urgently.

There must be lots of Daisy Andersons. That's what

Karen had told herself, having deleted the final message. It could be anyone, it didn't have to be *her* daughter. But the fact that the shootings had taken place in Southampton was unnerving, so Karen had quickly googled the incident. Details were still scant – the police playing their cards close to their chest – so, in frustration, Karen had shut down her computer and switched on the radio instead. The local BBC station seemed to have abandoned normal programming to focus all their attention on this sudden and unexpected calamity and, as Karen listened, more details started to emerge. Daisy Anderson *was* a local girl, who'd until recently attended Meadow Hall Secondary School and who lived with her father on a farm near the River Hamble.

Karen had listened in astonishment. The reporters seemed to be suggesting that the farm's owner had been one of Daisy's victims. Surely that wasn't possible? Michael had doted on Daisy and Daisy on him, to the exclusion of everyone else. Surely she wouldn't have attacked him?

Her first instinct had been to grab her mobile and call him. He hadn't changed his phone number as far as she knew, so . . . But then she'd chickened out. She hadn't picked up the phone to him in years and it somehow seemed wrong to be calling him now purely because she had heard some disturbing reports on the radio. It seemed ghoulish and unpleasant, so she had turned the phone off, fearful of the journalists who would inevitably be calling soon, opting to listen to the terrible news on the radio instead.

Her daughter was wanted by the police. Daisy was a fugitive. Still Karen couldn't compute it. She knew

Daisy had been in trouble before, had committed various minor misdemeanours, but nothing like *this*. In the matter of a few hours, she had become famous. No, she had become infamous . . .

Karen had snapped off the radio, preferring to sit in silence on the edge of her bed. The twins were asleep, which was something, but still Karen knew she would have to tell them something when they woke up in the morning. But how do you explain to two eight-year-olds that their estranged half-sister had just murdered six people in cold blood? How on earth do you put that into words? How she wished Bryan was here now. It was bloody typical that he should be away just when she needed him most . . .

Suddenly Karen jumped out of her skin. There was a noise coming from downstairs. A horrible repetitive, insistent noise. Crossing quickly to the landing, she listened intently. There it was again – someone was beating on the front door, demanding to be let in. Tiptoeing a few stairs down, she cast a wary eye at the door. The upper part was frosted glass and through it, she could just make out a shadowy figure, beating, beating, beating on it . . .

Her first thought was to turn and run. To call the police and lock herself and the kids in the bathroom. But something now made her pause. The figure behind the door seemed too tall, too imposing, to be Daisy. She had had an accomplice but he had apparently been shot and killed.

It was Bryan. It *had* to be Bryan. He had presumably heard the news and hurried home. Perhaps he'd been calling her, but stupid fool that she was, she'd turned the phone off. Yes, that's who it was . . .

Without hesitating any longer, Karen ran down the remaining stairs, flinging open the door. But it wasn't Bryan. Nor was it Daisy.

It was a tall woman in biking leathers.

114

20.29

'Are you sure, Karen? Are you *absolutely* sure?'

Helen and Karen were huddled together in the kitchen, talking in hushed tones so as not to disturb the boys upstairs.

'Of course I'm sure. I think I'd notice if someone had sprayed graffiti all over my house . . .'

Her voice was sharp, fear making her jumpy, so a breathless Helen softened her tone.

'No graffiti at all? Not on your car, at your place of work, Bryan's office –'

'No, nothing like that.'

'And you haven't received any abusive messages or seen anyone loitering nearby?'

'No, we would have called the police if we'd experienced anything like that –'

'And you've had no contact with Daisy of late?'

'None at all,' Karen responded, a little shamefacedly.

Helen exhaled and tried to fathom this unexpected development. As soon as Karen had let her in, she'd conducted a tour of the house, checking each room in turn. But Karen's room was clear, as were the spare room, the bathroom, the boys' room . . . The twins were sleeping peacefully and, like Karen, were completely unharmed.

'Ok, I want you to stay put. Don't answer the door unless you know it's me, not even to your husband. I'm going to do a circuit of the grounds. After that, I'll want to get you and the boys away from here. A protection unit will be assigned to you until Daisy is apprehended. Do you understand?'

Karen nodded mutely.

'Good, now go upstairs and wait for me there.'

Karen obliged, so Helen made for the front door, pulling her mobile phone from her pocket. Her mind was turning, trying to work out what she'd missed. All the evidence had pointed in Karen's direction – it wasn't possible that she had got the *wrong* target again.

Was it?

115

20.32

McAndrew hovered over him, imploring him to work faster. As soon as she had received Helen's call, she had raced to the tech suite. This was affectionately known to McAndrew and her colleagues as the 'locker room' because it was full of men and had a distinctive odour, but it was the place to be if you wanted to open up someone's digital footprint.

Most of the evidence from the farm was back at Southampton Central. It had taken the boys a little while to crack the password protection on Daisy's laptop, but now they were in – sifting her personal files, her internet history and her social media legacy, guided by an impatient DC McAndrew.

'Ignore all the stuff about the British Army, racist groups, the Probation Service. Focus on recent emails, recent searches . . .'

'Shout when you want me to stop,' the data operator replied, pulling up Daisy's internet browser and flicking through her searches in reverse chronological order.

Sites relating to home-made explosives, becoming a mercenary and mass shootings in America sprang up, as did internet news site articles on the murder of Jo Cox and the trial of Anders Brevik. Nestling in among these were more mundane searches, detailing commuter routes to and from Ashurst and the opening hours for Sansom's pharmacy.

'That's about ten days' worth. Do you want me to continue?'

'What about a Tor browser? Something she could access the dark web with?'

'Nothing like that. It's all pretty basic stuff on here.'

'Does she follow anyone on Twitter?'

'Nobody interesting. No one who's a realistic target anyway.'

'What about Facebook?'

'No. She's posted a few times, but that was months ago and anyway she has no friends, so nobody read it.'

'What about her email?'

They trawled through a few weeks of emails, but Daisy didn't really use email and most of the messages in her Inbox were spam. Frustrated, McAndrew stared at the screen, willing it to give her something – *anything*. If they were wrong about Daisy Anderson's choice of target, then she felt sure that her laptop held important clues. It was the only expensive item she owned and she used it pretty much every day.

'What about searches?' she said suddenly.

'We've been through her web search –'

'I mean her Facebook searches.'

'Well, she hasn't got any friends, so I don't see –'

'Have a look anyway.'

Shrugging, the operator opened Facebook.

'As you can see, her page doesn't have much on it, so . . .'

He pulled up the search box.

'Type in Karen Anderson.'

The operator obliged, but had only got so far as 'Kar' when the box auto-suggested 'Karen Anderson'. McAndrew held her breath as the profile picture of Karen Anderson's Facebook page appeared. It was a holiday snap of Karen, Bryan and the boys smiling at the camera.

'It won't let us get beyond the profile page as Daisy wasn't a Facebook friend of Karen's,' the operator added.

'Can we tell how often she's searched for this profile page?'

'Sure, give me a couple of minutes,' he replied, typing once more.

McAndrew had her answer in less than *one* minute and it didn't cheer her. Daisy had looked at Karen Anderson's profile regularly – two or three times a week for the last few years. Karen was a keen Facebook user and had changed her profile picture regularly during that time. So even though Daisy couldn't access her full page, over the years she had managed to immerse herself in the holiday snaps and personal pics of Karen and her new family – a family from which *she* was pointedly excluded.

116

20.37

Karen stared at herself in the mirror. Following her interview with DI Grace, she had gone upstairs, double- and triple-checking the boys were ok, before returning to her bedroom. It was still freezing, so she had hurried into the sanctuary of her cosy, ensuite bathroom.

This had always been her space. Bryan tended to use the family bathroom, leaving the ensuite to her. Their lives were so busy – they both worked and the kids were such a handful – that Karen always enjoyed retreating in here, to bathe, apply her lotions and potions, to have a bit of private time. Tonight, however, it afforded her no respite – looking at herself in the mirror she saw only an anxious, guilty woman staring back at her.

Slipping off her dressing gown, she grasped the hot tap. Then she hesitated, her hand suddenly stilled. She was in her nightdress now, her arms and shoulders exposed, and her eyes immediately strayed to the tattoos that were an unpleasant reminder of the wildness of her youth. She had got together with Michael Anderson when she was a teenager – young, rebellious and desperate to be away from her parents. He had introduced her to drink and drugs and for a while they had lived hard . . . until Daisy came along. That had changed *everything* – it wasn't planned and didn't bring them any closer to each other – and had made the tattoos they'd had done together seem juvenile, even a bit obscene. Now these same tattoos made Karen feel sick – especially the one of the serpent devouring itself, which graced the underside of her forearm.

As soon as DI Grace had mentioned the snake graffiti, Karen had wondered if this was the image she meant. She hadn't pressed the police officer for details – she didn't really want to know – but Daisy had loved that tattoo when she was a little girl. In fact, she'd wanted one just like it and had begged her mother to let her go to the tattoo parlour with her, but Karen had never sanctioned it.

Was this all her fault then? Was the graffiti signature Daisy's way of letting the world know that *she* was responsible? That six people had died because of *her*? She hadn't seen Daisy, hadn't spoken to her in over eight years and had little idea who – or what – she'd become. It seemed somehow impossible that the sweet little girl in pigtails had become a ruthless killer, but how would she *know*?

Karen could feel her world shifting on its axis, the sins of the past finally catching up with her. She wasn't scared for herself – DI Grace was doing a circuit of the house and they would soon be in protective custody – but she was worried for the boys. Their lives would be disrupted, their rose-tinted view of the world destroyed and they might even be in danger themselves – from a vengeful half-sister they had never met. The thought made Karen want to vomit. How could she have played her cards so badly? How could she have got life so wrong?

Bending down, she turned on the tap. She felt dizzy and tired and, as the water slowly felt warmer to her touch, she scooped great handfuls of it on to her face, revelling in its soothing caress. For a moment she felt calmer, losing herself in the simple luxury of it, before reality intruded on her thoughts once more and she turned off the tap.

Fumbling for a towel, she straightened up from the basin. Instantly, she froze. Looking in the mirror, she realized that she wasn't the only person in the room. A figure was now standing directly behind her.

The intruder was scrawny and shaven-headed with heavy bruising around a swollen, bloody nose. It took Karen a moment to see that it was a woman, a moment more to recognize the hazel eyes, the long eyelashes, the small dimple in her chin. It was Daisy, but not the daughter she remembered. The stick-thin wraith who was staring at her was somebody else altogether.

She was like an image from her worst nightmare and when she finally spoke, Karen felt her heart stop.

'Hello, Mum.'

117

20.41

She stole through the darkness scanning the shadows for danger.

Helen's mind was still considering the strange turn of events, but she was determined not to rest until she was *sure*. She had checked the front of the house then, slipping down a side passage, had headed towards the rear of the property. The house had a large garden: the back fence was a hundred feet or so distant and the nearest neighbours were a fair distance away too. Normally this seclusion would have been attractive, but tonight, in the gloom, the property's isolation made Helen shiver.

Padding across the concrete, Helen rounded the corner of the house, hurrying towards the back door. It too was secure – locked and bolted from the inside – so she continued her circuit. But there was nothing alarming. No sign of Daisy, no hint of the serpent graffiti . . . just nothing. Exhaling sharply, Helen turned quickly, heading to the end of the garden. She hugged the boundary fence, searching for signs that it had been penetrated, but it too was intact. The back gate, though easily scalable, was padlocked shut.

Helen walked back towards the house. There was nothing for it now but to wait for the cavalry, then return to base to set in train new searches for Daisy. But still Helen hesitated – she had been so *convinced* that Daisy would come here, it had seemed the logical conclusion of her campaign of violence. But was she mistaken? Had she simply projected her own feelings, her own emotions, on to someone else's madness?

The psychoanalysis would have to wait for another day. Shaking herself out of it, Helen started to jog, keen to be doing something useful. But as she got nearer the back of the house, she slowed down. Something *was* out of place. It took her a moment to work out what it was, but then she got it. One of the windows to the master bedroom was open – only a chink, but it was definitely open. It was a cold, wild night to be airing the room and Helen hurried closer, craning her neck upwards.

The window wasn't secured at all, swaying slightly as the breeze picked up, which alarmed Helen even more. Was it possible that someone had squeezed through it? She squinted, trying to make out scuff marks on the wall or windowsill, but at this distance it was impossible to see. There *was* a drainpipe nearby, which an intruder could have scrambled up, and as Helen examined it she discovered there was fresh mud on it. This didn't prove anything in itself, but Helen's mind was whirring now and, turning away from the pipe, her eyes fixed on something that confirmed her worst fears.

On the ground floor windowsill, directly below the master bedroom, was a single drop of blood.

118

20.43

'Do you need a doctor, sweetheart? Are you in pain?'

Daisy had said virtually nothing since her sudden arrival. She seemed to be enjoying her mother's terrified twittering.

'Daisy, love, come and sit down. Your nose is bleeding . . . I can fetch you some ice for that bruising, we can get you cleaned up . . .'

'Love,' Daisy finally responded, rolling the word around her mouth. 'That's not a word I've heard you use very often. Do you even know what it means?'

'Don't . . . don't . . . be like that,' Karen said soothingly, stuttering slightly as she did so. 'I just want to help you. I know what's been going on, what you've been through today. You're in a bad way.'

'I think that's a bit of an understatement, don't you?' Daisy laughed loudly. 'The understatement of the fucking year.'

Karen's instinctive reaction was to tell Daisy to keep her voice down, to avoid waking the boys. But she swallowed that thought. Looking at her eldest child, she now saw that her daughter was carrying a shotgun, which hung by her side. Karen was still struggling to take in this transformation – from the little girl she'd known to this shaven-headed monster – but there was no doubting that the later, more aggressive incarnation of her daughter was currently holding sway. She looked hostile, composed and utterly fearless.

'Look, I know you're angry with me,' Karen continued, just about managing to keep her voice steady. 'And I understand why –'

'Do you?' Daisy retorted. 'Tell me, Mum, why you think I'm "angry"?'

Karen faltered slightly, taken aback by the vehemence of Daisy's question.

'Because I wasn't there for you,' she eventually replied, her voice shaking with emotion. 'Because I left you with *him* . . .'

'Don't you dare bring Dad into this. He was a good parent, he looked after me –'

'He was a drunk, Daisy.' Karen was suddenly angry. 'Say what you like about me, but don't pretend that that man was a saint. He was violent, abusive –'

'Shut the fuck up,' Daisy spat back, taking a step towards her mother.

'I know you think he took care of you, but just look, Daisy, look what you've become.'

'He gave me a roof over my head, fed me, clothed me . . .'

'Did he? How many times did you have to get yourself breakfast when you were growing up? Find yourself some clothes to wear? How many times did you have to get *him* dressed because he was too drunk to do it himself?'

Now Daisy paused. Karen could see that her words had hit home.

'Look, love, I can see that you hate me . . . that you think you hate me . . . but please understand I never left *you*.'

'Bullshit.'

'I couldn't take it any more. The drinking, the abuse –'

'You were pregnant, bitch. Don't lie to me.'

'Yes, I had an affair, yes, I was pregnant, but why do you think that happened? Because my husband gave up on me, gave up on life, all he was interested in was where the next bottle was coming from, even as the farm slowly fell apart around us.'

'You're lying.'

'Bryan offered me love, a way out –'

'So why didn't you take me?'

Now Karen hesitated. Suddenly she felt crushed by guilt, overwhelmed by shame, years of repressed sadness catching up with her.

'I . . . I wanted to, believe me, I wanted to . . .'

Daisy was staring at her, angry and unconvinced.

'But Bryan, he . . . he didn't want someone else's child. I was already pregnant with twins and at that point he didn't have much money. He had a small one-bedroom flat, whereas the farm was so big, you were settled there.'

'You abandoned me.'

'I know, I know,' Karen replied, tears running down her cheeks now. 'And I wish I hadn't, I wish I'd had the strength to stand up to him, but I was in a bad place. I had to get away and at the time –'

'It was a price worth paying.'

Daisy's interjection was bitterly angry and Karen now hung her head.

'Yes,' she muttered eventually. 'But I've regretted it ever since. I really, really wish I could turn the clock back, be the mum I should have been.'

'Keep telling yourself that. But you and I both know the truth. I watched you walk away from the house, watched you all the way to the end of the track. And you *never* looked back, not once.'

'Please, love, put yourself in my shoes . . .'

'You didn't give a shit about anyone but yourself.'

'That's not true.'

'You pretended that I never even existed. I was your dirty little secret.'

'No, no, I often thought about you –'

'But I don't get a mention on your Facebook profile. "Mother to two lovely boys", it says.'

Once more Karen looked shamefaced.

'That was Bryan's idea, he thought it would be confusing –'

'Bryan, Bryan, Bryan. When are you going to realize that this is all about *you*, Karen? Blame him if you want, but it's *your* black heart that's the problem.'

'Please, Daisy, don't do this.'

'Funny how you want to talk to me now, isn't it? Daisy this, Daisy that. How many times have you said my name in the last ten years?'

'Many times. I've spoken about you often, I've prayed for you and –'

Daisy chuckled, shaking her head in amused disbelief.

'And I never stopped loving you. Never.'

Karen's tone was mournful, but insistent.

'I wrote to you.'

'Like hell you did.'

'I wrote to you every birthday, Christmas. Bryan wouldn't let me visit, but I wanted to let you know I was thinking of you –'

'I never saw a card.'

'I sent money too. I knew the farm was struggling and I didn't want you to suffer, so I sent £50 each week for clothes, books –'

'Don't lie to me.'

'We had so much and you had so little, but I'm guessing your father used the money for drink, instead of giving it to you –'

'Shut up, bitch! Just shut the fuck up!'

Enraged, Daisy raised her gun, pointing it directly at Karen. But as she began to squeeze the trigger –

'Don't do it, Daisy.'

Daisy spun round to see a breathless Helen standing in the bedroom. Immediately she charged out of the bathroom, heading directly towards the unwelcome intruder.

'I should have killed you the first time we met,' the young woman hissed, raising her gun.

'You had your chance, but it's over now. This is the end of the road, Daisy.'

'Like hell it is.'

'Come here, Karen,' Helen said firmly, turning to the terrified mother.

Karen hurried out into the bedroom, then suddenly froze, as Daisy's gun swung back in her direction once more.

'This is pointless, Daisy. You won't get away, so please, just give me the gun.'

Right on cue, police sirens could be heard. Getting louder, getting closer.

'Bullshit. I'll kill both of you and be away before they even get a sniff of me.'

'That's going to be pretty hard, especially as you've only got *one* shot left.'

For the first time, Daisy hesitated.

'You left the rest of your shells in Bray Road and you've already fired once, so . . .'

Daisy's eyes flicked from the police officer to her mother and then back again.

'Well then, I guess I'll just have to choose, won't I?'

As she spoke, she raised her gun, so that it was pointing at Helen's face once more.

'Eeny . . .'

She swung the gun towards her mother.

'Meeny . . .'

Then back towards Helen.

'Miny . . .'

Karen Anderson cowered, as the barrels swung back towards her.

'Moe . . .'

Helen didn't budge as the gun moved her way once more.

'Catch a . . . oh fuck this . . .'

Daisy now took aim at her mother's head. But even as she did so, Helen moved quickly across the room, placing herself in between mother and daughter.

'Get out the way.'

'I can't do that, Daisy.'

'This is about her, not you. She deserves to die –'

'No, she doesn't.'

'She deserves to suffer, to plead, to beg for her life and *then* to die. I want her to know what she's done to me –'

'She knows, Daisy, believe me, she knows, you don't need to punish her any more.'

'Someone has to pay, for my shitty life, for all the times I've been kicked and kicked and kicked again –'

'Then shoot me.'

'Get out of the wa—'

'I mean it. Shoot *me*.'

119

20.53

The shriek of the siren cut right through her. Charlie was already on edge, her anxiety levels rising steadily, and the piercing scream was only making things worse. In the past, she had enjoyed using the blues and twos – the strobing lights and that awful, insistent noise bullying motorists into moving aside – but tonight the familiar scream made her shudder. It sounded distressed, even mournful, as if presaging bad things.

She roared onwards, barely dropping her speed below eighty, despite the hostile driving conditions. She was at the head of a convoy of police vehicles tearing towards Karen Anderson's house. DC McAndrew's discoveries had been enough to convince Charlie that Helen *had* been right about Daisy's final destination, so she'd ordered all available vehicles to attend the remote location. She felt sure that the end was close and she didn't want Helen to face a pitiless killer alone.

So far progress had been swift and smooth, but now Charlie saw the raised rear lights of a tractor up ahead. She had left the B-roads in favour of single-track country lanes. On paper, this looked the quickest route to the Anderson home – but not if you were stuck behind a lumbering farm vehicle. Charlie punched the horn savagely, adding to the cacophony, and the driver raised his hand in acknowledgement, increasing his speed a little. It was too slow – far too slow – but despite her anger Charlie knew there was little else the driver could do. There was nowhere to pull over, so he would have to keep going, pushing his old tractor to the limits of its capabilities, as the police vehicles backed up behind him.

Charlie swore violently, slamming the wheel in frustration. What if Daisy was at Karen's house already? It wasn't in Helen's nature to hang back and wait for help. If Karen or the boys were in danger, she would act to protect them. She would confront the teen killer, alone and unarmed. And what then?

The tractor lumbered on, but now a desperate Charlie spotted her opportunity. Up ahead, a tiny track led off the road to a gated field. It was only a short strip of rutted mud, but for a few feet it would broaden out the road. Gunning the engine, Charlie waited and waited, then suddenly raced forward, darting to the right of the wide vehicle and speeding past it back on to the road. She made it by an inch, spraying the startled farmer with mud and stones, as she accelerated away down the road.

Charlie was convinced she'd heard him curse both her driving and her gender, but she didn't care. She was free at last – and racing towards Helen.

120

20.54

'I'm not fucking about. I will do it –'

Daisy jabbed the gun towards her face. But Helen didn't blink, her eyes fixing Daisy's. There was a strange calm about her now.

'Good,' she replied. 'I want you to.'

'That's bullshit. You don't want me to kill y—'

'Yes, I do.'

'Get real –'

'You think I'm bluffing, but . . . you have *no idea* what my life has been like . . .'

Helen's voice shook as she spoke. Daisy stared at her, unnerved by this sudden display of emotion.

'. . . and maybe you don't care. But my life has been leading to this moment. Leading me to you.'

'You mad? You don't even know m—'

'I have seen things that you couldn't even imagine. I've done things that would turn your soul black. And it's made me sick, Daisy. Sick in the head. Sick in the soul. So, please, do me a favour. Pull the trigger.'

Daisy threw a look towards her mother, then back to Helen. Slowly, she slid her finger around the trigger.

'I deserve it. I deserve to be punished for what I've done,' Helen continued quickly. 'And what's more, I want to be. I've had enough. I can't bear to look at myself in the mirror any more, I need some . . . peace. So I'm not asking you, Daisy. I'm *begging* you.'

'It's your funeral,' she hissed.

'It's my *choice*,' Helen replied quietly. 'So, do it.'

Daisy's eyes narrowed and she began to squeeze the trigger.

'Do it!' Helen roared.

121

20.56

Charlie took the corner at fifty miles an hour, the car skidding across to the wrong side of the road, before she yanked it back on course. Karen Anderson's house was just up ahead and she floored it for the last hundred yards, pulling up sharply at the end of the drive.

Flinging the door open, she leapt out and started towards the house. Helen had been radio silent for some time and, as she approached the house, Charlie noticed that the front door stood open.

Instinctively, Charlie knew something was badly wrong and broke into a sprint. But, as she did so, she heard a sound that stopped her dead in her tracks.

A single gunshot ringing out.

122

20.57

The explosion filled the room, bouncing off the walls. But now a new sound could be heard – a long, slow, agonized scream. Karen Anderson was stumbling backwards, clawing at the walls for support. She was terrified, in shock and coated in a thick spatter of blood, which clung to her face and body. She crashed into a chest of drawers and hung on to it for dear life, unable to comprehend the gruesome scene in front of her.

Helen was on the floor not five feet away from her. Her face was contorted, she was covered in blood and her hands were clamped to a huge hole in Daisy's neck. Time had seemed to stop as their captor squeezed the trigger, Helen bracing herself for the impact. But, at the last moment, Daisy had jerked the barrels away and upwards, ramming them into the soft flesh underneath her chin. Helen had lunged towards her, desperate to save the young woman, but she was a second too late. The gun had erupted and Daisy had crumpled to the floor.

For a moment, Helen had been disoriented and dizzy, the force and volume of the blast sending her reeling backwards. But recovering herself, she had rushed forward, throwing herself down by the injured woman. Blood was oozing from the impact wound, the torn flesh charred with the burn blast, and Helen had pressed her hands to the injury in a desperate attempt to stem the bleeding. But as she took in the brutalized body in front of her, her eyes settled on the terrible exit wound on the top of Daisy's head. Half of her skull and a good chunk of her brain had come away, catapulted to the other side of the room.

Helen continued to press down, unwilling to give up, though it was clearly pointless. The young woman was past saving – in truth she was probably dead before she hit the floor.

Often in her diaries Daisy had spoken about her desire for self-immolation, her need to end her painful, loveless existence. Now she had got what she wanted.

123

21.02

Helen walked away from the house. The modest drive was crawling with police officers and paramedics and they hurried to help her. Her ears were still ringing, her head was throbbing and she knew she looked a sight, but Helen batted them away. Charlie hadn't prevailed upon her to get herself checked out, so they weren't likely to convince her.

Helen didn't want to stay a second longer than she had to. She would do her duty, talk to the attending officers, but her work here was done. Karen Anderson was being treated for shock, the boys were being reunited with their father and Charlie could handle the clean-up operation. Helen didn't want to linger – she wanted to get clean herself, to wash Daisy's blood off her, even though she knew that the stain of this night would last for many years to come.

She had saved Karen Anderson, but she had failed to stop Daisy bringing her short, difficult life to a calamitous end. Was Daisy beyond redemption, beyond help? Helen didn't believe that and had wanted to give Daisy a chance to atone, perhaps even to heal. But in that split second Daisy had made a decision, opting for annihilation over arrest. And in so doing she had spared Helen.

Had Helen meant what she'd said to Daisy? In that moment, the words seemed to come so easily to her and it had certainly *felt* right. As she'd spoken, Helen had been back in a different space – transported back to a time some years ago when another person had pointed a gun at her head – and this time she'd been expecting a different outcome. She had certainly believed Daisy was going to fire and had stared down the barrels, grim with defiance and determination, but had she actually wanted her to pull the trigger?

Maybe it was an impossible question to answer. Perhaps she would never know. All that was clear was that Daisy had made the decision for her. And Helen would have to live with the consequences.

124

10.02

It was a bitterly cold day. Autumn had surrendered to winter – the leaves now dead and gone – and the temperature had plunged. Standing on the street corner, exposed and cold, Helen tugged self-consciously at her skirt. She always wore trousers, but a work suit was not appropriate today, so she had made an exception, despite her concerns about the way it made her look. She was even more worried about her make-up and pulled a compact from her bag, checking her face in the small mirror. Two weeks had passed since that terrible day and most of Helen's bumps and scratches had receded. The bruising on her face was harder to hide, despite her best efforts, and Helen took in her reflection with resignation. She had hoped to be looking a little better for Joanne's funeral.

It was a day she'd known was coming, but was nevertheless dreading. She had been keen to return to work straight away, to help with the follow-up investigation. But the Chief Superintendent had intervened, ordering Helen to take a couple of weeks off. As a result, Helen had hardly seen the team since Joanne's death and had had no chance to gauge their reaction to that day's traumatic events. Charlie of course had been a regular visitor in the interim and had assured her that the team were shaken, but defiant, resolved to carry on their good work in Joanne's name. Helen had been very grateful for Charlie's support, just as she was now to see her pull up at the kerb. She had decided to take a break from biking for a little while and had asked her old friend to pick her up.

'You're looking nice,' Charlie announced, as Helen took her seat beside her.

'There's no need to lie, Charlie. I look like a boxer in a skirt.'

'A very well-coutured boxer,' Charlie countered good-humouredly, as she pulled away.

They chatted on the way to the church, Charlie quizzing Helen about her recuperation and being gently interrogated in turn about the state of the investigation. Helen heard her responses, but couldn't fully take them in, her mind already scrolling forward to what lay ahead. She had agreed without hesitation to speak at the funeral, but wondered now if that had been the right choice. She was Joanne's superior, so it was expected of her, but how would her eulogy sound to Joanne's family, friends and colleagues, most of whom knew of the recent difficulties between them? Would they think her two-faced? Insincere? There could be no question of backing out – that would be beyond awful – but Helen wondered why she hadn't asked Charlie to do it instead. Charlie had known Joanne far better than she did.

The conversation lapsed into silence as they neared the church. People were standing three deep on the pavement, keen to pay their respects as the coffin passed by. Helen recognized some of the faces – clerical and support staff from Southampton Central – but many more were simply ordinary citizens who'd turned out to honour a fallen officer. It was a humbling sight and Helen sensed that it was affecting Charlie just as much as it was her.

Parking in a nearby car park, the pair walked purposefully towards the church. Experience had taught Helen that uncomfortable situations were best tackled head on, so she kept up a brisk pace, until they reached the steps of the church. Now they slowed and as Charlie laid a supportive hand on Helen's arm, she pulled back to allow her superior space to proceed. Picking up an order of service, Helen stepped inside the church's impressive Gothic interior.

Helen's antipathy to religion was well known, but even she was taken aback by how beautiful the church looked this morning. The mourners' outfits were colourful (as requested by the family), the candles plentiful, and pink and white lilies were everywhere. They were Joanne's favourite flowers and the scent and beauty they provided had a calming effect on Helen. And now, as she walked towards her place at the front of the church, she was surprised to see several friendly faces turning towards her. Pretty much the whole of Southampton Central was present, as were the mayor and other local dignitaries. She even spotted Emilia Garanita, who appeared sombre and respectful in her dark suit, no doubt mulling over how close *she* had come to death.

To Helen's surprise the assembled masses looked at her not with hostility, but with relief, even happiness. They seemed pleased that she was recovering from her injuries and was fit to lead the tributes to her fallen colleague. This goodwill extended even to Joanne's family – her father giving Helen a small, friendly nod, as she took her place in the second row. Helen was more moved than she could say, smiling back briefly, before burying herself in the order of service.

There were countless readings scattered among the traditional hymns and prayers, many of Joanne's friends, colleagues and relatives keen to celebrate a life lived with passion, purpose and determination. As Helen took this in, as she turned to look at row upon row of stricken but resolute mourners behind her, she couldn't help but reflect on the love and affection that Joanne inspired. In her darker moments, Helen had occasionally speculated as to what her own funeral would be like. If she managed to command even half the number of mourners that Joanne had she would be deeply gratified, for there was no longer even standing room in the packed church. Here then was evidence, if it was needed, of the amazing contribution that Joanne had made in her relatively short life. This was a woman who had lived, loved, fought and endured without ever losing her sense of purpose.

This was a woman who had made a difference.

125

10.48

The lone mourner stood by the graveside, looking down at the coffins below. Botley Parish Cemetery was a stone's throw from the farm where Daisy and Michael had lived and suited everyone's purpose, being small, discreet and out of the way. The vicar had initially bridled at the thought of burying a mass murderer with one of his victims, but Karen Anderson's impassioned pleas had eventually won him over. There was no question of forgiving Daisy or condoning her crimes, but Karen had argued forcefully that the small amount of love Daisy *had* received in her troubled life had come almost exclusively from her father and that it was fitting that they should be laid to rest together. She had ignored any claim that Jason Swift might have to her daughter – she didn't even want to *think* about him. To her, he was somebody else's problem.

The twins were at school, unaware of today's committal. They knew little of Daisy – they had gleaned more about their half-sister from the newspapers than they had during the previous eight years – and, besides, Karen didn't want an audience for this private duty. She knew that many people hated her, felt that the whole tragedy was her fault. To a large extent, she agreed with them and had been tempted to duck her duty, painfully aware of the hypocrisy of playing the loving wife and mother *after* the event. But, in the end, that was why she *had* to be here – her sin of omission, her absence from the family home, had been the catalyst for these terrible events, so it was her responsibility to honour those who had lost their lives, Daisy included.

She had opted for a joint headstone, to discourage people from vandalizing it, with just their names and dates on it. No quotation from the scriptures, no message, just a simple record of two people who had lived and died.

The service had been short to the point of bluntness, but the vicar had not been unsympathetic. Karen had been especially grateful for his discretion about when and where the service was taking place and his firmness in dealing with the handful of reporters who had turned up to gatecrash proceedings. They were waiting for her, just outside the gates, and Karen knew she would have to face them soon. But they could wait a little longer.

For now, she was needed here, to offer prayers for a husband and daughter who deserved better.

126

11.16

'DS Joanne Sanderson gave her life to save others.'

Helen kept her voice steady and clear, aware of the many faces that were turned towards her. She had begun her address with a personal message to Joanne's family, but now kept her gaze fixed on the back of the church, as she moved towards her conclusion.

'This was not done for personal glory, but because it was her duty. Joanne was not without ambition – which of us can claim that? – but she was never driven by it. For her, the important thing was to do her job. She was determined not to be found wanting, to stare down every crisis and danger without wavering, to preserve the life and liberty of those she'd been charged with protecting. She never shirked her duty, never put her own interests first – she was selfless, courageous and committed. She represented the best in each and every one of us and, though we miss her deeply, she continues to inspire us, reminding those who follow that our first responsibility in life is always to *others*, never to ourselves.'

Helen pondered these words as she joined the congregation at Joanne's graveside shortly afterwards. The last few months had been some of the darkest of her life and somewhere along the line she had become mistrustful, suspicious and angry. As a result, she had failed Joanne, perhaps costing her her life. Nobody else saw it this way, but for Helen Joanne's personal legacy was clear. If she was to continue to do *her* duty, as a police officer and a human being, Helen would have to learn to trust again. Only by doing so could she become a true leader once more.

It was time to turn away from the darkness towards the light, to embrace all that was good in others *and* herself. To do anything else would be the greatest betrayal of all, which is why Helen had resolved to become a better person, to recommit herself to the service of others, to fight the good fight.

She would continue to walk towards the fire.